NeNe Capri

Cover Design by Black Market Logos
Book Interior Design by Lashonda Johnson & Ghostwriter Inc.

The Pussy Trap 4

The Shadow of Death

By

NeNe Capri

DEDICATION

This book is dedicated to my Princess Khairah. Everything I am and everything I do is for you!

ACKNOWLEDGEMENTS

Thank you to the Whole Boss Lady Publishing and NeNe Capri Presents and Real Raw Radio Family. This Road is not going to be easy, but every sacrifice is well worth it. We got this..! There is no Limit..! ~ The Boss Lady NeNe Capri!

NeNe Capri

PROLOGUE

Six months had passed, and Kayson and KoKo were enjoying the married life. With all that they had been through, they deserved all the happiness in the world. Kayson relocated Goldie and the immediate crew, sold all the property in St. Croix, and then moved to another island in Dubai. Before Baseem went underground, Kayson put him on Detective Greg and Damien. With the help of Porcha and Shameezah, he did them real dirty; a perfect going away present for Mr. and Mrs. Wells. Once Kayson and KoKo were safe, Mocha released Yuri to Mr. Odoo with a stern warning; making him realize he was not untouchable. Forcing him to back the fuck up. Tyquan had gone on the run, leaving them one enemy unaccounted for, but Kayson vowed to continue his search. Keisha remained in their care while recovering, and yes, Mrs. KoKo was on house arrest again. Kayson had set their life on a new path and was working with KoKo on stopping the chase of the demons of the past.

"Oh shit!" Kayson moaned out as he slow stroked KoKo from the back. Shortly after, he released long and hard. He looked down at the sweat glistening on her back and placed soft kisses up and down her spine. Then he whispered in her ear, "Doggie in the morning. The breakfast of champions," he chuckled as he pulled out and stood up.

"You are so spoiled," she stated as he pulled her to her feet.

"Sheeit . . . I'm not spoiled. I'm blessed," he kissed her lips.

"Whatever, Mr. Spoiled."

Kayson admired her sexy body as she walked to the bathroom. He had missed her being pregnant with Quran, and was enjoying watching her belly swell. He was staying as close to home as possible so as not to miss anything this time around.

"What are we doing today?" she asked as she adjusted the water.

"I can't think right now. I'm fucked up."

"Get it together, Boss. You owe me a date. I want to have my last hurrah before your daughter invades my life."

"I'm trying to pull it together, but my nigga Trae said it best, 'Pregnant pussy is to die for.'"

KoKo laughed. "You are so stupid. Well, I'ma tell you right now, you ain't gonna have a bitch bloated every year, so get that shit outta ya head. I ain't Tasha Macklin."

"Whatever. You gonna do what I tell you," he said, coming up behind her and reaching around to rub her stomach. KoKo leaned back and rested her head on his chest.

"Thank you, baby," he said.

"For what?"

"Loving me."

"I told you I will love you a day past forever; and if I go first, I'ma haunt yo' ass for the rest of your life."

Kayson burst out laughing, "That's fucked up. How you gonna rest in peace?"

"You get another woman, it ain't gonna be no peace. I'ma be up in your house rattling shit and knocking shit over."

"That's selfish. You gonna let all this good dick go to waste?" he joked.

"No, 'cause I'm taking that muthafucka with me."

They both burst out laughing. "You crazy as hell."

"And don't forget it."

Within the hour, KoKo, Kayson, and Quran were so fresh and so clean, ready for a family day out.

Kayson smiled, watching as KoKo tried to keep up with Quran with her big belly.

After a few hours passed, their family day was just about over, and Kayson had KoKo drive him to the airport. He needed to meet up with Baseem to handle some business. Then he was going to be stationary until the baby was born.

"I'll be right back," he said, kissing KoKo on the lips.

"Bye, Daddy," Quran grabbed him around the neck.

"Why you always blocking?" he said, pulling him to the front seat.

"I'm not blocking," he giggled as Kayson tickled his neck.

He pulled his son into his arms and hugged him tight. "See you in two days," Kayson put his fist out. "You're the man of the house. Hold it down for me."

"Okay," Quran hit his fist and then crawled to the back.

Kayson leaned over and kissed KoKo again.

"Hurry up back. I think your daughter wants outta here," she looked down at her belly.

"Trust me. I will not miss this one being born," he hopped out and shut the door.

KoKo watched until he was inside the private plane.

"Mommy, what's blocking?" Quran asked.

"It's what your father does to keep me from being in charge," she smiled.

"Why you wanna be in charge? Daddy's in charge."

"Fasten your seat belt," KoKo shook her head and pulled off.

Quran shrugged his shoulders, buckled up, and looked out the window.

An hour later, Quran and KoKo walked into the house. She fixed them a snack and an ice cream sundae. Later that evening, she put Quran in the tub. Dressed in his pajamas, Quran joined KoKo in the living room for their movie night. The moment she saw his eyes closing in the middle of their Disney movie, she tucked him in her bed. KoKo picked up his toys and then cleaned the kitchen.

On her way to the shower, she checked the alarms, peeked in on her son, and placed her gun under her fluffy pillow. As KoKo lathered up, she felt a slight tightness in the bottom of her stomach.

"Don't you start, little girl. Your daddy is not here. I need two more days," she looked down at her stomach.

By the time she got out of the shower, she felt a few more pains, and they were sharper.

"Not now, momma," she walked to the closet and grabbed a sundress. She wanted to be dressed just in case.

KoKo laid down and dialed the number for the phone on the plane.

"Hey, baby. You miss me already?" Kayson asked.

"Yes, of course. But I think I'm in labor."

Kayson got quiet. "What happened?"

"When I got in the shower the games began. You know this is your fault."

"How is it my fault?"

"You and your doggie style."

"You and your 'not until six weeks.' The Enforcer don't play that."

"Whatever!"

"I'm on my way back. Keep me posted."

"Okay, baby. Hurry!" KoKo felt another sharp pain.

She tried to remain calm and fall asleep, but the pain and pressure began to take over. She got up and attempted to walk to the kitchen to get some water. When she turned the corner, she felt a heavy object hit her head, and then she saw black.

"Wake up, KoKo," she heard the soft, yet commanding voice say.

Struggling to open her eyes and lift her head, KoKo sat half way up and got the shock of her life. Keisha stood over her with a gun in her hand.

"What the fuck!" KoKo mumbled. She tried to move her hands, but they were cuffed to the pipe under the kitchen sink.

KoKo yanked her shackled hands, trying to break free. "What are you doing?" she asked, trying to bring her head to her hands. And as she did so, she pulled back a handful of blood.

"See, I tried to be patient. I tried to wait and see if the animals would wipe themselves out, but you are fucking relentless. I put Mo on you. I put Boa on you. I even put the cops on you, and for some reason...you just won't fade the fuck out!"

"What the fuck is wrong with you?" KoKo looked partly confused and shocked.

"You're what's wrong with me. You're the reason Malik did not love me. You're the reason why my daughter is gone!" she yelled.

"I am your daughter," KoKo tried to bring her back to reality.

Keisha laughed hard and loud while holding her stomach. "You are soooooo stupid. Didn't Tyquan tell you to open your eyes?" she leaned down toward her. "I am not your mother. Nine tried to tell you everything. I kept telling Mo, 'That bitch is smart. She is going to figure this whole thing out.' But Mo said, 'No she won't.' It was the death of her, but I ain't going out like that," she leaned in and held the chain in her face and with gritted teeth she continued. "You took my Star. She was all I had in this world. You owe me, and just when I was about to cash in, that nosey husband of yours fucked with the accounts. Now, I need you to tell me where my money is."

"I don't know shit about your money," KoKo said as the crease in her forehead appeared.

"I figured you would say that. So I guess I will have to go to plan B."

Keisha pulled a metal object from a bag and walked over to the stove. She turned the fire up high and placed the object on the flame.

"This is all about money?" KoKo asked as a sharp pain struck her stomach and back. Her head throbbed.

"It has always been about money," she leaned back down. *"They owe me. I sacrificed everything, and I want what's coming to me. They didn't give it to me, but you will,"* she stood and walked back to the stove.

KoKo could hear her phone ringing incessantly. She knew Kayson was calling her back to back.

"So, where did you say my money was?" Keisha asked, coming toward her with the hot object.

"Fuck you!" KoKo shouted.

Keisha stepped over her and placed the red, hot tip on her leg.

"Ahhh!" KoKo yelled out as the pain shot through her body.

"You still don't know?"

"I don't know shit!" KoKo spat in her face.

Keisha smiled, wiped the saliva away, and then burned KoKo again.

"Muthafucka!" KoKo screamed out this time. The pain was so severe her water broke.

Keisha went back to the stove. *"Let's see how much Kayson will love you with the skin burned off your pretty little face,"* Keisha placed the object back on the fire.

Tears came to KoKo's eyes, but she would not let them fall.

Keisha pulled up a chair and looked at her watch. *"I gotta let it get good and hot,"* she crossed her legs.

"Bitch, you better kill me!"

"Oh, don't worry. I am. But I want to do it real slow. While we wait, I want to tell you a few things. I don't know if you knew this, but Monique really did like your little orphan you're going to leave behind. We had so many arguments over if we should kill you or not. She was real conflicted. Thank God you got to her because she was really getting ready to fuck things up with her guilty conscience; especially when her son came back into the picture. And Boa, you must have been fucking him real good because he was flip-flopping. Mo had to pay him big time, and if Boa's suicidal girlfriend wouldn't have pulled her stunt, I would have been living free by now.

She paused and looked at her watch again. *"Oh well, water under the bridge,"* she rose to her feet, heading toward the stove.

Again, KoKo could hear her phone ringing off the hook.

"Bitch, you better hide good because Kayson will not rest until your grave is

cold."

Keisha turned toward KoKo. She squatted beside her to look in her eyes. "*I'm not afraid of your husband,*" she smirked. "*To be truthful, you have no idea who he really is,*" she stated, lowering her eyes. "*Let me ask you something,*" Keisha shifted her weight from one side to the other. "*When he crawls between your thighs and gives you all that power, inch by glorious inch, making you see what he wants you to see, hear what he wants you to hear, feel what he wants you to feel, rendering you incapable of thought and control,*" she paused. "*Can you really say you know who he is? You climbed into a dangerous game with some very powerful players. Each one led by their desires. Money. Power. Greed. Sex,*" she chuckled. "*I think they call it . . . temptation. And oh, it can be a beautiful thing in the hands of the right person; but in the hands of the wrong person, it can be deadly. And you, my dear, were dealt a very deadly hand.*"

KoKo stared in her eyes, unfazed by her little speech.

"*Finally, your smart ass mouth is closed,*" Keisha slowly stood up and headed to the stove.

KoKo's pains were coming faster and faster. She needed to say something to distract her.

"*The only thing worse than a greedy bitch, is a thirsty one. Bitch, you ain't 'bout this life. You ain't worthy enough to suck a dog's dick!*" KoKo looked at her with low eyes and flared nostrils. "*I didn't climb into this game. I walked in the front door and sat right down at the muthafuckin table. And I have been trumping you muthafuckas from day one,*" KoKo continued to taunt her.

Keisha turned the metal object over the blazing flame as she began to feel the sting of KoKo's words.

"*While you trying to keep up with who and what I know, Tyquan played the shit outta your dumb ass,*" KoKo said with a devious smile.

"*What the fuck are you talking about?*" Keisha picked up the hot object.

"*It's okay. He's that type of man. Fuck a bitch, then trick a bitch.*"

"*You don't know what the fuck you're talking about!*"

"*I can't tell. He's laid up with Deborah right now, while you're standing here broke. I guess your pussy wasn't as good as you thought it was,*" KoKo said, trying to throw her off her square.

Keisha thought for a minute.

"*Yeah, look at you. You're weak. He don't want no weak, broke bitch!*"

Keisha's breathing quickened with every word. She threw the object across *the room, barely missing KoKo's head.*

She reached in her robe pocket and grabbed her gun. Breathing heavy, she pointed the gun at KoKo's head. "You don't know what you're talking about. Tyquan loves me. He has always loved me!" she yelled.

"Bitch, you're weak!" KoKo taunted.

"You and that fucking Sabrina took everything from me!" Keisha stood, shaking and crying. "Now I'ma take everything from you," she pointed the gun at KoKo's stomach.

"You can take whatever you want. But the only thing I won't give you is my soul," KoKo closed her eyes.

When she heard the first shot, she braced herself for the pain, but didn't feel anything. Slowly, she opened her eyes and saw Keisha fall to her knees coughing up blood. Then her head hit the kitchen floor. When she looked past her, she saw Quran standing in his pajamas with her .22 tight in his grip.

"My daddy said I was in charge. He said, 'protect your mommy.'"

KoKo began to cry at the sight of her baby at the other end of a gun. A ton of emotions flooded her body at once: pain, fear, regret, and lastly, pride.

"Keep it pointed down and walk slowly to Mommy," she instructed.

Quran walked slowly around Keisha's dead body. When he got to KoKo's side, he stood next to her with his eyes fixed on the woman he had affectionately called MiMi.

"It's okay, baby. You didn't do anything wrong," she tried to sooth his little soul.

KoKo began pulling at the pipe in an effort to free herself. Then she heard keys in the front door.

Kayson opened the door and unarmed the beeping alarm. He frantically called her name. "KoKo! Baby, where you at?"

"I'm in here, Kay!" she yelled back.

Kayson ran to the kitchen and almost lost it at the sight of KoKo tied up, Keisha laid out bleeding with a gunshot to the back, and Quran standing with a gun in his hand. He rushed over and gently took the gun from Quran, put it on the safety, and laid it on the counter.

"Move over, son," he instructed as he began yanking at the pipes to free KoKo's hands.

"Baby, look in that bag," she said as she grimaced in pain.

He grabbed the bag, pulled everything out and turned it upside down. A key hit the floor. He unlocked the cuffs and then untied her feet.

13

"Ohhh . . . baby, be careful," KoKo moaned as he moved her leg.

Kayson ran and got a towel, rushing back to her side. He wrapped it around her, picked her up, and held her in his arms. Moving to the phone on the wall, he called 911 and waited for the fall out.

Quran grabbed onto his father's leg. "I kept her safe, Daddy. Right?"

"Yes, you did, son. Come on," *he said as he walked to the front door to meet the ambulance.*

"Baby, what the fuck happened?" *he tried to ask.*

KoKo lifted her head off his shoulder and looked in his eyes.

"As hard as we prayed that he would be better than us. He now has blood on his hands."

* * * *

A week later, KoKo was sitting in her bed watching Kayson smile as he looked at his baby girl, Malika Kah'Asia Wells. KoKo beamed as he held his daughter while little Quran sat next to his dad rubbing her tiny hand on his face. Even though they had everything to live for, the pain of the past would not allow her to give up the search. She was determined to be a woman of her word and make everybody pay their debt, and the sacrifice wasn't shit. She couldn't wait for the baby to get old enough, because she was going after whoever was left and their whole family. For every devilish temptation within their darkened hearts, all their jealousy, power, and greed, she would use against them to set a trap that would ultimately end in death.

* * * *

"Hello," *Tyquan answered as he ran on his treadmill.*

"You know we can't let that muthafucka live in peace, right?" *the cold, malicious voice boomed through his speaker.*

"Brenda, I got it," *he stopped the treadmill and grabbed his towel.*

"No, I got it. You have had enough time to fuck shit up. From here on…I'll handle it," *she abruptly disconnected the call.*

14

Chapter 1

Unfinished Business...

Brenda turned the streets of Newark with one goal in mind: death and a lot of it. She had sacrificed everything for the organization and the last things she was going to give up was Tyquan and the money. So many obstacles stood in her way for years, and it was time to move each and every one of them out of the way.

When she pulled up in front of Dutchess' house, she found a spot down the block to park, grabbed her gun, tucked it away and got out of her car. Brenda darted her eyes from one side of the street to other taking notice of the beautiful spring blossoms that were forming on the trees. Walking up to the porch filed her gut with flutters and her heart with agony and pain thinking about what all Dutchess could have revealed and how it would alter her plans.

Knocking lightly then a little harder, Brenda anticipated the look on Dutchess' face when their eyes met.

"Who?"

"Old friend," Benda yelled back.

Being naturally cautious, Dutchess moved to a small table next to the door, grabbed her .22 and gripped it tightly as she peeked out the curtain. When she saw the whites of Brenda's eyes, she cringed.

Pulling back from the window, Brenda tried to control her

breathing and gather some composure. She tucked the gun in the pocket of her lose-fitting pants and cracked the door. "Brenda?"

Brenda forced a smile. "Good Morning, Dutchess."

"What brings you to this neck of the woods?"

"Just thought I would stop by to check on an old friend."

"I don't have any old friends."

"Dutchess, I know we should have something left between us that warrants me being able to not have to stand on a porch and talk to you."

"There ain't shit between us; have a good day," Dutchess began to shut the door.

"I think there is KoKo between us," Brenda said, putting her hand out to catch the door before it closed.

Hearing KoKo's name made Dutchess' mouth fill with spit. "Don't come to me with that bitch on your tongue."

"Dutchess, please...I need answers," Brenda pleaded.

Dutchess thought for a few seconds. She too needed answers and maybe something would slip from Brenda's lips that would get her closer to her own revenge. "I will give you ten minutes and not a second longer," Dutchess firmly uttered, slowly pulling the door open.

Brenda stepped inside the foyer and eyed all the black art that adorned the walls. "Still pro black I see," she teased.

"You're working with nine minutes now; don't waste them licking my ass."

"You wish your ass was precious enough to feel my tongue,"

"Bitch, talk or leave," Dutchess grabbed the door knob.

"Look, I need to know what she came here for."

"Who told you she was here?" Dutchess asked with one brow raised.

"The same person who sent her here," she paused. "I know that she killed your son," Brenda announced, causing Dutchess to put her hand in her pocket closer to her heat.

"And that is your business how?"

"It's not. But we have a common interest and that is the death of her and that Kayson."

"I have no beef with Kayson. His wife, on the other hand, is at the top of my list. But since I don't trust you, you will have to work on her demise on your own," Dutchess stood firm.

"You don't trust me?" Brenda went into bitch mode. "You fucked my man…how the fuck could you let your mouth speak distrust against me?"

"If he was so much of your man why was he in my bed?" Brenda chuckled. "I don't know why I came here,"

"Me either, and your time is up."

"Just remember when they come for you, and oh…they will be coming, that I tried to help your sorry ass."

"Bitch, you trying to help yourself. You don't give a fuck about me and the feeling is mutual," Dutchess raised her voice and gripped the handle of her gun.

Brenda's nostrils flared as she gave her final warning. "I hope they kill you slow."

"I've been dying slow since the day I met all you bitches and the regret is the grave I live in daily. But I promise you this: the only hand that will deal my fate is my own. Good bye," she grabbed the door and pulled it open.

Brenda looked Dutchess up and down, and then turned her lips up. "Crazy bitch."

"And you're an evil one,"

Brenda grabbed her gun and slammed the door. Dutchess was not slow to the draw as she pulled hers.

Both women stood only inches away from each other with something hot at the other end of an unforgiving hand.

"I fucking hate you," Brenda yelled as she caressed the trigger with her finger.

"Don't be no punk, bitch…squeeze!" Dutchess yelled.

"I always hated your slippery tongue," Brenda spat with her arm fully extended.

"Your man always loved it; another one of my gifts that kept him cumming," Dutchess hurled back.

"This time you get a pass. But the next time, blood will spill."

"No time like the present," Dutchess growled.

Brenda thought about what was at stake and knew that if she pulled the trigger she would not make it to see KoKo suffer, which was the only thing that pumped blood through her veins. Slowly, she lowered her gun; a deadly mistake, but somebody had to be the first. "Stay out my way."

"You haven't crossed my mind in twenty years, but if you cross my path again, I won't be merciful," Dutchess spoke firm and held her gun even firmer.

Brenda grabbed the door knob, keeping a locked eye with Dutchess. Pulling it open enough to exit, she spoke the last words she would ever speak to Dutchess.

"When all this shit comes out and your rat ass is at the other end of Kayson's rage, remember that only a treacherous bitch is worthy of the grave he will put you in."

"Well, when he finishes with you, send him over here so he can be in the presence of a real bitch because your scandalous ass ain't worth his bullets," Dutchess spat, then slammed the door damn near hitting Brenda in the face.

Dutchess quickly moved back just in case Brenda wanted to strip some wood from the door. She watched as Brenda hurried down the street back to her car.

Brenda jumped in her car and grabbed her phone. "It's done."

"Was she angry?"

"Very. Make your move, she's off her square."

"Good. Bring all that heat to me, I need it."

"I'm on my way."

6 months later...

Brenda slowly moved Tyquan's arm from her waist and eased off the bed. The anxiety of having Kayson and KoKo out there and not knowing if they were hunting her, like she was hunting them, had begun to take a toll on her spirit. Even in her sleep there was no peace. She walked into the bathroom to take a look in the mirror to see just how much the stress was affecting her appearance. As she turned her head from side to side, a smile came across her face.

"Bitch, you ain't got shit to worry about," she said aloud, admiring her well maintained 5'5", 125 pound figure, chocolate brown skin, and sultry eyes; then she ran her finger along the bridge of her keen nose and full brown lips. At the age of fifty-two, she looked better than most twenty-year olds.

Brenda ran some water over her face, pulled her hair back into a ponytail and headed to the living room in her thong and tight t-shirt. She grabbed the remote and opened the blinds; they parted and slid across the floor-to-ceiling windows before settling in separate corners of the room.

Brenda grabbed a bottle of water from the refrigerator, put on her sneakers, and then climbed onto the treadmill and turned it on high speed. She looked out over the city as she ran; her mind busied itself with thoughts of money, power and revenge. The more she fantasized, the faster she ran. Sweat drizzled down her body as if she was cleansing herself of any feelings of love or regret. She needed to feel only pain and heartache with the only goal in mind…her enemies' heads as trophies on her shelf.

CHAPTER 2

TIME'S UP

KoKo laid the baby in her playpen and moved to the kitchen counter to place her call. As she dialed the numbers, her well-calculated plan played in her mind.

"Hello," Goldie answered as she walked around her living room rocking little Jarod in her arms.

"I see they finally sat our asses down," KoKo said, cracking a smile as she rested her body against the counter.

"Hell yeah, got my ass on double house arrest. I need more than Calgon to take me away," Goldie said as she continued to rock a cranky, teething baby.

"You feel like getting out and playing for a little while?"

"Hell yeah," Goldie bubbled up with excitement.

"I'ma send Bas to get you."

"A bitch will be on the curb," she joked.

"See you in a few days," KoKo disconnected the call.

When she hung up, she immediately called Baseem. "What it do, play boy?"

"Sheeeit...you know me, making these niggas pockets depressed," Baseem said as he kicked his feet up on the coffee table and released smoke from his lungs.

KoKo got quiet.

"Why you get quiet, you jelly because daddy won't let you out to play?"

"Kayson got two kids and I'm not one of them," she said, moving to the window and looking at the sun dancing on the crystal clear pool water.

"That's what your mouth say."

"Whatever, nigga. I need you to go get Goldie."

Now it was Baseem's turn to get quiet. After a brief silence he spoke clear words. "Do Kay know?"

"What the fuck am I...five? Just take care of it for me," she stated firmly.

"Don't get in no shit, and most importantly...don't get me in no shit,"

"Love you too," she disconnected the call, placing the phone on the counter before staring out the window for a few seconds. When she turned around, Kayson was standing right behind her, causing KoKo to jump.

"What was that about and why yo ass so jumpy?"

"Why you always sneaking up on me?" she quickly moved to where he was standing and hugged him tightly, kissing him softly on the lips, then slipping her tongue into his mouth. Kayson squeezed her tightly, enjoying her tongue play. When she pulled back, his mouth was happy and his dick was hard.

"Don't try to distract me with all this ass and titties," he said, gripping her firmly in his hands. "Why you sending Bas for Goldie?"

"I miss her and the baby and we haven't seen them in a while," she stated, kissing him again, and then pulling back from his embrace.

"Don't get fucked up," he smacked her ass as she moved toward the sink.

"I have been a very good girl," she replied, rinsing off Quran's lunch dishes.

Kayson moved to the sink, coming up behind KoKo and wrapping his arms around her. KoKo continued to wash the dishes as she could feel the heat coming off of Kayson's frame.

"I need you to be more than good," he gently warned.

KoKo looked forward, not wanting to say anything that would reveal her hand. Lying to him was impossible, but the truth could be deadly.

"Baby, I would never do anything to harm our family," she stated in an attempt to soften his mood.

"Turn around," he ordered.

Reluctantly, she turned and looked up in his eyes.

"I'm not asking you. I'm telling you. Don't get caught up in this war. I have done everything in my power to keep you and the kids safe. Behave yourself," he gave her an intense stare through his hazel eyes.

"I promise," she said, trying to even convince herself.

Kayson just raised his eyebrow at that statement. He knew his wife well. The children had gotten older and her thirst for revenge was getting stronger. It was only a matter of time before she was going to get away and get her feet back in the streets.

Kayson held their gaze for a few more seconds. "Yeah, a'ight. Call Mariam up here to look after the children and come upstairs and give the Enforcer a long, wet conversation," he said, then kissed her lips.

"You are so spoiled," she responded, giving him a smile.

"I am supposed to be. Let's go." He tapped her butt and walked off.

When Kayson walked out the kitchen, KoKo dropped the smile from her face. She knew that she was about to do the total opposite of what he had just asked and she could only pray that he would find it in his heart to forgive her.

CHAPTER 3

DEADLY REIGN

"Hold that nigga up," Baseem ordered Pete and Chucky.

They each pulled at one side of the man's body in effort to keep him steady on his knees.

"Baseem, please…" Mo pleaded, looking up at him with sweat running down his face. He twisted his wrist in the tight restraints that held his arms behind his back.

"Nigga, you tried to fuck me," Baseem flat out accused, tilting his head slightly to the side.

"Nah, I swear on my kids yo. I ain't do it. I have always been loyal to you and Kayson," he tried to plead his case.

"Shut the fuck up!" Baseem yelled, causing his voice to echo around the empty room.

As Baseem moved closer to Mo, the intensity of his anger poured from his spirit as his shadow danced on the walls in the dimly lit room.

"Baseem, I swear. I didn't cross you," Mo said one more time as urine began to seep through his clothes. He looked down at the sharp knife tightly gripped in Baseem's hand; tears rolled down his cheeks and all he could do was pray.

"I can respect a cheat, may even have love for a gullible ass nigga, but a snake…all I can give him is death."

Mo had made a grave mistake. He had crawled in the bed with one of Baseem's sexy, but deadly, informants and then his tongue got slippery. Baseem tilted Mo's head back as he stared down into his frightful eyes.

"You of all people should have known better; when you climb up in some deadly pussy, the only thing you're supposed to do is moan. Not snitch!" Baseem said with his teeth gritted tight.

Without hesitation, Baseem began stabbing Mo in the throat repeatedly. Blood poured from his veins as flesh tore from his neck. Baseem released Mo's head and it bobbled to the side. Pete and Chucky released his arms, causing his body to slam to the floor in a puddle of blood.

"Damn, nigga...you got blood everywhere. Nigga got on his good shit," Pete said looking down at his bloody clothes.

"I had to stab that nigga in his throat; maybe in the hereafter, he will learn how to shut the fuck up. Let's clean this piece of shit up. I got a trip to make."

Chucky and Pete pulled out two huge butcher knives and began to dismember Mo's body; limb by limb.

Baseem turned to the exit. He had another mission to complete; Goldie. As he got in his car he said aloud, "One down, many to go," he started his engine plotting his next kill. He and Kayson were on a mission. Kayson was working from the top and Baseem was working from the bottom. They were going to run the rat into the middle where he would have no other choice but to reveal himself. The only fear they both had was KoKo, and if her search would get in their way. The last thing they wanted was for KoKo to end up at the wrong end of their deadly reign.

CHAPTER 4

SNEAKY

Baseem drove in silence from the airport to KoKo and Kayson's house. The sun was beaming and the feeling of tranquility came over him as he passed all the colorful flowers and tall palm trees. Every time he visited them, he could feel the calm that KoKo always described as orgasmic.

As he passed the many crowds of people in the market place, he occasionally glanced in the rearview mirror at Goldie and the baby. He had to admit, she was beautiful; all the baby weight was gone and her pretty smile gave him a sense of comfort. Goldie's dreads were neatly twisted and pulled back into a bun and her soft golden brown skin was flawless. He could definitely see why Night had snatched her up.

Baseem drove up into the hills to Kayson's hideaway thinking about what he and Kayson had planned and he wondered what KoKo and Goldie were up to. Pulling to the gate, he had to admire the setup. The walls around the small compound where at least fifteen feet high. Security was out the ass; gun men and cameras everywhere, Kayson had it all covered. Baseem entered the gate and pulled to the door.

Stepping out the car, he looked up and took in some sun. He popped the trunk and sat the bags on the ground, then headed to the back door to assist Goldie with the baby. When he opened the door and looked at little Jarod, his heart thumped because all he saw was Night.

"Can you take this for me?" Goldie asked, passing him her bag.

Baseem took her bag and moved to the side allowing her to exit the car. Goldie clutched Jarod in her arms and headed up the walkway.

Baseem watched the perfect jiggle of her ass as she walked. He just shook his head as he refocused is vision. Goldie positioned herself at the door so she could see KoKo first. It had been months, and she needed this vacation bad; but she knew her Boss and that KoKo most definitely had some shit on the burner. She was ready to execute a well-calculated plan.

When KoKo heard the bell, she placed little Malika in her chair and headed to the door. When she opened it, Goldie was smiling big with her handsome chocolate bundle in her arms.

"Damn, you look good; let me find out that Cali air got a bitch glowing," KoKo said, opening the door wide for them to pass. "Look at this little chocolate drop," KoKo squeezed the baby's cheeks.

"Girl, I be chillin'...smoking that ohhh wee," Goldie said, giving KoKo a half hug. "Plus, you know Wadoo won't let us out of his sight."

"Shit, I know that's right, he has specific orders," KoKo let go of Goldie and shot her eyes at Baseem. "Why yo face always tight?" KoKo asked as he passed her.

"'Cause I smell some bullshit in the air."

"Boy, shut up. Ain't nobody doing shit."

"Yeah, a'ight," he responded, walking to the seating area and placing Goldie's bag beside the couch. "Where is Kay?"

"He's downstairs in his hideout. Can you send Quran upstairs when you get down there, its lunch time," KoKo said, looking at her watch. "And stop acting like somebody trying to do something to you," she shot him a side-eye.

"It's not me I'm worried about. Don't make my brother fuck you up," Baseem walked off headed downstairs.

"Ain't nobody scared of Kayson," KoKo called out as she heard the door shutting.

"Where would you like these, Ms. KoKo?" her butler asked, holding the two duffle bags he had retrieved from outside.

"You can put them upstairs in the guest room at the end of the hall," KoKo instructed. As the butler moved up the steps with the bags, she waved at Goldie to follow her.

As Goldie walked into the large, all white living room she began, "You know they gonna be all over us, KoKo," Goldie took a seat on the couch.

"Well, they better get real close because I'm about to act the fuck up," KoKo stated as she entered the living room.

"That's why I fucks with you," Goldie chuckled.

"We gotta go up to my little hideout. I am sure the ears are pressed to the door," KoKo walked to the intercom and summoned Mariam to the main floor to look after the children.

Within seconds, Mariam came from one direction and little Quran ran from the other. "Mom you wanted me?" he asked, running past her and straight to Goldie, taking the baby's hand in his and shaking it back and forth.

"Yes, you need to eat," she raised her eyebrow.

"I'm not hungry. I want to go back downstairs with daddy."

"No. He is taking care of business," KoKo spoke firm.

"So was I," he said, turning in her direction and giving her the same intense stare Kayson gave when he wasn't playing.

KoKo locked eyes with him and tilted her head to the side. "You better do something with those eyes," she ordered.

After a few seconds, he blinked back his gaze and turned back to the baby. KoKo had been having a few problems with him and his small attitude. What he didn't realize was that his mother was a crazy bitch and was being very patient with him. But KoKo saw that she was going to have to get him straight because what she was not going to have was a man child putting his foot in her ass.

KoKo held her glare in his direction, then turned to Mariam and gave her instructions for both babies and Quran while she and Goldie headed upstairs to her bedroom.

"If I ask you again, there will be more than a problem," KoKo said as her eyes pierced the side of his little face.

Quran looked up into KoKo's unwavering eyes, and then moved toward Mariam, keeping his lips pulled tightly together.

"I have it, Mrs. KoKo," Mariam assured as she took Jarod from

29

Goldie's arms.

Goldie smirked as she watched Quran walk off full of attitude. "He is his father's child," Goldie said, rising to her feet.

"Yup and just like his father, I'ma have to show him who's the boss. Let's go blow these trees," KoKo said as she walked off shaking her head.

* * * * *

Baseem sat comfortable in a thick, suede lounge chair sipping his drink and pulling on a blunt. Kayson was seated across from him stroking his chin as he processed the information that Baseem just gave him about the new crew in New York and Jersey and the new connect. Shit was tight, and with their absence, the young boys were getting out of hand causing Chucky and Pete to lay a few niggas down; bringing unwanted heat on the trap spots.

"Sounds like to me, I need to take a trip," he smoothly stated, staring at Baseem.

"You know me, Kay…I'm ready to put some niggas on they ass," he pulled hard on his blunt.

"I had the feeling that my presence was needed. I was trying to let these niggas earn their titles, but with me and KoKo off the scene, niggas comfortable," he stated smoothly as he began to devise a plan.

Baseem nodded his head. "Whatever you want to do, I'm down," he took another deep inhale. "I see your wife got some shit brewing," he chuckled taking his drink to his mouth.

"Yeah, her ass thinks she slick. I'ma let her wet her feet a little. You know KoKo is the toughest nigga in the crew," Kayson cracked a semi smile.

"Yeah, we just gotta make sure she put her nose in the place that don't have her in our shit."

"Don't worry; I got enough stuff lingering to keep her busy. And you know me; I can always find some shit to throw her off my scent," Kayson stated with confidence.

Baseem just sat back and pulled the thick smoke into his lungs, he had a new energy flowing through his veins. He was ready to reclaim the streets and putting niggas on they ass was at the top of his list.

* * * * *

Goldie and KoKo were sitting on the floor in the walk-in-closet smoking a blunt like two high school girls cutting class.

"So, what's up, Boss?" Goldie asked, taking some deep pulls.

"I got to get back to the A and straighten shit out, and then we gotta go to New York and restructure. I heard that the crew is getting a little out of control. Last, I gotta find out who is behind all my demons. I will never be able to rest until I get all my questions answered," KoKo said taking the blunt from Goldie's hand.

"I understand. I feel the same way. So, what you got planned?" Goldie asked, rubbing her hands together.

"I got a crew of bad ass bitches that are ready to make a nigga bend and fold," KoKo said, squinting her eyes.

CHAPTER 5

FIRST ENCOUNTER

"I need you to make sure my money is doing what it is supposed to be doing," Baseem stated, giving Steven a firm eye.

"I got you. I have to make sure we cover our asses," Steven tried to reassure him.

"I pay you enough money to make sure my ass and every fucking thing else is covered," Baseem's voice rose slightly, catching the attention and glares of a few people in ear shot.

"Let's go upstairs and talk numbers," Steven looked around the huge lobby as his colleagues began to fill back in after lunch. Baseem's voice had already alerted the woman at the desk and the security at the check point.

Baseem stared at Steven for a few more minutes and then agreed to go with him. They moved to the elevator and hit the up button and waited. Just as they were about to step inside, a woman flew out the doors running right into Baseem, sending her files flying into the air and scattering all over the floor.

"Damn," she mumbled as she kneeled down to collect her paperwork.

"My bad, ma," Baseem bent down to help her.

"No, it's my fault," she said, not looking up as she snatched at the paperwork. She was running late and small talk would only hold her up.

"You always starting trouble," Steven accused as he stood back

33

in his charcoal brown Armani suit, watching the two of them scramble to retrieve the documents.

"Oh shut up," Simone hurled at Steven. He was her biggest competition at the firm and had a way of rubbing her more than the wrong way.

"Clumsy ass," Steven mumbled as he straightened his tie.

Once all the papers were back in her hands, she looked up and met eyes with the man that she had almost knocked down. When he shot her a pretty warm smile, her heart jumped.

"Do you make a habit of knocking people down?" Baseem asked smoothly as he rose to his feet, extending his hand.

Simone was lost for words as his comforting voice settled against her eardrum. She put her hand in his, allowing him to pull her up.

"No, I was running a little late," she said, trying to settle her breathing and collect her thoughts.

Baseem looked at the small amount of cleavage that showed off her soft breast. Her light brown hair draped the sides of her face accenting her brown eyes and soft pouty lips. His eyes moved over her curves that were perfectly pronounced in her dark grey pencil skirt.

"I guess it was my fault," he proclaimed, bringing his gaze back to hers.

"Maybe we should just both watch where we are going," she slightly flirted.

They stood in an eye lock, caught up in each other's smiles until Steven cut in. "Excuse me, but we gotta go," he announced as he held the elevator doors open and stepped inside. "You can holla at Mrs. Stuck up later," he said, holding his finger on the open door button.

Simone dropped her smile and shot a hard stare at Steven. "I hope you blow up," she hurled in his direction, and then began to walk off. "Thank you and enjoy your day," she coldly said to Baseem putting pep to her step.

"Can I ask your name?" Baseem yelled out as she put more distance between them.

Simone kept moving, turning the corner headed to her

destination.

"Damn, why you blocking nigga?" Baseem asked as he stepped on the elevator.

"You don't want to fuck with that stuck up bitch. She evil as hell," Steven spat as he recounted in his head the many times he tried to mess with her and she damn near spit in his face.

"Fuck what you heard. Evil pussy taste like sugar," Baseem spat with a smirk on his face.

"Well, her evil ass must be diabetic sweet," Steven said as they exited the elevator.

"Let me warn you. I don't give a fuck about none of this fancy suit and upscale building shit. If you fuck with my money, I will blow your fucking head off," Baseem said as he locked eyes with Steven.

"You can go in conference room one while I grab your profile," Steven swallowed his spit hard as Baseem's words echoed in his mind.

"Yeah, you do that," Baseem said as he walked off headed to the first glass-enclosed room. His mind was focused on his money, but his dick was tapping his zipper reminding him of how good the mysterious woman's ass looked as she walked away. Baseem didn't give a fuck what Steven said, he was going to make sure he snatched her up first chance he got.

NeNe Capri

CHAPTER 6

THE COUNCIL

KoKo stood by her candy apple red Mercedes watching as the two cars she waited for pulled on to the private airport blacktop heading in her direction. She had a foolproof plan and was about to kick it into full effect. As the cars came to a stop, a slight smile turned up at the side of her mouth. Each driver moved to open the door to release KoKo's deadly council.

Goldie jumped out the back seat grabbing her purse, and then she threw on her shades. Her golden dreads were twisted back neatly into a bun. She stepped hard toward KoKo in her white skin-tight jeans with her booty bouncing just right with every step as her heels clicked against the pavement. Goldie glanced over at the other vehicle and watched as the females exited one by one. She took note of their appearance from head to toe. Wordrobe was on point hair and skin flawless and curves that made a man wanna answer questions he wasn't asked. Goldie nodded her approval. They looked prepared for the occasion, but she still wondered who these new bitches were, and what the boss had up her sleeve.

"What's up, Boss?" Goldie asked, giving KoKo a smile and then taking her position next to her.

"We about to find out," KoKo responded, keeping her eyes on the newbies.

Both women moved from the vehicles dressed in all white as requested, with a small overnight bag over their shoulder; exuding the same strength and confidence as Goldie. Just like her, they took no shit and were prepared to put a nigga on their ass if he breathed wrong. Neither woman spoke a word as they approached, focused on their mission.

"What it do, KoKo?" Adreena asked, stopping a few feet way.

"I'm on your time, you tell me!" KoKo shot back.

"What's up little mama you ready for my big world?" KoKo asked Breonni, looking her over.

"Does a dick love to go deep?" Breonni shot back.

KoKo smiled at Breonni's slick tongue; for the first time, she had a replica of herself. "That's why I fucks with you," KoKo said then turned to the steps leading up to the plan.

"Ladies this is Goldie. Goldie this is Breonni and Adreena." The ladies shook hands and exchanged a few words. "Let's board," KoKo said turing to the steps.

The woman filed a single line and followed her onto the private jet.

KoKo took her seat; Goldie and Adreena placed their bags down and took seats across from her and buckled up. Breonni looked around at the interior and was mesmerized as her bag slid slowly to the floor. Everything seemed to bling. The soft, tan leather looked like butter and the shiny silver that draped over the arms sparkled. She had flown many times, but being on KoKo's private jet make her feel like a celebrity. Breonni took the seat next to KoKo, fastened her seat belt and prepared her mind for takeoff.

When the plan was at the proper height, the seat belt sign was turned off; and as if on cue, the flight attendant brought them each a tall glass of white wine, and then sat a black marble ashtray with a small golden box on the table next to KoKo.

"Thank you and we won't be needing anything else," KoKo looked up into the flight attendant's eyes.

"Yes, ma'am," she nodded and walked off, closing the cabin door behind her.

KoKo looked over her shoulder, waiting a few moments before she began.

"Now that I finally have us all together, let's take this shit up a notch," KoKo announced, bringing her drink to her lips. After taking a few sips, she sat it down, opened the box next to her, grabbed a blunt and lit up.

"The first order of business is to keep my business in your head and never let it slip from your tongue," she spoke firm, releasing a thick stream off smoke from her mouth. "Remember, if a muthafucka turns the tables on you, you better kill yourself before you turn on me because I don't know mercy. But that bitch, murder…she is my best friend," KoKo looked in the eyes of each woman for weakness or doubt.

"I fucks with you the long way. I am tried and tested. You all I got," Goldie locked eyes with KoKo to show her sincerity and allegiance. She had reservations about the other two bitches; but she knew, without a doubt, that KoKo had her back and for that she was ready to give her life for her.

KoKo picked up on Goldie's insecurity and addressed it immediately. "Goldie, questioning your loyalty was never my intent. Yes, Adreena and Breonni are new to the team and they too have been tried and tested. And make no mistake, each person that I have chosen, I didn't do it with my heart. I chose each of you because you are best for the job," she paused and relit the blunt. "Goldie, yeah, you are official and together we can kill a few muthafuckas; but we can kill a whole lot more if they can't see which one of us deadly bitches has the gun."

"Salute," Goldie said as she raised her glass.

Breonni and Adreena raised theirs in agreement. KoKo raised her glass last and smiled before giving her final warning. "Death is the only thing guaranteed when you play with the big dogs. Be careful."

They brought their glasses to the center, and then threw the drink to the back of their throat. "I can't wait for y'all to meet Lu; that nigga crazy," KoKo chuckled, then passed the blunt.

"Who is Lu?" Breonni asked, reaching over for the pass.

"My secret weapon," KoKo sat back, crossed her legs and smiled as she saw her plan coming into full play.

NeNe Capri

CHAPTER 7

DUTCHESS

"Come see me," the oh-so-familiar voice boomed into Dutchess' ear.

"For what? Whatever you can say to me could be done with this phone call," Pashion applied lotion to her hands as she tried to calm her mood.

Dutchess paused and gagged the silence.

"Just meet me at our usual spot; seven o'clock sharp, not a minute after," the woman gently warned.

"Pashion, you clearly have not learned who I am after all these years. I don't bend to threa—"

"They know," Pashion cut her off from her rant.

Dutchess sat silent as Pashion's words moved through her mind and a slight chill eased up her back.

"Seven o'clock sharp," Pashion said, then disconnected the call.

Dutchess stood still for a minute before placing her cell phone on the kitchen counter. She took her cup of tea in her hands and sipped slow as she put together a plan. She knew that this day would come, but looking it in the face caused the heat to slowly drain from her body.

Dutchess placed her cup in the sink, turned on her heels and then went into action. She grabbed some sheets from the hallway closet, covered the furniture, and then hit her safe; grabbing passports and documents. Dutchess moved around pulling out draws and gathering her jewelry. She then went through the pockets of a few jackets in her hallway closet, pulling out small rolls of money and stuffing them in a small black attaché case. Once she had her money tucked away, she grabbed a few items of clothing and packed them in a medium travel case and headed to the back door.

Dutchess sat her bags at her feet, reached in her pocket to release the safety on her gun, gripped it tight in one hand and released the latch on the door with the other. She took a firm look around then grabbed her bags and moved down the concrete walkway and to her car. When she pulled out the drive way she was on a mission. Everything had gone full circle and KoKo's mercy on Dutchess was either going to be a blessing or a curse. She had no idea if KoKo would come back and this time be ready to take her life. Either way, she was going to be prepared and she damn sure was not going to let them strike first.

Dutchess pulled into Pashion's driveway then quickly moved to the front door. She rang the bell then tucked her hand in her pocket, gripping the butt of her gun. The locks clicked and the door sprung open. Dutchess hesitated; looking into the opening with caution. When Pashion showed her face from behind the door, Dutchess forced a slight smile then proceeded inside.

Pashion closed the door hard, causing Dutchess to jump. "Don't worry, I would not have invited you to my home if there was danger in sight," Pashion made clear her intent. She walked into a small office off from her foyer and walked around her desk then poured herself a drink.

"I'm not worried. I'm just curious as to why you would try to help me," Dutchess went right to the point. She stood eyeing the many diplomas and certificates along with family photos on the walls as she tried to figure out Pashion's angle.

"If you know anything about me, then you should know I am not trying to help you. In fact, I cannot stand you," Pashion also went straight to the point.

"Then we can end this shit right now!" Dutchess turned to walk away.

"If you walk out that door, you are going to lose more than you're willing to sacrifice," Pashion said as she took a seat at her desk.

Dutchess stood still for a few seconds then turned back in Pashion's direction. Her eyes roamed over Pashion's brown face; her smug grin and squinted eyes let her know it was some bullshit in the game and she was not in the mood to play any games.

"What do you know?"

"It's not what I know that is important. It's what they know," Pashion brought a cigarette to her lips, lit it up then pulled deep. "Please. Have a seat," she directed.

Dutchess moved to the soft yellow chair and perched her small frame on the edge.

"Speak."

"Five-hundred thousand," Pashion spat, taking another pull on her cigarette. The ashes fell to the desk and with a swat of her hand, she blew them to the floor while holding a firm eye with Dutchess.

"I haven't seen you in twenty years. Have not spoken to you in over fifteen, and with a straight face you have the guts to try and stick your hands in my pocket," Dutchess rose to her feet. "Bitch, fuck you and them! And don't contact me anymore," she turned to the door.

As Dutchess gripped the knob and turned the lock, she heard the heat blow out of Pashion's mouth. "They know who your other son is, you already lost one."

Dutchess released the door knob and headed back toward Pashion.

"I thought so. Now I am the only one who can help you," Pashion paused and sipped her drink.

Dutchess cracked a smile then went in. "Unlike the rest of you bitches...I know what this is. My sons have me running through their veins; so if they have to die for what they believe in, then that choice is theirs. You are the dirtiest woman I have ever met; and when the shit hit's the fan, I pray it fly's right in your face." Dutchess headed out this time with no intent on returning.

43

As the door began to close, Dutchess yelled back, "Remember you have kids too!" she slammed the door tight and began to sprint to her car.

Pashion sprang to her feet and ran to the door. She pulled it wide, only to catch the tail lights of Dutchess' car. "Shit," she hurled as she slammed the door.

She thought that by now, Dutchess would be ready to fold; but her swiftness to deliver a deadly blow might turn out to be the shovel that would dig her own grave. Pashion turned over her plan in her mind, then she thought about her own son who was tied up in the web of deception that they had all carefully weaved before the children were born. Now, each child's life was dangling in the balance with all of them living on borrowed time.

CHAPTER 8

SECRET WEAPON

KoKo and her team rode in the back of the limo in silence; their eyes danced over and beyond the vast fields. The land stretched its arms out into the horizon as the glow of the sun began to soften over the fields of corn and grass. Each woman had an idea, but didn't really know how their lives were about to change. KoKo had been plotting her plan for years and she finally had all the pieces she needed. And even though she had been warned many times over the years to let it go, she could not rest until every hand involved in her parents' death paid with their life.

"Where the hell we at?" Adreena spoke, seizing every ones attention.

"We in 'The Hills Have Eyes' territory; this where them psychos eat a nigga for dinner mufuckas be camped out at," Breonni chimed in.

"Oh shit, are the doors locked? I hope it's enough gas in this bitch," Goldie looked in their eyes. "Bullshit if you want to, I'm about to pull out my mace," she reached for her bag.

They all stared back at her going through her purse and busted into laughter.

"Them crazy muthafuckas drink that shit for breakfast. They come up in here, we gonna put something hot in they ass!" KoKo pulled out her diamond handle Tiffany & CO. and turned it back and forth in her hand. "You can spray that mace on them for good measure."

"Oh shit," Adreena put her fist out to Bre.

Breonni shook her head and looked back out into the distance.

They laughed and chopped it up as the limo pushed on to its destination. Within an hour, the car was pulling up to a log cabin surrounded with beautiful willow trees and assorted landscapes of flowers. The driver jumped out, opening the doors for the ladies. KoKo stepped out first, then each woman took her turn.

Breonni settled her gaze on some deer antlers that were affixed to a nearby tree. Her nose flared as she thought about the head they once rested on. "Who the fuck kills Bambi," she mumbled.

KoKo turned slightly to give her a raised eyebrow.

Breonni nodded then put the silencer on her lips.

Adreena looked around as the feelings of uncertainty moved through her gut.

The door came open and a big white guy began to wave them over. Goldie eyed his red lumberjack shirt with no sleeves, off black jeans and cowboy boots then chuckled.

KoKo gave her the eyes then turned to walk up the steps.

When the door shut tightly behind them, the man walked past them and toward the back of the cabin. KoKo took in the warm feelings of the room. She enjoyed the smell of the fresh cut wood and lavender candles. She smiled at a memory she held dear of her and Kayson having one of their getaways up there, and how the big, soft furniture always made you feel at home. Breonni admired the modern and country mix of earth tones that set off the décor. She could tell this nigga, Lu, was situated.

"Why are you standing in the middle of my floor like we don't share the same man?" Lu came walking from the back with her long, light brown hair blowing with every stride. She walked over to KoKo and opened her arms.

"You know I don't do all this mushy shit," KoKo said as Lu put her arms around her.

"Oh please, you know your ass is a big old softy. And how is the Boss?" Lu said as she let her go.

"You better stop trying to get with my man too," KoKo joked.

"You know I love me some Kayson, but his swag can't match my Bull," she twisted her lips.

"You crazy as hell," KoKo said as she took a seat in the high-backed lounge chair.

"We'll fight over men later; let me get to know the girls," Lu turned her attention to the ladies. "Welcome to my home, make yourselves comfortable. You want something to drink?"

"I do," Breonni said, taking a seat on the matching couch across from KoKo.

"No, thank you," Goldie and Adreena said in unison then took a seat on the side of Bre.

"I know what you want, KoKo," she walked off into the open kitchen, poured Bre some sprit, and gin and grabbed a small brown box and a bottle of water.

Goldie and Adreena looked over at each other and shrugged. Everything had just changed, KoKo was planning on attacking these niggas from all sides.

"Okay, let's get it cracking," Lu passed out the drinks then opened the box, pulled out a long, fat blunt and passed it to KoKo. A smile hugged the corner of KoKo's mouth as she reached out and took it from her hand. Lu put fire to the end and sat back as KoKo took a deep inhale.

"Alright…when we leave this room, everything that is said stays in this room," she paused, knocked off the ashes and continued. "This shit right here that we are about to get into needs to be handled with caution and extreme suspicion. Anybody could be your enemy. I've seen muthafuckas turn on themselves in tight situations."

KoKo passed the blunt to Goldie.

"If your heart ain't in this get out now, because I don't do cross. I will not be merciful to a trader." She locked gazes with each woman to make sure they got the point.

"KoKo, you know that you have my loyalty. And if they are an enemy of yours, then they are an enemy of mine," Goldie also looked each woman in the eye.

Meeting the team for the first time, Lu took in each woman's character. Breonni…well, Lu felt that she could feel her pain and a life time of betrayal. Adrenna seemed like a problem child who had ran away to be in the circus and ran into a bad bitch named KoKo. Goldie's personality held a tone of emptiness and there was a

47

darkness behind her eyes; it was the kind of blankness you get after really seeing death. She knew KoKo had some real woman on her team that had lost parts of themselves; parts that would allow them to kill without prejudice or remorse.

Each woman was also checking Lu out. She was a little white woman with a whole lot of spunk and judging from her attitude, she was ready to lay a nigga in the dirt at a blink of an eye.

"Everybody down?" KoKo asked for the last time.

"You already know," Goldie answered and everyone else nodded in agreement.

From this point on, the plan was in full motion and there were two options: succeed or die.

CHAPTER 9

TAKE IT FROM THE TOP

Simone sat comfortably at her table sipping herbal tea and reading the stock report. She turned the pages and money over in her head, jotting down notes to share with her clients.

"Hey, beautiful," Baseem said in her ear, causing her to jump and spill her tea as she tried to place it down on the saucer.

"Why would you do that?" she asked, dropping her paper and clutching at her chest.

"My bad, beautiful. I didn't mean to scare you," he waved over the waitress who quickly moved to them and wiped up the spill and refilled her cup.

"Why are you here?" she tried to compose herself.

"I needed to see your pretty face," Baseem said as he took a seat. "Why you always spilling things when you see me?" he joked, giving her a sexy smile.

Simone maintained a stiff face as she stared at the sexy persistent man sitting in front of her. "How did you find me?" she asked, crossing her hands in front of her.

"I have my ways," he sat forward. "I am a man that always gets what he wants."

Simone picked up her small recorder and it record. "Fire my assistant," she said then laid it back on the table twisting her lips in disgust.

"Don't be mad at her. She was just trying to help a desperate brother out."

"I bet she was, but I don't play mixing business with pleasure. I am very serious about my job."

"I know and you need to be more serious about your play time too," he looked down at the plumpness of her breast sitting up in her peach button up blouse.

"Um, hello," she waved his attention back to her face. "Real woman want to be taken seriously and my breast is not my serious part," she gave him a firm eye.

"I am looking forward to getting to meet all your parts," he flirted.

"What do you want from me? I am way out of your league we have nothing in common."

"Let me have a date and I can show you what we have in common," he went straight to the point.

"Sorry, but I don't date your kind," she took her cup by the handle and brought it to her lips.

"What is my kind? Young, confident, rich with a dick game that keeps a woman's panties wet even when I'm far, far away," Baseem spit that slick shit.

"Look I am not a quick bone and I don't date drug dealers."

"Damn," he sat back and grabbed his chest. "You just gonna label a man? What happen to innocent until proven guilty?"

"Whatever. I am about to eat and don't want your bullshit to spill all over my meal."

Simone responded, as the waitress came to the table with her spinach salad. "Will there be anything else?" the woman asked.

"No, that is it for now," Simone answered, looking over her plate.

"Anything for you, sir?"

"No. He is about to leave," Simone answered for him.

"What night can I pick you up?"

"You just don't quit?"

"Nope."

Simone looked at him for a few seconds then gave in. "Okay. I will have one lunch with you. Next week...Wednesday, here at one o'clock and be on time. After that you can go on to the next female that you want to try and conquer," she stated slickly as she took a folk full of salad to her mouth.

"I'll take it. See you then," he stood up peering down at her.

"Wait?" she asked with attitude.

"You are the sex as hell with that smart-assed mouth."

"I bet I am, have a good day."

"I will." Baseem reached in his pocket and dropped a few hundred on the table. "Enjoy your lunch," he walked off not allowing her to respond.

Simone smiled a little at his cockiness as she turned to watch him walk out the restaurant. Her heart raced thinking about being in his presence once again.

* * * * *

Breonni walked into the bike club and eyed the room looking for her mark. She moved toward the bar as her eyes danced over the crowd; just as she was about to order her drink, she spotted the man from the photograph. She placed her order and took it to the head before having another. Bre slammed a bill on the counter and headed to the pool tables.

Magic caught a glimpse of Bre from the corner of his eye then turned to weave through the crowd to get a better look.

Bre grabbed a stick and chalk and moved around the table, trying to lay down a bet with a few guys. When one accepted, it was on. The short, plumb man racked the balls and she broke em'; after calling her balls, she began to sink one after then next.

Magic got up and moved a little closer to watch her technique and the fact that she was tiny with pretty brown skin just the way he liked them was not hurting his investigation. Bre stood back and allowed the gentlemen to hit a few in, then she moved in for the kill; sinking her last three balls and the eight ball in the side pocket.

"Good game, you can leave my money right there so I can spank another rookie," she spat then waved the waitress over.

"Fuck you mean, rookie. Little girl, you out ya league, ma. I ain't paying you shit." Curt said and turned his back on Bre and began talking shit to some dudes who were sitting around watching the game.

Magic crossed his arms and watched to see how this was going to play itself out.

"You really think it is at all possible that you would be able to walk out that door without paying me my money?" Bre's chilling tone rested on his shoulder.

Curt turned around. "Bitch, I ain't giving you shit!" he hurled in her direction.

Bre went into her vest and pulled out her baby girl. "Say that hot shit one more time," she pulled one in the chamber and moved toward him.

"Bitch, is you crazy?" he put his hands up in an effort to get her to chill.

"That's two bitches; anything else you want to get off your chest?" she asked then squeezed one off hitting him in the shin.

"What the fuck is wrong with you?" he yelled out as he went down in pain.

The bartender drew his weapon and Bre posted up. The other guest in attendance moved to the side.

"Put that shit down," Smit yelled out from behind the bar.

"Fuck you," she hurled back, pointing her gun in his direction.

Magic had seen enough. "Relax Smit," He said as he walked toward her slowly, waving his hand at Smit to lower his weapon. "Let me take a minute to introduce myself. I'm the owner, my name is Magic. I'm sorry you have been inconvenienced. I assure you we can rectify this real chill like," he continued.

"This bitch ass nigga needs to pay his debt and apologize for his disrespect then we good," she lowered her weapon and rested it by her side.

"Fair enough," Magic said as he moved beside Curt. "How much do you owe her?" he gritted.

"Five large," Curt moaned out from the pain.

"Pay her!" he ordered.

Curt struggled to pull his money from his pocket; the pain from the open wound in his leg was sending burning sensations all throughout his body. He passed the money to Magic then threw up all over himself.

"Apologize," he barked at Curt snatching the money from his grip.

Curt looked up with venom in his eyes. He stared at Bre as if his eyes could shot lasers. He held his hand on his stomach as rage rose up in his gut. Apologize? I wanna spit in this bitch's face, he thought while trying to muster up the energy to part his lips and speak the words.

The music had stopped playing and every man stood still and watched with a cautious eye. Magic looked over at Bre then back at Curt. Then he pulled out his gun and blew Curt's head back as if Curt's silence toward him yelled kill me! "You took too long, muthafucka," Magic spoke through clenched teeth.

"Y'all clean this nigga up and get the fuck outta here!" he ordered then walked over to Bre.

The crowd scattered, moving about their task careful to not say or do anything to heat shit up. Bre held his gaze. She watched in her peripheral as everybody cleared out of the room, leaving her alone with Magic and the guy behind the bar. When she heard the doors lock, she took a slow, deep breath and embodied the character.

"Ya' nigga was a bitch," she smirked, tucking her gun back in the holster.

"Why you say that?" Magic asked, tucking his gun away as well.

Breonni took a minute and looked him over. His chocolate skin was smooth and when he smiled his teeth blinded a bitch. He was tall and slim and built to perfection in all the right places.

"First of all, he's a fucking cheat; second, he is a coward. He should have at least called me one more bitch on his way out," she leaned up against a nearby pool table and crossed her feet at the ankle then folded her arms over her chest.

Magic rested his eyes on the thickness of her hips and the pout of her light brown lips which caused him to lick his own.

"Is that what you think? He's a coward because he would rather die than apologize," he paused to let the rhetorical sink in.

Bre gave him the I'ma hold my ground stare, tipping her head slightly to the side.

"That man just saved your life," he stopped and let her take that in also. "If he would have apologized, I would have had to kill you," he moved a little closer. "There is no way I would have been

53

able to let you live knowing you took the heart of one of my soldiers," he searched her eyes. "Tonight he died because he hesitated on a command which lets me know he would fold. At any rate, you owe him a thank you," he softened his face by giving her a slight smile.

"Maaan…Fuck that nigga! He learned two lessons tonight: don't cheat, and don't hesitate. That's all he's getting from me."

Magic passed Bre her money. "I would like to apologize for his behavior. Please stay as my guest. You intrigue me; I would like to say some private things to you," Magic went into get em' mode. She had an attitude that was rare for a female and he wanted to test her gangsta.

Bre held a calm, firm appearance; but on the inside, her heart was jumping and her stomach was doing flips. She had gotten him to open the door and she was about to step right in.

"What makes you think I would give you more of my time?"

"Don't worry. I'ma make it worth your while. I want to hold on to you for a couple of days. No strings…just be my guest and let me enjoy that tongue," he walked over and took her by the hand.

"Won't your woman be looking for you?"

"You let me worry about that. Ain't nothing going to be between you and me but us. Come sit with me so I can talk to you," he pulled her to her feet and began leading her to a booth in the back of the club.

"I will have one drink with you and then I'm out," she slipped her hand from between his fingers.

"That's fair. Give me two hours, and if by then I don't convince you to give me some time, then I will let you go; we part as enemies," he extended his arm so she could slide in the booth first.

"Fair enough," Bre softened her mood as she slid into her seat.

Magic ordered a bottle of campaign and they sat and talked. He asked every question that he thought would trip her up, but she was on point. Breonni had learned from KoKo to say what was necessary and let them bate themselves. In that short period of time, she learned his strengths and his weaknesses. He had a strong team, but some may not respect him. Breonni already knew she would accept his offer, and he had just given her the bullets to put in the gun.

"So, what do you say?' he asked, pouring the last of the bottle between their two glasses.

"I will give you a few days of my time. Everything is on my terms and you will not be getting any pussy, so cross that shit off your list."

"Please believe me, pussy is given to me. I never have to take it. But I'm not trying to fuck you. I can fuck any bitch I want. I just want to hang out with you for a few days to see where your head is at," he stretched his legs out and parted her feet with his. "But before our time is up, you might have to let me taste it."

Bre moved her feet to close her legs.

"You would have to come up off of a real good time in order to even sniff at this pussy," she said softly.

"I can already smell it. It has a scent of, I need to be held down and fucked real good, but that is not my business," he threw up his hands in surrender.

"Oh shit, you ain't right," she laughed.

"See, we gonna have fun. Let's roll. I don't want to waste a minute of my time," he slid out the booth and reached for her hand.

Bre stood up and gave him the side-eye. "I better not end up on 'Return our Missing'."

"I got you. Quit acting like you scared. How you gonna be a killer and be scary?"

"You playin', I watch Lifetime."

Magic had to laugh. Her cute and tough attitude was what he was looking for. He was gonna hold onto her for a few days while his people ran her background, and if she was foul, she would be dead before they landed.

* * * * *

"Hello."

"You're late," Baseem looked down at his watch.

"I'm sorry Baseem, I can't make it. I have an emergency meeting. We had a company merger and several of my clients are going crazy worrying about their money," Simone moved papers from one folder to the next as she prepared for her meeting.

"Did you think about what I asked you last night?" he asked smoothly into the phone.

"Yes, I did," Simone blushed at the memory of how nasty Baseem spoke to her last night.

"And?"

"And my answer is still no," she said as she stacked her files and grabbed her thumb drive.

"I think I can change your mind," he got up from his seat at the restaurant and headed to the door.

"Well, that will have to wait until our scheduled evening call; I have to go. Talk to you later,"

"A'ight," Baseem disconnected the call then handed the valet his ticket. When his car came around, he jumped in and headed to Simone's office.

"Hold all my calls please. I have a meeting in a little over thirty minutes, I need to prepare," Simone said into the intercom as she sat in front of her computer and forwarded several emails to herself and checked her client's accounts and profiles. She tapped away at her keyboard looking back and forth at the clock.

"Ten minutes, Miss Bivings," her assistant's voice rang through the intercom.

"Okay," Simone replied then called her accountant to make sure all the figures where updated.

As she stood to gather her documents, she looked up to see Baseem walking into her office. Her eyes moved over his frame as he got closer to her desk.

"What are you doing here?" she mouthed as he moved closer.

"I came to collect on my investment," Baseem mouthed as he walked up on her turning her to face him. He stepped between her legs and parted her feet with his.

"Stop," she mouthed to Baseem. "Yes, Mr. Yates, I'm here. Yes, please send them to my assistant," she said as Baseem's hands roamed over her hips then squeezed her waist then he placed her up on the desk.

"Baseem, don't," she whispered, placing her free hand on top of his.

"Pay attention."

"Yes, I agree," she responded to Mr. Yates' statement while watching Baseem's hands slide up her inner thigh.

"I need to go," she tried to hurry her talkative business partner. When she heard him say one more thing, she thought that she would pass out.

Baseem reached up and grabbed at the string of her thong and pulled her panties down.

Simone gasped for air as she watched him rock up. She placed her hand firm into his chest and pushed him back.

Baseem grabbed her wrist and pulled her to the edge of the desk and pressed his heat against her throbbing clit.

Simone squirmed as he grinded, feeling the steam that was emitting from between her thighs. "You feel so good," he whispered as he released her wrist to feel the slippery liquid that began to drip from her lips. Baseem leaned in and kissed her collar bone.

"Baseem...don't," she rested her hand on his chest.

"Let this shit happen," he reached up and ran his hands through her hair then kissed her deep as his fingers searched for that special spot.

Simone received him into her mouth as she tried to concentrate on the man on the other end on the phone.

Baseem continued to heat her up. "You had a lot to say on the phone last night. You ain't bout that life," he teased as he continued.

The man on the other end continued to ramble, to which she could not pay attention as Baseem brought her to the edge of no return. Her breathing picked up and just as she was about to release, Baseem moved his hand and backed up.

Baseem tasted his fingers and shook his head. "You sweet as hell," he whispered.

Simone panted as she watched him move to the bathroom and close the door.

"I will call you back after the meeting," she cut the man off then hung up. Simone pulled her skirt down then covered her face with her hands.

Baseem emerged from the bathroom drying his hands and

smiling at the condition he had just put her in. "You good?" he asked, snatching her panties from the desk and sticking them in his back pocket.

"I can't believe you did that," She looked at him shaking her head.

"That was your fault. Don't talk shit and I won't have to test that shit," he leaned in and kissed her cheek.

"They are waiting for you, Miss. Bivings," Megan's voice boomed.

"They waiting on you," Baseem teased.

Simone grabbed her files a she tried to gather her thoughts. When she opened the door, there stood her boss and several clients with black suits and very serious faces.

"Are you ready, Miss. Bivings? We're waiting for you," Mr. Connors asked.

"Yes, sorry for the delay," she answered, feeling frazzled as she tugged at her skirt.

Baseem walked out of her office and looked each man over. Stevens' eyes almost busted out of his head when he saw him emerge from behind her.

"Mr. Baseem," Mr. Connors stuttered a little shocked at his presence.

"Good afternoon. I hope you are taking good care of my money."

"Yes, sir…we are on top of it all."

"Good. Have my accounts transferred to Miss. Bivings. I feel safer with her handling me," he looked over at Simone's blushing face.

"Right away, Mr. Baseem. Steven, have all the accounts transferred to Miss. Bivings and give her a full report after our meeting," he looked at Steven with a stern eye.

"Thank you, Miss. Bivings. I'll call you later for an update," Baseem said as he began to move pass the men. "Y'all enjoy the rest of the day," he looked in Steven's face and smiled at his surprise.

"You do the same, sir," Mr. Connors replied and all the men turned to watch Baseem walk away.

Steven's eyes lowered into a small slit as he looked down at the red lace panties tucked partially in Baseem's back pocket. Simone caught what everyone else was looking at, and her pretty brown face turned beet read.

"Are we ready, gentleman?" she tried to compose herself, and then walked off toward the conference room.

"I guess you better, 'step your game up' as they say on the streets," Mr. Connors joked.

Steven could feel his blood boil as the money he was making off of his golden goose slipped through his hands and fell in between Simone's legs.

NeNe Capri

Chapter 10

Thank you so much...

"I am so happy you're here," Goldie said as she closed the door behind Baseem.

"I had to come, you sound like you were about to jump from the ledge," he said moving smooth down the hallway.

"This damn Ikea furniture is for the birds. I done read the instructions forward and backwards."

"I got you ma," Baseem said, placing his tools on the floor and pulling his shirt off. Then he removed his watch and pinky ring. He stood in his t-shirt, staring at Goldie and waiting for her to lead the way.

Goldie's eyes moved all over the muscles in his chest and arms. She shook her head then turned toward the bedroom.

Baseem grabbed his black tool bag and followed her down the hall. He came up behind her and eyed the dimples in her lower back that peeked out slightly from the top of her stretch pants. Goldie stood looking at all the different pieces that needed to be assembled and just slowly shook her head.

"Where you put the instructions?"

"They are over there on the window seal," Goldie pointed to the big bay window to the left.

Baseem moved past Goldie, grabbed the instructions then went to work.

"Let me get the baby bathed and settled and I will come back and help you," she said as she exited the room.

"Nah, I'm good. You can hook a brother up with something to eat though," he rubbed his stomach and smiled.

"Oh, I got your back. You just saved my life," Goldie walked off to get the baby straight and then hit the kitchen.

Baseem listened to Pandora on his phone and bopped his head as he put each piece together perfectly. His stomach began to growl as his nostrils were filled with the aroma of steak, onions and biscuits. He could barely concentrate; he stacked each piece and when the last one was in place, he stood back and filled his chest with pride.

Goldie walked in the room all cheese with her hands folded on her chest.

"I told you I had yo back; you owe me one," he looked up and smiled.

"Wow. This is so nice. Thank you, Bas," Goldie spoke in a high-pitched tone and threw her arms around his neck.

Baseem caressed her back, inhaling her fragrance.

Goldie closed her eyes and enjoyed the touch of a man. Momentarily, she felt a surge of guilt and pulled back; fidgeting with the sides of her shirt. "You ready to eat?" she asked, looking around the room at the way the dark blue and red bunk bed set with the slide was positioned in the room.

"Let me wash my hands. I'll meet you in the dining room," he slid past her, heading to the bathroom.

"Okay," Goldie walked swooped up the trash then headed to the kitchen to prepare their plates. She placed the juicy meat over the white rice with gravy and put the cauliflower and cheese on the side. Last to hit the plate was buttery corn on the cob with Obay seasoning. She topped it off with homemade mash potatoes with ranch dressing and mushroom and onion gravy.

Baseem walked over to the table and his mouth watered as each scent eased into his nostrils. Taking a seat, he rubbed his hands together with anticipation.

Goldie put his food on the plate and sat it down in front of him.

Baseem filled his lungs with hot-flavored steam. "Damn, ma...you ain't playin'. These homemade biscuits? Let me find out," he picked up his folk and dug in.

"Uh, yes. I'm a real woman. I'm not your Kentucky Fried Chicken eating bitches you mess with from the club," Goldie shook her head as she poured them a glass of wine and took a seat.

"I hear you, ma," he chuckled then continued to fill his mouth with the tender meat and potatoes and gravy.

Goldie and Baseem sat and talked awhile about some of the events they had gone through in the past year. Some were joyful and some were painful; but they both had to be thankful for making it through.

Baseem smiled as Goldie filled their glasses and filled his plate with more of the tender meat and rice. He dipped the biscuit in the warm gravy and sucked it down like he had not eaten in years. Goldie was filled with joy as she watched him chow down and lick his fingers. When they were done, Goldie stood and collected the plates and took them into the kitchen. Baseem walked to the bathroom and washed his hands and face. On his way back, Goldie met him right outside the kitchen door.

"Thank you for all your help today," she stated, not looking up.

"I told you I got your back, and I mean that in every way. You need something...you or the baby, come to me first," he gave her a firm gaze.

Goldie looked up and smiled. "I know you got me," she reached out and grabbed his arm.

"You better be careful where you put your hands," his heart jumped a little.

"Boy, please...you ain't thinking about my hands, you know all those bitches be on you. But, thank you for being a good friend," she kissed him on the chin. "You want something else to drink?" she said, turning back to the kitchen.

"Nah, I'm good. Thank you," he headed to the living room. Baseem grabbed his shirt and pulled it over his head.

Goldie came back into the room with a drink in each hand. Passing him one, she took a seat on the couch.

"Nah, I'm straight, ma."

"You gonna just leave without having your last drink?" she extended her arm holding the glass up to him.

"I'ma have this one. But don't be trying to take advantage of me," he took a seat next to her on the couch.

"Ain't nobody thinking about you; you are safe up in Goldie's spot," she put her hand up in surrender.

"Oh, I'm safe?" he asked, taking the drink to his lips.

Goldie felt the tension building between them and she quickly ducked it. "Anyway, Mr. Baseem...what's on your agenda for the evening?" she asked, taking few sips.

"You know me...always on the grind," he responded, looking in her eyes.

"Indeed. Let me ask you something," she paused and took another sip. "Do you ever get tired?"

Baseem gripped his glass and took in a little air. "To be honest, no. It's like I was born with this hand and no matter how many times they reshuffle the deck, I keep getting the same cards," he continued to stare in her eyes.

Goldie felt a lump rising in her throat as her next words fought to be freed from her lips. "I thought I could never get tired until I had to clean Night's brains off my skin," An onslaught of emotion stole her moment and a tear escaped her eye.

Baseem reached over and ran the back of his hand gently over her face catching her tears. "You're going to be a'ight; you're built for this shit. Plus, little man is going to keep you on point," he flashed her that sexy smile.

Goldie forced a smile to her face then wiped at her eyes. "Thank you, Bas."

"I told you, I got you. Come walk me to the door," he patted her thigh placed his glass on the table then stood up and pulled her to her feet. "Let me know if you need anything." he leaned in and gave her a firm embrace.

Goldie closed her eyes as she felt the strength in his hands pulling her closer. It felt as if every muscle in his arms caressed her back.

"I sure will," she inhaled him as she pulled back; Goldie enjoyed the way she felt in a man's arms, but she knew they need not cross that line. Goldie gripped his hand and gave him a smile. "Thank you," she said then headed to the door.

Baseem's eyes roamed over her body as she walked off. He just licked his lips and rubbed his hands together at the visuals that played in his head.

Goldie opened the door wide and as he passed her, she took another deep breath.

"Lock up and get some rest," he kissed her on her forehead then moved swiftly toward the elevator, keeping the boundaries of their relationship intact.

"Be safe, Bas," she yelled out.

"Always," he said as he stepped on the elevator.

Goldie closed and locked the door, set the alarm and headed to her room; stripping along the way. She needed a cold shower and quickly.

Chapter 11

Out of Your League

Breonni stood back while Magic ordered three plane tickets. She had no idea where the nigga was taking her. A little fear set in as she watched him take the tickets in his hand and head in her direction. Bre pulled a lollipop out of her pocket and popped it in her mouth.

"You ready?" Magic asked, looking at Bre like she could be dipped and licked at the same damn time.

"Maybe. Are you going to be a good boy?" Bre asked, rotating the candy in her mouth.

"I am always good, are you ready to be everything I need this weekend?"

"I don't know about everything, but I will try and accommodate your appetite," she teased, tightening her jaws.

"That tongue is slippery. I need to see what that mouth do," he took her by the hand and headed toward the gate.

"If you had your own shit you might have found out," Bre teased.

"Oh, don't worry; I've got some big things planned for your little world," he gave her a wicked grin. "Thank you for seeing me on such a short notice," Brenda headed to a seat in front of Mr. Fucciano's huge mahogany desk.

"Good Afternoon," he rose to his feet as she sat down. "I don't really know how I can help you, but I will listen," he said as he sat back resting his arms on the chair.

"We have a common interest and I am interested in removing that thorn from both of our sides," she clutched her purse in her lap and crossed her legs.

"You will have to speak plain words so there is no confusion," the calmness of his deep, Italian accent played well against her ear drums.

Brenda took a deep breath then put it on the table. "Mr. Wells needs to be removed from the equation. I know you have business with him, but I know someone who can fulfill what he is bringing you and double it," she stated confidently.

"You are so way out of your league, Miss Watson. My relationship with Kayson is not one of finance, it is one of trust; and you, my dear, I do not trust."

"You trust a man that allows his wife to make decisions on his behalf? I thought you were old school," she hurled an insult in his direction.

Mr. Fucciano chuckled. "Aren't you someone's woman that they sent on the front line to try and negotiate?" he stood up, fastening his jacket. "If you will excuse me, I have a meeting to attend," he came around the desk and stood by her side.

Brenda stood up speaking her final words. "You are making a huge mistake."

"And so are you," he returned word play, placing his hand against her back and lead her to the door. "Have a nice day," he escorted her to the hallway.

"You do the same. Wish we could be meeting under different circumstances," Brenda said as she walked off.

Mr. Fucciano didn't respond; he watched her walk onto the elevator then he turned toward the conference room. As he walked, he thought about Brenda's proposition. A father moving in on his son is not too un-common, but to have this woman in the middle, what is the purpose of that, he thought as he approached the glass enclosed area.

He paused when he looked in and saw the slim and curvy, dirty blonde haired, white girl with legs for days. They seemed to extend from the bottom of her short skirt and planted themselves into the ground with every step. The woman moved around the boardroom, commanding everyone's attention as she spit out numbers and time frames.

Fucciano pushed the door open slow and stepped inside. Jill, his assistant, looked up and saw him standing there and interrupted the presentation to announce his presence.

"Uh, oh hold on. We have a very special someone in the room; please welcome Mr. Fucciano,"

The room erupted in applause and Jill pulled out a chair for him at the top of the conference table.

"Thank you. Please…as you were," he stated, waving his hands to calm the team down.

"Mr. Fucciano, this is Luanne Veizades. Luanne, this is the boss," Jill made the introduction.

"How are you?" Luanne moved forward with confidence and shook his hand firm.

"Please to meet you," he looked over her features. "Sorry I missed your presentation. I would be honored if you would come to my office and bring me up to speed on the subject."

"Sure, no problem," she accepted, gathering her briefcase and paperwork.

"Jill, please send something over for us to drink in celebration of this new venture. Have the team review the business plan and send me a report," he instructed then rose to his feet and opened the door wide as he watched her glide past him.

Once in his office, he watched her go into action and speak about money and ventures like she had the master plan.

"So, do you think you can turn all that into a profit in the next six months?" he cut in as soon as she took a breath.

"Absolutely, and then some," she spoke straight and direct.

"Okay, well send the budget and project overview to accounting so we can analyze it and set a start date."

"Great," she said, jumping up out of her seat and organizing her things.

"Leaving so soon?"

Luanne looked up. "Absolutely, I want to get everything into your hands today," she closed her briefcase and straightened her jacket.

"Yes, I agree, but the day has already been long; let me take you to lunch and then you be will nice and relaxed to work, yes," his smooth accent suggested that she had no other choice.

Luanne paused, thinking about his offer. "Okay, lunch might be good," she said, giving him a slight smile.

"Great," he rose from his seat and came around the desk. "I am so bad with names, my dear. What do you prefer to be called?"

"You can call me Lu; all my friends call me Lu," she said, heading to the door with a wicked grin on her face.

"Friends it shall be," he turned off the light not realizing he had just stepped into a world of darkness.

As they walked, his boy – Ledger – held a low-eye gaze on his face. He didn't trust that bitch and hated it when Magic brought random bitches so close to the organization. He didn't have a problem with a nigga getting some pussy, but it would cost them more than a nut if one of them bitches were deadly.

Magic turned briefly to check out his boy and gave him a quick lift of the brow to get him to chill. Ledger nodded that he understood; but was keeping a close eye on Bre. He had made a few calls and if any came back sideways, he was going to rock her to sleep himself.

As they boarded the plane, Bre made sure to brush her fat ass, wrapped in tight jeans, against his dick. Magic gave the first accommodations by allowing his dog off the chain. Breonni arched her back a little as she felt that rock. Damn, she thought as she took her seat in first class. Magic took his seat and ordered a few small bottles of Jack. Bre crossed her legs and enjoyed the rest of her lollipop as she watched Magic get right.

"When we land, I want all that ass right in my face."

"What makes you think a bitch will bless you with all that?" she looked in his unwavering eyes.

"Oh, don't worry. When I get finish, you will be begging me to eat everything on my plate," he held her gaze.

"Why me?"

"You intrigue me and I need to see why this heat exists between us. If by the end of this weekend it's nothing...then I will hit you off with a small stack for your time and let you leave me with some great memories."

"We will see," she turned her head and looked out the window.

Magic sat back in his seat and turned over his plans. He needed to cuff a bad bitch and Breonni's attitude had him convinced that she could be the one. But as she had just stated, we will see.

Magic and Breonni talked and shared a few ideas about the game and Magic became even more fascinated. Breonni spoke freely about her thoughts and passions which was rare outside of most females he encountered. She had passed all his little test, he was convinced by the end of the flight that she was who he needed on his team.

As the plane came to a stop, Breonni took a deep breath, stretched her legs and got ready to take in the Florida sun.

"You ready?" Magic put his hand out and pulled Breonni up from her seat.

"Why you keep asking me am I ready like you about to show me some shit I've never seen before," Breonni asked, giving him the side-eye.

"You may have seen it, but you never seen Magic do it," he gave her a firm gaze.

"I hear you, playa," she slid past him and gave him another display of what was to come.

Magic just shook his head; he knew that Bre had no idea what she was in for, quickly they moved through the airport and to the car that awaited their arrival. Bre sat in the back of the limo staring at all the pine trees and the pretty blue water as they approached the port. The car came to a stop and they were escorted to a yacht and helped aboard. Bre's eyes danced all over the deck taking inventory. There were two upper level decks and one lower level. The main deck had a huge Jacuzzi and several lounge chairs with thick pillow top cushions on one side and a white marble table with six chairs and an umbrella shielding it from the hot Florida sun. The mahogany wood and gold accents had everything popping.

"This little boat is nice," she said as she ran her hand along the edge of the deck.

"Little, huh?" Magic chuckled.

Breonni moved to the table and took a seat as she watched Magic and Ledger talk off to the side. Ledger had an evil look on his face and he kept staring at his phone. When the call came in,

Ledger held a tight jaw as he stared in Bre's direction. Her heart began to race as she tried to remain calm.

Ledger disconnected his call and whispered into Magic's ear. Magic looked over at Breonni then headed in her direction. Breonni tightened her fist as she thought about where she would hit him first in order to get away. Magic kept his eyes on Bre's expressions as he got a little closer. When he was about to part his lips, Bre rose to her feet.

"I want you to go get right so we can be alone. I have something really nice planned for you once we take off," Magic said with a smile then pulled her into his arms. "Let me get rid of my boy so I can have you all to myself."

Breonni put a smile on her face then pulled back. "Yes, I can't wait to have you all to myself. I need to see if your actions can back up your tongue."

"I love when a woman has doubts. It makes her screams sound even sweeter."

"We will see," Bre said as she slid past him. "This way?" she pointed the double door.

"Yes, take your time; they are preparing lunch."

Magic walked behind her watching the jiggle of her ass in her jeans. He stopped at Ledger and relieved him of his post.

"You sure? We didn't find shit yet, but I don't feel safe leaving you here with her."

"It's all good. I got it. I will see you in two days. Have fun and try to get that nut off your back; you're starting to get bitter, nigga," Magic joked.

"I like being bitter; that way I don't have to worry about putting my dick in something lethal," Ledger responded.

"I have seen those bitches you fuck with. I'm surprised you don't have to piss sitting down," Magic joked. "See you in a few days," he dropped his smile and moved toward the cabin doors.

Ledger stepped off the boat and on to the dock feeling like he was signing his boy's life away. He watched as the boat took off, then he picked up his phone to make his last call. It was something about Bre that he didn't trust and he was going to find out what it was.

* * * * *

Breonni moved around the room opening drawers and checking under the mattress. She needed to locate something she would be able to defend herself with in case the nigga got outta line. She sifted through her purse and came up empty. She had to admit, the nigga was on point. That commercial flight stopped her from being able to carry anything; giving him the edge. She sat on the bed and looked over at the bathing suit and silk wrap that he had laid out, and then she reached for her phone and dialed KoKo.

"Hello," she whispered.

"What's good, ma? You straight?"

"Yeah, I'm good," Breonni said, rising to her feet and continuing to walk around the room.

"Where you at?"

"On a boat."

"A boat? Where?" KoKo sat up in her seat.

"Florida. I'm good for now. I will hit you back in a few. I'ma turn this phone off, you know he's on my ass."

"A'ight. Be careful,"

"I will," Breonni said, then erased the call and turned off her phone.

She gathered the items from the bed and headed to the bathroom. When she entered and saw the glass and gold shower with several showerheads, a calm came over her mind. Breonni stripped down, regulated the water, and then hopped inside. As the warm water rained over her body, she fixed her mind for the journey ahead.

* * * * *

KoKo sat her phone down and looked over at Baseem.

"What's up, sis?" he asked picking up on her sudden mood change.

"It's nothing; just weighing some shit," she said, turning her seat to face the wall.

Baseem sat there for a minute then spoke plain. "I know you got some shit brewing. I need to caution you that Kayson is not playing when it comes to you staying away from this war," he got quiet allowing his statement to sink in.

73

KoKo turned back to him and took in the seriousness on his face.

"Look, I fully understand what is at stake and I won't risk mine or the family's safety," she assured.

"Are you sure about that?" Baseem asked, knowing that KoKo had been sneaking around and using Goldie to help her do it.

"What is that supposed to mean?" she sat forward holding his gaze.

Baseem thought for a minute then answered. "KoKo, I love you. You are more family to me than the bloodline I was born into. However, I am most loyal to your husband and I will be slow to speak about what I can, but I will not hide anything from my brother," he spoke firm then stood up.

"I won't cause you to have to make that decision."

Baseem nodded his head then headed to the door. "Let your husband lead, ma. There is a dark side of that man that you never want to see," Baseem said, giving KoKo no time to respond as he opened the door and walked out of her office.

KoKo turned back around in her chair and watched the monitors. She couldn't help but think about the possible danger she had put Breonni in, but she had to tuck that shit; each woman had made their choices and she had put too much into the mission. She also had to acknowledge Baseem's warning. There was definitely a side of Kayson that she didn't want to see; however, she too had a side no man wanted to run into.

Chapter 12

Never Cross the Line

Goldie moved around her apartment cleaning and packing her and Jarod's bags. She had to drop him off at KoKo's house with the nanny then catch a flight to Atlanta. She had just placed her swifter and cleaning supplies in the hall closet when she heard a knock at the door. She turned the radio down, cranked up the baby swing, and headed to the door. When she looked out the peephole and a smile came across her face. Goldie pulled the door open and a bigger smile was on Baseem's face.

"Why yo ass always take so long to open the door?" he asked moving through the space she provided. "You better not have no niggas up in here," he joked looking around.

"Boy, please…the only man in my life and my bed is six months old," she stated, closing the door.

"Yeah, a'ight," Baseem said, taking a seat on the couch.

"You always starting something. Don't you have some work to do, trouble maker?" she asked, taking a seat across from him on the loveseat.

"You are my work. I gotta make sure you and my little friend are straight," Baseem said looking in her eyes.

"Well, don't worry…we're good. You want something to drink?"

"Yeah, hit me with some hen and coke," he said, rising to his feet. "Let me run to the bathroom real quick."

"Make yourself at home," Goldie responded heading to the kitchen. "Oh, and the spray is under the sink," she giggled.

"You got jokes. I didn't even say anything when you farted in my car," he said heading down the hall.

"Shut up, I did not. That's nasty," she yelled back, grabbing a glass from the cabinet.

When Baseem returned his drink was on the coffee table on ice. He took a seat and began to handle his afternoon pick-me-up.

"Damn, what the fuck! Did you put soda in it?" he asked, looking at his watch. "It's one o'clock in the afternoon. Yo ass be in here getting fucked up!" he looked at the glass then sat it down.

"What...you can't hang?" Goldie said, perching her lips to the side.

"Sheeiit...I was doing this when you were in an A cup," he responded, taking the drink to his lips and downing the rest.

Goldie watched him take the hot liquid to the head and place it down. Her eyes roamed over his body. He was defined in all the right places and from what she could tell, he was hung like a pony and his swag said he knew how to use every inch of it. She was caught up in the middle of her fantasy when her better judgment kicked in. He was Night's friend and even more than that, he was a friend to her and that was a line she did not want to cross. Her mind and her pussy were in a strong argument when she heard a loud voice in her head say, Bitch you better not. Goldie shook her head and then stood up.

"Let me go get dressed real quick. Do you need anything else?"

"Nah, I'm good," he looked up and saw the fat print in her booty shorts staring back at him.

"I'll be back."

"A'ight," he sat back and rested his arms on the pillows.

When Goldie turned to walk out the room, his eyes settled on her ass and his dick pulsated against his zipper. He grabbed his little friend, "Be cool," he mumbled, causing Goldie to turn back around and catch him with a handful of that steel.

Goldie turned back toward the room and kept it moving. But on the inside, she died a thousand deaths. When she got to her room, she closed the door and sat on the bed. She looked over at a picture of her and Night in Vegas and a few tears welled up in her eyes. Goldie covered her face and tried to shake off the feelings

76

that had taken control of her mind.

"Baby, I miss you," she said out loud as she lost the fight with the water that forced its way from her eyes. "I will always cherish what we had and I will not violate it," she picked up the picture and held it to her lips. She gripped it tight to her chest and took a deep breath. Goldie placed the frame back on the desk and headed to shower and got dressed.

Baseem put his head back on the couch and reflected on the feelings that appeared every time he was in Goldie's presence. His loyalty to his boy was ironclad; yet his feelings for the woman he left behind could not be denied. He was at war with his lust and his love; and on top of that, he had a special place in his heart for Night's son. Baseem played with the ideas that had taken over his thoughts and when he opened his eyes, Jarod was staring at him with a little smile.

"What's up, little man?" Baseem got up from the couch and moved to the swing.

Once Baseem had him in his arms, Jarod put his head on his shoulder and grabbed his shirt tight. Baseem's heart felt warm and he was honored that he could be here for his boy's son. He took a seat on the couch and began his ritual of bouncing him and making crazy faces to make him laugh.

Goldie emerged from the back fully dressed in all white. Her jeans hugged every curve and her shirt sat at the top of her hips, accentuating her tiny waist and curves. Goldie sat the small overnight bag for the baby and her purse next to the door as her heart, too, became heavy watching Baseem with her son. Goldie again got choked up. She smiled to push back the emotion.

"You ready?" she asked, walking over to take the baby out of Baseem's arms.

"Yeah, I'm ready," Baseem stood up and straightened his shirt.

Baseem stood close to Goldie and a little heat rose between them.

Goldie moved from his side toward the door. She needed to put some much needed space between them. Baseem picked up the bags and followed close behind her. As he looked over her shoulder at little man, he decided he was going to keep the relationship the way it was. He knew that the pussy would be worth it, but the trust would be compromised and the one thing he didn't want was to cause her any more pain. Baseem tucked his feelings, deciding to be a friend and continue to help as much as he could.

Goldie had a similar struggle; however, the fact that she had not had sex since the day before Night was killed was clouding her vision. The ride over to KoKo's was quiet, but in those moments of silence, they both vowed to never cross the line.

* * * * *

Breonni exited the bathroom fully dressed and ready to give Magic the distraction he needed to drop his guard. She took a deep breath, grabbed her shades and then headed back to the upper deck. When she got closer to where Magic was sitting, she got a tingle between her thighs as she eyed his glistening eight pack. She tipped her shades and let her eyes dance over his frame. When she caught a glimpse of that print, her stomach buckled. She shook her head and moved over to where he sat.

"I hope I didn't keep you waiting too long," Bre said, rubbing her hand along the muscles in his back.

"You are well worth the wait," Magic eyed her sexy brown curves as she took her seat.

"What's on the menu?" she asked, taking the napkin from the table and placing it on her lap.

"I got the chef hooking us up something real official. You eat seafood?"

"Yes, I love it," she perked up thinking about the possibilities.

"Let me find out you do tricks for fish like Shammo," Magic joked.

"Hell yeah, but that nigga has nothing on me. I'm about to fuck something up, land…" she looked at his dick. "…and sea," she said, biting into her bottom lip.

"Come sit on my lap," he directed.

Breonni got ready to accommodate him until she looked up and saw the chef coming with a platter.

"Oh, that is going to have to wait," she sat forward rubbing her hands together.

78

"Damn, it's like that?"

"Yup, get ya life. I have work to do."

Magic laughed at her doing a little dance in her seat as the food arrived.

The chef placed a tender piece of steak — fresh off the grill — onto her plate, and then he placed grilled clams in garlic butter and Cajun lobster tail right next to it. Next he dressed Magic's plate with the same and poured them both a tall glass of white wine. Once he stepped away from the table, they dug in.

Magic laughed as Breonni chowed down and spit sexy one-liners at him. He smiled as the ends of her lips turned up and the gleam in her eye sparkled when the flavors touched her tongue. Butter and seasonings were all over her hands and she didn't give a damn. She dipped her seafood and put big pieces of steak into her mouth paying him no mind. Baseem had brought several women out to his little getaway, but she was different. Breonni was unfazed by his money or his aim to impress her; she had a chill button he wanted to stroke all night long.

When they were done, Breonni went to the bathroom and brushed her teeth. She then leaned against the sink and just stared at herself in the mirror. Slight regret seeped into her soul and she thought about what she had traded in for this new life that was far from glamorous. She tugged at her bathing suit and tightened her wrap at her waist, then she returned and sat back looking at Magic with a hazy glimmer in her eyes.

"Wooow…a bitch need a nap."

"Can I put you to sleep?" he asked.

"I know you don't think that I'ma give you some pussy cause you gave a bitch lobster and steak," Breonni asked with her head tilted to the side.

"Obviously you didn't do your homework before you came all the way out here," he responded.

Breonni paused. "And you must have not done your homework either before you drug me all the way out here."

Magic chuckled then stood up. "Come with me. You got too much air in your lungs; I need to take some of that."

Breonni stood up and gave him a raised brow.

"Don't worry I got you," he said, taking her by the hand.

Magic lead her to the Jacuzzi and hit the jet causing the bubbles to percolate. He stepped inside then put his hand out to help her in.

Breonni dropped her wrap and stepped in to the warm water. "It is so beautiful out here," she said as she looked out at the clear blue water and tall trees in the distance.

"Yeah, I love the water. I try to come out here every chance I get," Magic said looking in the direction of her gaze.

"So you're a concrete teddy bear," she teased.

"All niggas can be soft when they need to be. You just have to know when to be soft and when to be rock hard," he put his hand down and gripped his dick.

Breonni put her arms out along the edge and waved her feet in the water as she stared at him intensely. "So, what are your plans for Miss Bre?"

Magic stared back as he responded. "I am very curious about you. You have me very intrigued. I want to hold onto you for a while."

"Hold onto me for a while? What am I...lose change?" she put her hand out to the side.

Magic smiled. "Nah, nothing like that. But that's the shit that keeps a nigga interested."

"I guess so. On the real...I'm just me. I like what I like and do what and who I feel. Life is too short for regret or to miss great opportunities when they are staring you in the face."

"I feel that. Can you let me have an opportunity to be something you won't regret?"

"Maybe," Breonni flirted, lowering her eyes.

"I think I can convince you with this magic," he again stroked his steel.

"Pussy ain't pancakes, nigga; you can't just flip it and get it sticky and a bitch gonna fold."

"I don't want to flip it. I just want to taste it," he moved closer to her placing himself between her legs.

Breonni held eye contact with him as he cuffed her legs under his arms.

The passion in his eyes caused flutters in her stomach as Magic pulled her pussy up to his face and nibbled along the top of her bathing suit. He inhaled her scent then tugged at her bikini bottoms with his teeth until he exposed her clit. Magic caressed her pearl between his lips then ran his tongue gently back and forth until her breathing slightly increased.

Breonni squirmed in his arms as he slowly pleasured her clit. Magic moaned lightly as her clit hardened against his slippery tongue. Breonni gripped the edge of the tub as Magic slithered his tongue along her lips. She bit into her bottom lip as the length of his tongue slipped inside her; pleasuring her depth.

"Ssss..." she moaned as the feelings of pleasure increased as he worked his magic.

Breonni's eyes rotated open and closed as she felt her energy rising. She leaned her head back and rotated her hips against his face. Magic looked up at her perky breast as they bounced. She moved gracefully in his mouth and his dick rocked to capacity. He placed her legs over his shoulders and stroked his heat. Eagerly he moved his tongue back to her clit and lapped at her juices as her moans caressed his eardrum. Breonni moved back a little as she felt the intensity of his power take over her body.

"Cum for me," he whispered then put his full attention on her throbbing peal.

"Okay," she moaned, opening her eyes and positioning one hand on his head to hold him in place.

Magic caressed her clit between his lips and tongue and gave her gentle, then firm, sucks until he felt her body make its first jerk. She glanced up and saw the chef peering down on them as she rode Magic's face. She held eye contact with him as she felt her juices begin to flow against Magic's lips.

"Ahhh..." she cried out as the heat took over her movements causing her pussy to jump and contract.

Magic stroked his dick and sucked her clit until they both hit the edge of no return. Bre released his head and held the tub tightly then gushed all over his lips and chin. Magic gave himself a few more firm strokes and released just as he rubbed his lips, nose and chin in her sweet nectar.

"Shit," he moaned as both their bodies quaked with pleasure.

Breonni held the gaze with the strange man in the window until he moved from her sight, then she looked down at Magic's glistening face and the hunger in his eyes.

"I need to feel you baby," he said as he stood up towering over her.

"Let me go get right," Breonni said, reaching down and pulling up her bikini bottoms.

"Let me holla at the staff then I'll meet you inside," he said as he helped her to her feet.

Breonni disappeared inside and Magic moved to the captain's quarters to pass out instructions. When Breonni got to her room, she closed the door, grabbed her cell and moved to the bathroom. She quickly turned it on to check for any messages or instructions and as soon as it powered up it began to ring. When she saw Unknown pop on the screen, her heart started to pound.

"Hello," she said into the phone as she moved to lock the bathroom door.

"Hey, li'l mama," the voice rang out like music to her ears.

"Hey, baby," she said with a huge smile on her face.

"You okay? I miss the shit outta you," he said as he moved around his cell.

"Yes, Long. I'm fine. I miss you too."

"Can I see you soon?" he asked with a heavy heart.

"I'm not sure. I'm outta town. But when I get back, I will try. You know the situation."

"Yes, I do and I live with my choice every day."

"It's all good, no regrets; right?" Breonni said in an attempt to lift his mood.

"I love you."

"I love you too," she said, closing her eyes and allowing his words to touch her soul.

Just as she started to say her goodbyes, she heard the door to the room open.

"Baby, you ready?" Magic asked, knocking lightly on the bathroom door.

"Yes, here I come," Breonni answered.

"I gotta go," she said and tried to disconnect the call, but the damage was already done.

"I bet you do. I'll catch up with you," Long hung up not waiting for a response. He sat on the bottom bunk and tossed his cell phone to the side. He needed his team to hurry up and move shit around he had to get back on the streets.

Breonni looked down at her phone and then turned it off. Her chest felt tight as she moved to open the door. Quickly, she tucked her feelings and focused on the mission at hand. When she opened the door, Magic was standing there completely naked with his long, thick, steel in the palm of his hand. Breonni tossed her phone on the dresser then took Magic by the back of his head and kissed him deep. She was ready to fuck her pain away.

"Nah, ma...I gotta take this shit slow. I need you to feel all this power inch by inch," he reached in and gently removed her top, then he placed his mouth over her nipple and sucked softly.

Breonni fought back the tears as Magic walked her to the bed while setting her body on fire. She wanted him to hurry. She wanted him to fuck away her shame, but he had a different menu in mind. Magic held his breath as he slid into her tightness. He stroked slow and sucked her nipples gently as her fingers pressed against his spine. He pushed all the way in and pulled back easy. Breonni's legs shook each time he hit the bottom and eased back.

"I'm about to make you mine," he whispered as his tongue caused her nipples to tingle with excitement.

With every pleasurable stroke of Magic's dick, her heart broke at the pain she caused Long. Tears escaped her eyes as thoughts of Long filled her mind. Breonni pulled Magic close and fantasized about the next time she would be able to feel her one and only love as she threw her pussy to Magic as if it was his; while filling the room with passionate groans. Magic clutched the sheets in his fist and bit into her neck; stroking her tight pussy from every angle. Breonni gave him everything he needed; and he gave her the same. She allowed her body to react and release at his command while focusing on the hour that she would be able take his life.

* * * * *

Goldie entered the back of the country club and eased past the wait staff in her black and white uniform. She grabbed an apron and small order tablet then headed toward the dining area. She moved around the open, airy room from one table to the next trying to get close to where Rock would be sitting. As she arranged a few sets of napkins and silverware, she saw Rock entering the double glass doors across the room. Goldie slowly turned her back and moved to a table a little further away, setting it and watching his every move.

Rock took his seat then looked around the room. Fresh flowers in glass vases were set nicely on each table. He looked out the window past the patio and took in the beauty of the wide open golf resort while waiting to have his order taken. Goldie moved around the perimeter of her dining area, carefully watching and waiting to see who the mysterious person was that he was meeting. Goldie watched the perimeter, checking the comings and goings of each entrance when she looked up and saw Baseem coming through the same double doors Rock had come from. She ducked behind a pillar and peeked out.

Baseem scanned the room spotting Rock then took a seat not too far away from him. Goldie watched as Baseem settled into his seat.

"Shit," she mumbled as she looked over at the other entrance to see how she could get away without him seeing her. She watched as the waitress came over to take his order when she was positioned in front of Baseem, she took a deep breath and moved swiftly to the exit. As Goldie reached for the door handle, Baseem looked in her direction, wrinkled his brow, completed his order and rose from his seat. Carefully he moved across the dining hall.

Goldie walked quickly down the hall stopping at the coat check booth. "I need to come in there real quick," she said to the young white girl.

"Mr. Zipperman said we are not allowed to have the staff mix in this area. I'm sorry."

"Please. I just need to come in there real quick," Goldie reached her hand over the counter and released the lock.

"Ma'am, I am going to have to ask you to step back on the other side of the counter," the young girl got a little upset.

Goldie grabbed her arm, dropping the smile from her face. "Please. He is here and he hits me," she looked to the side with tearful eyes.

The young girl pulled her in and closed the counter. Goldie slide down in the corner, ducking completely out of sight

Baseem walked out into the lobby huffing and looking in both directions. He walked down in one end of the hall then the other. When he got back to the coat check area, he paused, looking around.

"Did you see a young lady with blonde dreads?" he asked, leaning on the counter.

"Not that I can remember," the young girl looked him over, eyeing his tattoos and high-end watch. She looked back up into his face and a scowl formed on hers. "You shouldn't stalk women; it's against the law," she said, folding her arms over her chest.

"What?" he said, taken off guard.

She just twisted her lips and looked up in his eyes. Goldie rolled her eyes at the naïve young lady. Baseem gave the young woman a raised eyebrow, and then moved away from the booth looking out into the parking lot on his way back into the dining area. When the doors closed, the young lady waited a few seconds then waved her up and opened the half door.

"Thank you," Goldie said then peeked out. Feeling secure, she moved swiftly along the wall and out to the parking lot. She ducked down, heading to the back of the building. When she jumped in her car, her hands shook as she tried to fit the key into the ignition. Pulling out of the lot, her mind raced with the idea of almost getting caught, but the real issue was still at hand: who was Rock meeting and now why was Baseem there?

Baseem's eyes darted around the dining area in search of Rock. The empty table where he once sat held two full wine glasses but no sign of him or the person he was supposed to meet. He walked over to the far window and looked out over the patio and grounds but there was no sight of Rock. Baseem headed back to the exit. When he got in his rental he pulled out his phone and called Goldie.

"Hey, baby," she answered on the third ring; windows open,

music rocking.

"What's good mama, where you at?" he listened intently to her background.

"I'm still outta town. You okay?" she said full of energy.

"Yeah, I'm good; just checking on my baby girl."

"Awww…you are so sweet. I'm good. I guess I will see you when I get back," she pouted.

"You already know. Travel safe. Hit me when you get back to the city."

"Will do; be safe," she said disconnecting the call.

Goldie breathed a sigh of relief placing the phone on the seat next to her. The smile melted into regret as she realized things were getting a little serious between her and Baseem. Working so closely behind each other's backs was creating an explosive situation. Unsure if he had seen her, her mind raced with the consequences.

Chapter 13

Put it on the table

Luanne moved about the cabin setting the table for the crew. She lit a few candles and put the music on low. When she saw the head lights coming up the road, she walked out on the porch enjoying the moonlight on her face. The headlights dimmed and the truck came to rest. The driver jumped out and opened the doors so KoKo could get out. Goldie, Bre and Adreena followed behind with solemn faces; everybody was about business tonight.

"Hey, Divas. How was your flight?" Luann asked, putting her arms around KoKo.

"You gonna stop all this free love shit. Only the boss gets to caress this chocolate," KoKo said, moving back a little.

"Whatever, Luanne nudged KoKo's arm and moved to hug the other girls. "Come onI have everything set up for the ladies," Lu turned and lead the way.

They woman settled in pulling off their light fall jackets and sitting them down on top of their bags.

"Yes, I am so hungry," Breonni announced as she walked toward the table. "Let me wash my hands, I am ready to eat the table and all."

"Hell yeah," Adreena agreed, following Bre to the bathroom off from the kitchen.

"Thank you, Lu. You always make us feel at home," Goldie said, taking in the aroma of the baked turkey wings in gravy, steamed ginger asparagus and carrots, spicy yellow rice with shrimp, and diced lobster topped off with hot buttery Hawaiian

87

rolls.

KoKo stood back watching the joy on her team's faces for the simple things. Shit was about to go to a dangerous level and she knew that moments like this were needed when it got rough on the battlefield. Once the ladies returned to the table, KoKo moved to the bathroom freshened up then rejoined them taking her seat at the head of the table.

"Well, I would first like to say thank the Lord we all made it back safely and may we move forward with mercy for our sins," KoKo announced, taking her drink in her hand and raising it to the middle of the table.

Each woman followed suit and raised their drink high.

"Salute," Lu said and then they took a sip in unison.

The glasses touched the table and it was on. Lu stood carving the turkey and placing it on the plates then smothered it in thick brown gravy. Goldie put on the rice and Bre put on the vegetables. When the plates were filled with each dish, they sat down and dug in. KoKo thought about what they would reveal about the mission and then how she would guide the team from here. The woman chowed down getting seconds and finishing two bottles of red wine. When they were done eating, they cleared the table and retreated to the big comfy couches in front of the fireplace. KoKo was the last to take a seat. She perched herself in the high back lounge chair and crossed her legs.

"Roll something up. I need to give y'all the real tonight." KoKo looked over at Lu.

"That's what the fuck I'm talking about!" Lu jumped up and went for her secret box. KoKo was on deck and she wanted to lay out the red carpet. She sat down, pulled out a small, glass water pipe and a block of compressed weed from Thailand. She sat it in the bowl and lit it up. Pulling deep on one of the arms, the thick smoke filled her lungs and eased her mind. She passed it to KoKo and sat back waiting for that heat to drip from her lips.

KoKo pulled deep and nodded her head. She pushed her tongue to the roof of her mouth savoring the sweat and sour taste of the bud. She pulled on it hard several times then passed it on. After each woman took their turn, the whole atmosphere changed.

Lu jumped up and grabbed each of them a bottle of Corona with lemon before sitting back down.

"Reports," KoKo went right to business.

Lu looked around the room. "I guess I can go first," she said, then got started.

"Well, Mr. Fucciano is like a teddy bear; he just wants company and to buy me expensive gifts. Plus his dick don't work, thank God," she said and wiggled her pinky. "I have been with him when he has taken calls, but I can't tell who he is talking to. He is very careful about how he moves."

"Okay. Is that all?"

"He does have a meeting coming up with someone and it seems real urgent. The other night he was talking to someone and he got a little upset; then he walked to the bathroom and closed the door. On his way back to the room, I heard him say, 'Friday...seven sharp' but that was all I heard before he hung up," she shrugged her shoulders.

"I need to know how he is moving that money around. That is your main objective. Find out who he is filtering the money through."

"Got you," she sat back plotting.

"All right. Bre..."

"I spent the weekend with Magic. He was cool; he flew me to Miami we did the little boat thing then he got us a villa. On the real...he was a gentleman, very respectful. He mostly wanted to talk and feel me out. Then that nigga licked and slow fucked my brains out," she said, then chuckled.

"Gave you that magic stick," Adreena said laughing along.

"That nigga ate my pussy in twenty-five different ways. I almost put a barcode on my ass and hopped on the shelf, I was that nigga's meal plan," she added and they all busted out laughing. All except KoKo. She sat, watching their reaction to the information.

"Anything else?" she said with a firm voice, snapping everyone back to business mode.

"Not really, he is also very private. He rarely uses the phone, but when he does, it's to one person. Unknown pops up and he leaves the room. I just fell back and acted like I was in my own world," she said, then got quiet gaging KoKo's mood.

"I need that connect info as soon as possible." KoKo pulled hard and inhaled deep. "Sometimes it's not them that will give you the information. You gotta impress the crew when they know he is sweet on you and you come around, they want to show their position so you will put in a good word. But be careful you don't want him to feel like you in his boys faces."

"I'm on it," Breonni said then took a few sips of her beer.

"Adreena, what you got?" KoKo asked sitting back in her chair.

"Magic did tell his boys he was feeling little mama when he got back. There is no change in activity from what I can tell. Their shipment is still coming in on the same day. Everything else is pretty much the same. Baseem is on your ass, what ever Kayson has him doing keeps him running into one of my people."

"Is he questioning them?"

"Not really but I had to move around some people I have in place so he wouldn't get suspicious."

"Okay. Be careful. You know Baseem will sniff some shit out, fall back a little and watch from a distance. What else?" KoKo gave her a firm eye.

"Gotch you. Golden Paradise is bringing in that money and Chico seems to be keeping the team organized. I haven't heard any complaints," she gave her side of the card.

KoKo nodded then looked at the next in line.

"Goldie?" KoKo said, looking at her and knowing that there was something heavy on her heart.

"The club is doing well as usual, to confirm what Adreena reported." she sat up and grabbed her bottle of beer from the coffee table. "Chico is keeping everyone in line and payments been coming in a little above the mark."

"What else?" KoKo probed.

Goldie took a deep breath and put the facts together, she was afraid that her revelations could cost Baseem his life but not revealing could cost her her's.

"I followed Rock to the country club from the lead. I was posted up, waiting to see who he was meeting and guess who walks through the door?" she asked the rhetorical.

"Who?" Bre jumped for the challenge; neck to the side.

"Baseem," Goldie paused, looking at KoKo.

"Was he alone?" KoKo asked.

"Yes, he came in and sat a few tables away and it appeared like he was watching Rock too. I don't know who Rock met. I was stuck behind a fucking pillar and as soon as I saw an opportunity...I was gone. I had to duck in the coat room."

"Did he see you?"

"I don't think so. He called me right after, but I threw him a curve."

KoKo sat quiet. Then she took a few pulls of the bud. The water bubbled below in the glass enclosure as she took in the sweet smoke while processing, her thoughts. She replayed each lady's report and then formulated her orders.

"Lu, pull back a little...make him need to have you around. Make that nigga crave you so he can get comfortable in your presence."

"I'm all over that shit," she agreed, putting her game plan in mental motion.

"Adreena, stay in the shadows and watch Bre's back. Keep your eyes and ears open."

"Got you, Boss Lady," she leaned in and grabbed her Corona.

"Bre, let me ask you something," KoKo said then paused to take another hit. She blew the smoke high in the air then looked into Bre's eyes.

"You like Magic?"

Bre locked in and gave KoKo honest raw answers. "Yes, I do."

KoKo nodded her head. "You like fucking that nigga?" KoKo was forward.

"I enjoyed testing that ride."

"Let me explain something to you. If you gonna give that nigga some pussy don't play with it," KoKo pulled on the bud and eased into her alter ego; it was time to make sure they were on track.

"This shit we in ain't no fucking joke. The same way you watching that nigga, he watching you. You think you good because he likes to lick pussy? Bitch, please! He loves to eat pussy. That is his thing. You ain't special," KoKo sat forward. "You on a fucking mission; don't get caught up. And if you gonna fuck that nigga, you make that pussy put that nigga in a certain mood. Don't even mention the weekend. Let him bring it up, and when he do, you act like that shit was just okay. Then he gotta prove his shit is boss. It's called resetting a nigga's agenda. Now he fucking you with a specific purpose and you give him the pussy so good that it make that nigga's dick feel virgin like it's his first time."

"Damn," Adreena said, blinking her eyes and clutching her chest at the thought.

Breonni took in KoKo's words.

"Y'all can't be playing with these niggas. These dudes are not like your high school crush. These crazy niggas will open your chest up; female or not. Stay alert and approach your role in full character at all times," KoKo paused and looked at each woman. "I have buried some good men. I don't want to bury any one of you," she stared at them with great intensity. "If you can't do this, I understand; but if you are going to move forward after this day, don't fuck around with it. These niggas ain't playin'. They will cross your ass faster than rabbit pussy gets fucked. They do this shit!" her voice raised a few octaves.

Chills went through Goldie's body as she thought about quenching her thirst for revenge.

Adreena sat nodding her head, holding eye contact with KoKo.

Bre felt a fire in her belly to go. Her nostrils flared slightly and sweat beads popped up on the tip of her nose as she embraced the energy of the moment.

Lu's foot shook back and forth as anticipation grew inside her about her next move.

KoKo rose to her feet. "Everybody in or do I have to call in replacements?" KoKo looked at each woman.

"I'm down," Goldie was the first to answer firmly, then Bre, Lu and Adreena took up the rear. It had been decided; and from this day forward, the main goal was to complete the mission at any cost.

"Good. And remember, the only way to play the game is to play it for real."

Chapter 14
Checking in...

Kayson looked at the security as Baseem pulled into KoKo's bike club. He didn't make a habit of coming down there, but not seeing his wife all week let him know she was up to something and he needed to find out what it was. Plus he had caught some word that in her absence a few niggas were setting up side gambling. He needed to make them feel his presence.

Baseem stepped out the truck and spoke to a few men who looked in Kayson's direction, then hurried to his door to let him out.

"Good evening, Boss. The Boss Lady is up stairs; you ready?" They moved to secure him.

Kayson looked the men over then said, "I got this, do what she pays y'all for. These niggas know better," he stepped out the vehicle.

"Yes, sir," the head of security said as he moved back.

Kayson eyed the many cars and bikes as he moved toward the elevators. His all-black attire and stone cold face matched his heart. They got on the elevator and as they rode up to the top level, some activity on the gambling floor caught his eye.

"Stop this shit real quick," he ordered.

He stepped off the elevator with Baseem right on his heels. He caught the attention of a few regulars who stared as he and Baseem passed. Kayson gave them no energy he had an example to set. He headed to the corner where he saw the offence. Kayson gave the men a hard stare while they continued their transaction as if they weren't standing there. When dude with the most flex finally acknowledged that Kayson's presence he got huffy and stared him down.

"The fuck wrong with your eyes?" Kayson spat at the man with the hardest gaze.

"Excuse me?" the man returned, not knowing he was in the presence of a killer without a pause button.

Kayson wasted no time showing him. He pulled out his gun and pulled one in the trigger, then he shot dude in the knee, sending him to the floor in agonizing pain.

"What the fuck?" another dude yelled out, causing Baseem to pull out and security followed suit.

"Back the fuck up," Baseem growled.

Kayson moved toward the bleeding man and stood over him. "What was it you wanted to be excused from?" he peered down on him with his gun firmly by his side.

Dude looked up with fear and panic in his eyes. Silence stole his words; he held his knee tight as the blood pushed its way through the spaces between his fingers. Kayson took the beat from each man's heart, then raised his weapon and put two in his chest. The small crowd paused as they watched Kayson take the man's last thoughts and breath.

He scanned the faces of his punk ass friends then taught his lesson. "I learned two things in life, don't ever put your eyes on a man you ain't prepared to put your hands on. And never put your gun on a nigga you ain't ready to kill. You muthafuckas understand me?"

They nodded their understanding.

"Good put this nigga where he belong and put these niggas with him," he instructed as he tucked his weapon. "Baseem, I'll be right back," he said as he stepped on the elevator.

"Nah, keep yo ass right here, go secure some shit," he instructed the bouncer. "Some shit gonna change around this muthafucka," he hit the up button, giving KoKo's security a hard stare as the doors closed.

94

KoKo watched the monitors as Kayson approached her office. She tried to pass out instructions to Chucky and Pete, but could barely keep her mind focused knowing Kayson was about to go crazy. She hit the button and opened the door as he stepped up to it. Kayson walked through the door like he owned it.

"Y'all niggas is dismissed," he spoke firm, looking right in KoKo's eyes.

Chucky and Pete jumped up and headed out the door.

"Why the fuck you got cameras if you're not going to watch what niggas are doing?" Kayson went straight to the point.

"Well good evening to you too?" KoKo said, raising her brow.

"Don't get cute with me," he stood firm.

"Baby, I was watching everything. That nigga been coming here all week moving a weak ass piece of product and I had people on him. I was waiting for his connect to come to a special invite so I could handle that nigga," she paused. "Does that answer your question?"

Kayson stood for a minute. "First of all, watch your fucking mouth. Secondly, I don't like the way you moving. And third, when I ask you a question, I already know the answer. I checked that nigga two days ago; so unless you were going to dig his ass up for info, you wasn't about to uncover shit."

KoKo looked up into Kayson's eyes and got a little choked up for words.

"I never interfere in your business...please let me handle mine."

"All this shit is my business. You're my wife and I love you to death, but you work for me; never cross the two."

"What are you saying to me?"

"I always speak clear. You know how I roll. I share my throne with you, but you don't rule it," he gave her an unwavering gaze.

"Anything else, Boss?" KoKo asked as her blood began to heat up.

"When it is, I'll let you know," he spat back.

KoKo bit the side of her tongue to keep from saying the wrong thing.

"And where were you at all week?" he asked.

"I guess I was out trying to be an employee," she stood up and shuffled some papers on her desk. "Now, if you're done...I have a lot of work to do. I wouldn't want to make you miss your money," she looked at him then headed to the wet bar to get a drink. She was ready to cuss Kayson out.

Kayson put a slight smile on his face. He watched as KoKo stood back on her sexy bow legs. He could tell she was trying to keep calm as she sipped her drink.

"You mad at daddy?" he asked then pulled out his gun and laid it on the table.

"Don't talk to me right now," KoKo said, keeping her back to him.

Kayson's phone rang as he approached KoKo.

"Hello," he answered, seeing that it was Baseem.

"You straight?"

"I'm about to be. I'll be down in a minute," he responded then disconnected the call.

Kayson stepped up behind KoKo, allowing the heat from his anger to flow out his lips onto KoKo's neck.

"Please move," she said, pushing herself up against the marble counter.

"Or what?" he asked, pressing against her.

KoKo didn't respond; she just looked at him in the mirror above the sink with rage in her eyes. Kayson took the glass from her hand and placed it on the counter. KoKo folded her arms over her stomach and watched as his hands began to move along her body. Kayson slide his hand up her breast and placed it around her throat and squeezed lightly, tilting her head back against his chest. His intense gaze heated her on contact. He carefully unbuttoned her jeans and slid his hand along the top of her panties.

"I always know why you're acting up. And I definitely know how to check that shit," he said as he slid his hand down into her panties and began caressing her clit.

KoKo remained silent as she watched the boss touch the places that gave her intense pleasure.

"Why you been hiding daddy's pussy?" he asked, applying pressure to the situation.

"I haven't," KoKo whispered.

Kayson bit into her neck and squeezed a little tighter on her throat. He decorated her neck with soft kisses and firm nibbles as he circled her clit. KoKo allowed slight moans to escape her lips as Kayson played with Miss Kitty, bringing on one contraction after the next. She pressed her butt against his steel as she griped the edge of the sink. Kayson circled faster, increasing her breathing as he held her neck and watched the passion on her face.

"Kayyy…" she purred as she felt the warm liquid release into the palm of his hand.

"Let me have that shit!" he growled in her ear.

KoKo dropped her head breathing heavy as Kayson pulled down her pants, forced her legs apart, and pulled out the Enforcer. He tugged roughly at her thong until it met her jeans at her ankles. He pushed her forward and spread her checks, then rested the head of his dick at her slippery opening. KoKo felt him pushing in fast and braced herself for his inches.

"No, baby…do it slow. I want to feel every curve of daddy's dick," she moaned, looking over her shoulder into his sexy, hazel eyes.

Kayson pumped long and slow, watching the pleasure and pain on his wife's face. KoKo gripped tighter with every forceful stroke.

"Hit daddy's spot," she cooed as he held her hips and tapped that G.

"Is this what you needed?" his deep voice sent chills up her back as he pushed his stiffness deep inside her.

"Yesss…"

"Make this pussy obey me," he taunted as her walls gripped his dick.

"I will," she surrendered unto him what he needed.

"Convince me," he picked up speed.

KoKo made eye contact in the mirror as she threw the Boss his pussy; drenching his dick with every movement.

"That's what the fuck I'm talking about!"

He held her stare and matched her moves. Her muscles strangled him as he deep stroked; not missing a wall on the way in or out.

"Daddy," she moaned as the waves of electricity took over her

97

body and her mind.

"Say that shit and cum on this dick," he moaned as he felt his knees buckle.

KoKo pushed back faster into his every stroke; filling the room with loud sexy moans as she began to come all over him.

"Daddy, daddy, daddy!" she screamed out as she lost all control.

Kayson showed no mercy. He picked up his pace and fucked her good. KoKo leaned forward on the counter and placed one hand on his stomach to slow his push.

Kayson grabbed her wrist and pinned it to her back.

"Nah, baby...you wanted to be in charge, now take what comes with all this power."

"Kayson...wait."

"What I'm waiting for?" he asked, stroking deeper and faster.

KoKo closed her eyes and put her head down.

Kayson released her hand and grabbed a handful of her hair. He pulled her head up so he could see her face without missing a stroke.

"Nah, baby...watch my throne," he teased.

KoKo struggled to maintain eye contact as he hit the spot deep inside her that made her surrender her soul. Kayson reached down and spread her cheeks wider and moved to the side to hit her angle of understanding.

"Do what I tell you, KoKo," he commanded as he watched her pussy glaze his dick. "Shit," he moaned as he felt his temperature rising.

"I'ma do better, baby. I promise," KoKo confessed as she again gave the Boss what his dick craved.

Kayson stroked a little faster as he released long and hard. He stood in place; steadying his breathing then pulled back looking at KoKo's juices coating his thickness.

"You know you are my everything; right?"

"Yesss..." KoKo panted as he turned her to face him.

"I need you to pay attention and be careful. And never forget who's in charge."

"I know you're the Boss, baby; and I love ruling beside you. I love you," she said as he covered her lips with his.

Kayson tongued KoKo intensely; stealing her breath as he palmed her soft ass.

"I love you more," he pulled back.

"Impossible," she replied, tasting his lips.

Kayson smiled as he felt her hands caressing his dick. "Rock up. I want to taste The Boss's power."

She squatted in front of him taking the mic into her hand so she could check it.

"Handle your business, Boss," Kayson stared down into her lustful eyes.

"I intend to."

KoKo took the Enforcer into her mouth and gave the Boss that royal tongue treatment. Kayson watched as his wife pleased every inch of him. He knew what kind of woman he had and he loved everything about her. He also knew that Boss dick didn't mean shit if it wasn't attached to a real Boss.

Remember: when good pussy has been mind fucked you don't even have to touch it for it to obey; but if your pussy ain't happy, your whole empire will crumble.

Chapter 15

Fed up

Brenda walked into her and Tyquan's penthouse apartment and threw her purse on the couch feeling defeated. She plopped down on the sofa and put her face in her hands trying to collect her thoughts.

"You okay?" Tyquan asked, entering the living room in his thick black robe.

"I need this shit to be over," she spoke with a solemn defeated tone.

"It's almost over. But you gotta hold your shit together. You of all people should know my son will not bend or fold."

"Is it that he won't bend or that you don't have the power to make him?" she looked up and waited for a response.

Tyquan walked over to Brenda and slapped her on to the floor. "Don't you ever challenge my power," he stood over her looking at her as if she was dirt. "I run this shit. It will be over when I say it's over; until then, stay in your place and play your role. Unlike me, you are replaceable," he stepped back, tightening the belt on his robe.

Brenda rose to her feet and wiped her mouth with the back of her hand then licked the blood from her lip. She locked eyes with him and spoke firm. "You get one because unlike the rest of your team…I'm built for this shit. And I won't be satisfied until this right here…" she showed him the blood on the back of her hand, "…is leaking from both Kayson and KoKo," she turned her back on Tyquan and reached for her bag. "Remember this if nothing else, the monster you create is the one that will destroy you," she moved to the door and slammed it on her way out.

Tyquan thought about the words she had spoken, and then moved to his room to get dressed. He had been sitting in the background too long and now was the time to hit the trenches and put an end to all this shit.

* * * * *

"Hello," KoKo answered on the third ring while trying to get the children ready for bed.

"Hey, sexy," Kayson said as Baseem turned the corners. The night air was crisp and his mood was welcoming to it.

"We miss you," she said into the phone as she watched Quran gather his toys from the carpet.

"I miss y'all too. I'll be home in a few days. I need you to put together a dinner party with the team and their wives at the mansion."

"Dinner party?" she asked.

"Yes, I need to have a sit down and I want you to get acquainted with the other wives."

KoKo took a deep breath then agreed. "Yeah, alright," she said as she passed the baby to Mariam.

"Thank you, baby; see you in a few days."

"Okay, I love you."

"I love you too," she said then ended the call.

KoKo moved to the closet and got dressed. She had some things to settle before Kayson got back.

* * * * *

KoKo pulled up in front of Golden Paradise and parked in her VIP spot. She eyed the crowd and counted her money as it headed through the doors. A smile turned up at the corners of her mouth as she checked her guns before stepping out of her vehicle. KoKo was flawless in her emerald green jumpsuit that hugged every curve. She switched hard, clicking her black stiletto knee high boots against the concrete.

"Hey, Boss Lady," Chico said, opening his arms as she approached the velvet rope.

"What it do, playa?" KoKo said, leaning into his embrace.

"Damn," Chico's boy said, looking KoKo over.

Chico looked over at him like he was crazy. "Watch your fucking mouth!" he said with distain.

"My bad; no disrespect," he threw his hands up in surrender.

"Get your staff in line, Chico. They need to respect who writes the checks," KoKo stepped past the men and entered the club.

Chico looked over at his boy and shook his head. "Go find some shit to do," he ordered.

KoKo kept a firm look as she eyed the crowded club. Every section was filled and the waitresses were busy passing out drinks and keeping the men very happy. She moved across the floor nodding her head to the music. Meek Mill was blasting and she was feeling every word.

Lil nigga, we don't rock the same clothes, fuck the same hoes;
Cause it's levels to this shit.
Lil nigga, we don't drive the same whips, we don't fuck the same chicks;
Cause it's levels to this shit.
Lil nigga. we don't get the same paper, you a motherfuckin' hater;
Boy, it's levels to this shit.

As KoKo moved smooth to the beat, a few females came up to her with reports. She nodded and kept it moving. Goldie watched as KoKo approached the staircase. She jumped up to greet her.

"Welcome, Boss," Goldie said from the top of the stairs.

"Roll up. I need to get these lungs right," KoKo said as she moved up the steps.

"It's already done. You know how I do."

"My nigga," KoKo joked as they headed into the office.

Goldie pulled out the chair from behind her desk, allowing the boss to have the best seat in the house. She took the seat on the other side of the desk and lit the end of one of the blunts.

KoKo took the strawberry-wrapped loud and pulled deep and exhaled thick smoke before she began.

"Let me see the money," she requested and Goldie got up and turned the wall safe and brought out several stacks. She grabbed the adding machine and sat it down in front of KoKo.

"Let me see the books," she asked, continuing to pull the tasty smoke deep into her lungs.

Goldie handed KoKo the books and she moved back to her seat. KoKo passed her the blunt and went over the numbers. She put each stack into the machine and tallied up the totals.

"This shit don't match."

"What you mean?" Goldie asked, looking at KoKo with a raised brow. She jumped up and went beside KoKo. Goldie picked up the books and examined it against the totals that KoKo had.

"Hold the fuck up. This shit right here is whited out," Goldie said, scratching at the paper. "I swear, KoKo...I did not see this," Goldie confessed as fear rose in her gut.

"Who was responsible for the last drop?"

"That was Carlos. He is Chico's right hand," Goldie reported.

KoKo nodded her head then lit the other blunt. She turned to the monitors and looked out at the crowd then focused on the door. "Rock is coming here in a minute. Go greet him and bring him to me, then I want you to bring them to me."

"Got you."

"Goldie, I need you to put together a better team; I know your heart and your movements, so I won't blame you this time. But I am very unmerciful to a theft," KoKo warned.

"I understand and trust and believe it won't happen again," Goldie confirmed as she headed to the door to get Rock.

KoKo grabbed the stacks of money and placed them in the bottom drawer. She closed the books and placed them on top of the money; then she sat silent; plotting and awaiting Rock's arrival.

"Hey, Ms. Sexy," Rock said as he entered the office.

"Good evening my friend," KoKo got up from her seat and walked to where Rock stood.

He opened his arms and wrapped them around KoKo's sexy body and enjoyed the heat and scent that rose from her skin.

KoKo pulled back and gave him a wide smile.

"You are excused Goldie, go watch the floor," she instructed, taking Rock by the hand and leading him to the seat across from the desk.

KoKo sat up on the desk and stared Rock in his eyes. "So, what you got for me?" she asked.

Rock went into his suit pocket and pulled out an envelope and passed it to KoKo.

KoKo took it into her hand and pulled out its contents and read it over. "Is this evertything?" She read it to the end then folded it back up and placed it on the desk next to her.

"Yes it is."

"Thank you."

"No thanks needed; I told you I got your back."

"I appreciate all you do," she spoke softly to his kindness.

Rock licked his lips then stood up. He placed his hand on the side of her face and looked into her eyes. "I will always be here for you," he vowed.

KoKo reached up and put her hand on his. "I know. And I got you too."

Rock placed a single kiss on her forehead. "Call me if you need me."

"I will. You need me to see you out?"

"Nah, I got it. I'ma get a drink on my way out. Stay beautiful." He hugged her tightly.

KoKo closed her eyes and inhaled his scent. "Be careful."

"I'm Rock, baby. They better be careful," he smiled, then headed to the door.

KoKo watched that suave, well-dressed man walk out the door and she could not help but reminisce about the one time she was in his bed. After a few seconds of reverie, she popped right back to business. KoKo dropped her smile and moved to the desk, she slipped out of her high heels and grabbed her stomp a nigga's ass boots then loaded the Judge. She called Goldie's cell and had her bring Chico and Carlos around to the back. KoKo locked up the office and headed to the back door. When she emerged, she saw Chico with a look of fear and concern. He knew well how she got down and a meeting in the back could only mean one thing. Goldie stood to the side and watched KoKo as she paced with her heat in her hand.

KoKo stepped in front of the two men then lit a blunt and inhaled deeply; her silence was thick in the night air causing more panic to set in.

"Chico, I left you in charge; right?" she asked looking into his eyes.

"Yes, you did," he answered.

KoKo nodded her head then paced a little more puffing smoke into the night.

"Let ask you something. If I put you in charge and you hire this muthafucka and he robs me, then whose ass do I take it out of?" she asked, pulling back the hammer.

"I ain't take shit from you," Carlos raised his voice, looking down on KoKo.

"Never mind, Chico...the muthafucka with the sticky fingers just stepped in line," she turned to face Carlos.

"Do you know me, muthafucka?"

"Bitch, please. I don't take orders from women. I work for and with him. I don't give a fuck who you are."

KoKo put her head to the side. "Is that right?"

"Yeah, it's fucking right!" he spat in front of KoKo's feet just missing her boots.

KoKo looked over at Chico then shot Carlos in the stomach.

Carlos reached around his back and pulled his .45. On his way to the ground, he let off two shots hitting Chico in the leg and just missing KoKo's side with the other.

Goldie pulled out and put three in Carlos' chest. Carlos labored his breathing as tears escaped the corners of his eyes.

KoKo stood over him peering down; a smirk came on her face as she watched him gargle blood bubbles while struggling to hold on to life.

"I bet you give a fuck who I am now, muthafucka," she stepped on his arm; pinning it to the ground. She shot him in the hand; detaching several of his fingers.

Carlos cringed in pain as his eyes rotated in his head. As he took his last breaths, KoKo gave him her last words.

"On your way to hell remember me, muthafucka!" she spat, then put one in his forehead.

KoKo looked over at Chico who was lying in a puddle of blood holding his hand on his leg.

"I'll take care of your wife and kids. You're too stupid to lead them," KoKo let off, hitting Chico in the throat.

He put both hands up to his neck as he shook in pain.

"I don't do short dick; and I damn sure don't do short money. Clean this shit up. I can handle my dick, you make sure my money don't come up short," she said to Goldie as she headed back inside.

"I got you, Boss Lady," Goldie said, taking in some air. She looked at both Chico and Carlos and realized that under no circumstance, did she need to cross KoKo.

NeNe Capri

Chapter 16

Even Strategy

Kayson and Baseem moved in sync toward the restaurant where they were to meet Mr. Raja. There had been a call for peace between Kayson and Mr. Odoo, and knowing that the blood had gotten way past bad, they decided to send in a neutral party – Mr. Odoo's most trusted friend.

Kayson's eyes moved around the room pinpointing his men before he proceeded toward the table. With everyone in place if shit got bad, he settled into his mood of negotiation. He walked over to the table and took a seat across from the small-framed, well-dressed man. Baseem took a seat on the left, facing the door, and focused his eyes forward; showing he was basically there as a witness.

"Thank you for meeting with me, Mr. Wells," Mr. Raja's course accent past smoothly through his lips.

"The pleasure is mine. I have heard many good things about you," Kayson responded, sitting back in his chair.

"And I have also heard very good things about you too," he responded then took a sip of his water. Bringing the glass back to the crisp white cloth he continued. "The thing I like most about all that I have heard about you is that you are a very intelligent man; and loyalty is not a word of tongue, but of heart and character," He locked gazes with Kayson, feeling him out.

Kayson was also searching Mr. Raja's soul for any deceit. "I am a very good judge of character and it is my belief that you are not

109

only here for Mr. Odoo but also for yourself. Would I be wrong in my thinking?" Kayson sat forward, folding his hands and awaiting the response.

Mr. Raja gave a small chuckle at Kayson's forwardness; but he had to respect Kayson for getting straight to the point. "Your question seems to be is this about money. Well, I say this. My money is old money. So that is not what I am after. I need to have friendship," he paused, taking another sip and gaging the temperature of the room.

"Continue," Kayson encouraged.

"May I speak freely?"

"Please do."

"I am very loyal to my associate. I would never cross him; but I believe he had a rare diamond in his hand and treated it like broken glass. I believe that diamond goes by the name of KoKo," he said very calmly, being careful not to awaken the beast inside of Kayson.

"Chose your next words wisely," Kayson warned.

"I mean no disrespect. Your wife is a brilliant woman. In a very short period of time she made you a fortune and a solid confidant. I would love to have her settle a few scores and make me some new friends," he put his offer on the table.

Kayson took in a little air and processed the words that left Mr. Raja's lips. It was clear that he was not here to make peace for his friend, but to try and recruit his wife like she was for sale.

"Let me get this straight...you called a meeting so you can exchange goods and services for my wife?" Kayson's head titled slightly and his eyes squinted into a creased brow.

"Listen, there is a very large offer from our Japanese associates. They are sorry about the misfortune between you and Mr. Odoo, but they want to call it even and get back to the business. They want to deal in very large amounts of currency; they are ready to go, but they want to work with your wife," Mr. Raja sat back rubbing his fingers together as if he could feel the money flowing through them.

"Is that all?" Kayson spoke slow as he tried to silence his gut feeling that said kill everything in the room.

Baseem looked over at Kayson, then back forward.

Mr. Raja extended his hand out as a jester for Kayson to continue.

"I am going to warn you and all these muthafuckas that I'm not afraid to die. Therefore, I am definitely not afraid to kill a muthafucka. Never attempt to bargain with my wife. If they want to do business, then they do it with me as they have been doing it or they can suck my dick; either way, I'm good," Kayson rose to his feet. "Tell Mr. Odoo shit between us is settled; but he has to do business with someone else, he can never eat off my work again. Tell the Japanese if they want me, find me and we will talk figures," he nodded at Baseem and when he rose to his feet, they rolled out.

Mr. Raja sat looking at the door to the hotel room as it closed. He knew that he just had a man in his presence that was unbreakable and if he could win that kind of loyalty from him, he could flip the whole game on every player involved. A smile formed on his face as he thought of the perfect weapon.

* * * * *

"Kayson, can I see you?" Yuri's voice serenaded his ear drum; but even with sexy dripping from her vocals, she warranted no respect from him.

"Why are you on my phone?" Kayson asked as calmly as he could.

"My words left my mouth as a question, but they are more like a demand," she moved about her hotel room holding different dress up to herself in the mirror.

Kayson had to chuckle. He knew she was well aware that he was not to be played with yet she still tried. "Is there anything else?"

"Yes. Be at my favorite hotel in an hour and I will let him go unharmed. Be late, and I will deliver a body part every hour that I am kept waiting."

"And who is it that you want me to believe you have?"

"You're going to have to count your sheep. See you in an hour," she hung up, not waiting for his response.

"Who was that?" Baseem sat forward.

"Ain't nothing. Let me make a run right quick."

111

"You need me to roll with you?"

"Nah, I got this. Check on the men, have everybody lock in at the safe houses and call in on the emergency lines only, and be brief. Hit me so I'll know the count is cleared and make everybody stay put until you hear from me. If you don't, you know what to do." Kayson pulled his drawer open and grabbed his nine, then he stood and put it in place.

Baseem hopped up and went into general mode; hitting their territory securing the team.

Kayson made his way to the parking garage, jumped in his truck and headed uptown. Thirty minutes into his drive, Baseem called and just as Kayson had suspected, she had someone on the lower end; a pawn. Yuri knew him well enough not to touch his best; nevertheless, she had touched one of his family. He didn't know what she had planned, but with the new deal that was put on the table, he needed some eyes on the other side. Miss. Yuri Odoo had just put herself in the line of fire.

As he headed inside, his phone rang with instructions on where to meet her. He pulled up to the Valet and handed him a few hundred dollars on his way out of the truck. "Keep my shit right there," he pointed at a spot a few feet from the entrance.

Kayson stepped with caution, watching every movement and every hand. He made it to the elevator and rode to the top floor. When he arrived at her suite door, he took his nine into his hand and tapped lightly on the door with the handle. Seconds later, he saw a shadow in the peephole. The door came open and there Yuri stood with all her curves on full display. Her peach, off-the-shoulder body dress hugged every inch of her tightly.

"Thank you for coming, this shouldn't take long," she said as her eyes roamed over his frame. She settled her sight on the Enforcer for a few seconds longer, then connected gazes with him.

"Please, come in," she moved back so he could enter.

"After you."

Yuri's smile lit up her face as she turned. "Follow me," she said over her shoulder as she headed to the sitting area.

Kayson's eyes moved over her body. Her soft, brown calves tightened with every step causing her ass to bounce and sway.

Yuri's long, curly black hair hung past her bare shoulders and down her back. He just shook his head and followed behind her, enjoying the view.

"Would you like something to drink?" she asked, heading to the bar.

"No, thank you. State your business so I can roll out," he positioned himself in the middle of the room and then looked over each door.

"You won't need a gun, Kayson. This is going to be a very friendly meeting," Yuri assured him as she walked over to the couch, took a seat, and crossed her legs.

"What do you want?" he stated, giving her a hard, cold stare.

"Always right to the point, Mr. Wells; well, let's get to it. I want in on the Japanese deal; and for you extending that to me, I will in turn give you anything you want," she stretched her arms out along the couch.

"Where is my people?"

"Oh, he is perfectly safe. He's down the hall with the best piece of pussy his hands and mouth will ever experience," Yuri opened her laptop and turned it for Kayson to see Little Spank tied to a bed blindfolded with some chic riding his dick.

Kayson nodded at the confirmation of his boy being safe and sound.

"See...no worries. Why don't you have a seat so we can talk money."

"Nah, I'm good. But you can talk," Kayson stood firm in place.

"My dad will never forgive you, but I do. I know what happened was business and not personal. I am the next one up for the throne and I want to take this family to the next level," she held eye contact with Kayson and the power in his stare caused her clit to jump.

"What about your brother?"

"My brother is weak. He folded for the first piece of pussy that settled in his nostrils. No disrespect to your wife, I respect her brilliance; but let's face it, she ain't me."

"Anything else?" Kayson was ready to go.

"Think hard about this. I can move twice as much money for

113

you through my father's connects. I have several associates who need clean money and I am willing to share them with you."

"At what cost?"

"I will give you a week to think about my offer and then I will start shaking shit up," she stood up and headed in his direction.

"This is a very dangerous game you're trying to play," Kayson looked down in to her eyes.

"I want your kind of danger," she said a little over a whisper, taking in all that heat he was sending her way. "Unlike everyone else in your world, I am not afraid of you," she slid her hand down the length of his dick. "It's a shame that all this dick belongs to a bitch that doesn't deserve it," she moved her hand and turned to the door.

"Good night, Mr. Wells. Your boy will be put back into place before you get back," she opened the door wide.

Kayson moved toward the exit. "You know you have set some shit into motion; right?"

"That was my goal. I will be looking for your call in a week."

"Don't hold your fucking breath," he moved past her and out the door.

"One week, Mr. Wells," she repeated as she closed the door.

On his way to the elevator, Kayson formed a smile on his face. He was considering the Japanese deal, but didn't want to risk his men or his money. With Yuri stepping forward, he could use her men and her money. "Yeah, a'ight...she think this shit is game. Well, we about to play hard as hell," he said as he entered the elevator.

Kayson had Baseem pick him up after he returned from the hotel. He briefed him on the meeting, and then told him to send someone over to look out for Little Spank. Baseem looked forward out his front window as he drove and digested what Kayson said about their boy being laid up in that room while Yuri tried to call herself infiltrating with her pussy.

"Remind me again why we didn't kill that bitch," Baseem said as he felt heat rising in his gut.

"Because even a man with blood on his hands, lives by a code," Kayson looked over at Baseem. "You see...a woman who thinks she can trap a man with pussy is a bitch who knows she can't; but I love to watch them try," Kayson said, reclining his seat. Yuri had just handed her father's money over to Kayson without threat or coercion.

Chapter 17

The Turning Point

Baseem pulled up in front of Simone's house at exactly 7:30 p.m.; being late was never an option. He had been running hard and tonight it was going to be all about her. He eyed her quiet block then deaded his engine. When he reached for his cell phone to call inside, Goldie had sent him a text message with a picture of her and the baby being silly with a message that read, We miss you, be safe. He closed the message with a big smile on his face. He was briefly distracted from his mission. Baseem though about how soft Goldie felt in his arms and her pretty smile. He also thought about how each day he saw little man, it changed something in his heart. Baseem tucked the feelings back and dialed Simone. Once she picked up and confirmed she would be out in a minute, he clicked off and called Goldie.

"Hello," her voice boomed through the line and he could tell she had a big smile on her face.

"What's good, ma?" Baseem returned the greeting with a smile plastered on his face to match hers.

"Nothing much in here; playing with your little friend and I swore I heard him say, 'Call Baseem'," she spoke in a baby voice.

"You so crazy," he busted into laughter. "Y'all straight though?"

"Yes, we are fine; just checking on our special friend," she said, putting the baby in the playpen.

"As long as y'all okay, I'm good. I'll be by there tomorrow

afternoon."

"Negative. I have to leave town, but I will hit you when I get back," she pouted in the phone.

"A'ight, be careful."

"You too," Goldie hung up just as Simone opened the door to get in the car with Baseem.

"Hey, beautiful," Baseem switched his mood, greeting Simone as she took a seat.

"Hey Mr. Baseem," she leaned over and gave him a kiss on the check.

"Oh, so I'm mister now and I get a kiss on the cheek?" he gave her a slight smile.

"Yes, you are mister because you are a bully."

"Whatever. You ready to get bossed around for the next few hours. I got something special planned for us."

"Ohhh...I like special treats," Simone rubbed her hands together. "One condition, all of our clothes stay on," she said, raising her eyebrows.

"Yeah, they gonna be on alright. On the floor," he looked over at her then put his hand on her knee. "But don't even worry about that. That's for me to worry about. You just keep looking sexy," he turned his eyes to the front and put the car in gear.

Simone had to close her mouth before she caught something in it. She just shook her head and sat back. She had finally agreed to go out with him on his terms, and now fear and regret had taken over. She tried to calm her nerves as he hugged the corners like the streets owed him money. Simone looked over at his game face and knew besides everything else he had planned, digging deep into her sacred places was going to top off the night.

"I feel you all scared over there," he looked back in her direction then hit the satellite radio to break up some of the tension in the car. "Clear your mind. Sitting over there trying to imagine what I'm going to do will only make you tense up and run. And when this nigga smells fear, he tends to get outta control," he spat some slick shit and kept it moving.

"I am not worried about you," her mouth said, but Simone's stomach was now in sailor knots, she wanted to jump out at the next light. She could feel the danger of his presence, but was intrigued by the side of him that was sweet and loving; that part that told her he was a good dude. That was the part that calmed her nerves. But at the end of the day, no matter how calm she was, she knew that he was going to eat her ass alive.

Baseem pulled up to the hotel and Simone's face grew into a frown. She knew he was trying to get into her silky thong, but she at least thought that he would let them make the decision together. Baseem jumped out, spoke to a very well-dressed, clean-cut man, then hopped back in the car. He moved quick and silent. When he parked in the alley next to the side door, Simone looked up at the fire escape and then down at the big garbage cans at the end of the alley. He became unnerved.

Baseem stepped out and came to her side of the car. He opened the door and took her hand. Noticing the look on her face he immediately addressed it.

"Relax. I got you, baby," he assured as he led her up the metal staircase. He hit the car alarm and tapped on the door. The door came open and he was greeted by a friend who owed him a favor. The gentleman waved them inside and closed the door.

"Welcome and I hope you have a great evening," the man said as he led them down the long corridor.

Simone's heels clicked along the hallway as they were led to the back of the hotel restaurant. Baseem entered and first looked around the kitchen, then shook his head in agreement. When Simone could see past him, her eyes lit up. Baseem had the head chef set up a table for them in the corner of the kitchen. It was like a little fantasy.

"Awww…baby," she squeezed his hand and whined when she saw the crisp white table cloth with beautiful gold plate settings and a fresh bouquet of red roses in a pretty glass vase. There were three black gift boxes in different shapes stacked up with a red ribbon tied around them on a plate which made the ends of her mouth turn all the way up.

"I told you I got you," he looked down at her causing her heart to flutter.

Simone reached up, taking him by the back of the neck and

pulled him toward her so she could taste his lips.

Baseem wrapped his arm around her waist and enjoyed the softness of her lips and tongue as she slipped it between his lips.

"Thank you," she pulled back looking at him through glossy eyes.

"You more than deserve it," he said smoothly then led her to the table.

Simone floated over to her seat and positioned herself front row and center for the show.

Baseem grabbed an apron from the counter and tied it around his waist. "Real men cook and don't be hating on my apron either," he moved back to the table.

"No hate here, baby," she spoke softly, looking up into his eyes.

"Open your gifts," he instructed.

Simone wasted no time. She pulled the end of the ribbon, smiling all the way. She grabbed the big one first, placing the two smaller ones to the side. Simone reached inside and pulled out at diamond necklace and rocked a little in her seat. Baseem walked over, stood behind her, and pulled her hair back and fastened it around her neck. Simone rubbed her hand on his leg then grabbed hold of the medium-sized box and pulled out a diamond bracelet to match. Baseem carefully took it into his hand and closed it on her wrist; then he leaned down and kissed her lips, sucking the bottom one enough to cause her kitty to tingle. Simone crossed her legs as she ran her tongue over her lips.

"Go ahead before you end up on the menu," he stated smoothly.

Simone felt the temperature rising and obeyed, turning her attention to the smaller box. When she opened the last box, her eyes almost popped out of her head when she saw the canary yellow stone surrounded by little princess-cut diamonds. She looked up at him.

"I don't know what to say," she put her hand up to her mouth.

"Don't say anything. It's just something between me and you. I'm not asking you for anything but to ride with me. If we find something pure and true to hold on to and build on, we will take it from there. If not, you'll have some fly ass jewelry," he joked and gave her a reassuring smile as he slid the ring on her right hand instead of her left. "If it gets real, I know where to put it," he pulled her to her feet.

"You always seem to amaze me," she said, wrapping her arms around his neck.

"And you always amaze me." He hugged her tightly. They stood in a strong embrace as Baseem tried to control his dick from rocking up with all the smoke signals her pussy was sending him.

"A'ight, they got a brother paying by the hour; let me hook you up," he let her go and went to work.

"Alright. Alright. I have a front row seat; hook a sistah up," she sat down and folded her hands, taking in all the sights.

Baseem was a natural in the kitchen. He was chopping vegetables and seasoning everything just right. They joked, laughed and talked between him letting her taste different sauces.

Simone's mouth exploded with every sample he provided. He began serving her one dish at a time. He made her a nice spinach salad with a homemade vinaigrette and a glass of red wine.

Simone chopped away at her salad while she watched Baseem sauté some broccoli and tri-colored peppers. On the side, he had sliced very thin pieces of filet mignon marinated in teriyaki and ginger. After he seasoned them well, he stir fried them in garlic butter then added the tender meat to the vegetables. Baseem placed the steamy entrée on a plate and brought it to the table, placing it in front of her.

Simone was smiling from ear to ear. Baseem was doing things for her that no man had ever done and she loved every second.

"You are so good to me," she said as he looked at her like she was the only one in the room.

"You deserve it," he picked up the folk and placed a piece of meat into her mouth.

Simone closed her eyes and enjoyed the flavors as they danced on her tongue. "Mmmm..." she said, savoring each herb and spice.

"Yeah, fuck with ya boy," Baseem bragged.

"This is so good. Are you going to eat something?" she asked as she began to dig in.

"Later," he responded then moved to the stove to put away his tools.

Baseem washed his hands, removed his apron, and then took a seat across from Simone. He poured himself a drink and took the smooth liquid down his throat as he looked at all her features.

"You are so beautiful," he said, looking into her eyes.

"Thank you. You're not too bad on the eyes either," she joked as she finished her last bite and pushed her plate to the side.

"I will take my thanks and my meal later," he smiled.

"Fair enough," she returned, looking at the hunger in his eyes.

"You ready to go?"

"Yes, where is the ladies' room?" she asked as she rose to her feet.

"I'll escort you," he stood as well, taking her hand. Baseem leaned in and kissed her lips then lead the way.

Simone switched with every thought as she caressed the ice on her neck then looked down at her ring. "Thank you, baby," she said, squeezing his hand.

Baseem didn't respond, he just smiled and fantasized. He was planning on getting thanked real good all night.

When they reached her apartment their bodies where like magnets. Baseem pulled at her clothes freeing her breast then he covered her nipples with his mouth.

Simone's kitty felt his steam pushing its way between her thighs.

Baseem pinned her against the wall and guided his hands between her legs. His warm kisses hardened her nipples as an onslaught of feelings rushed through her at once. Just as Baseem reached for his zipper his emergency phone vibrated against his thigh. He paused and retrived it.

"Speak," Baseem said tryng to gather his breath. He listened as his orders were read off to him then the call went dead.

"I'm sorry baby, I have an emergency. I want you to get some rest. I'ma call you before I go to sleep." He kissed her lips one last time. Baseem helped her adjust her clothes then they walked soundlessly to the door.

Simone closed it tight then rested her head against it. "What are you doing?" she said out loud then pulled her shirt together and walked to her room. She hopped up on her bed and pulled her comforter up to her chin. She closed her eyes as she tried to control the wet tingle between her thighs.

Chapter 18

Taking the Lead

Brenda stepped hard through the lobby in her two-piece dark red suit. She moved right past the receptionist, head held high and on a serious mission. Exiting the elevator, her heels clacked along the shiny brown marble floor as she headed to Luccini's office. Brenda turned the knob hard, causing it to hit the wall with force; she stormed inside and slammed the door behind her.

"What the fuck is this shit?" Brenda threw a few contracts on his desk and folded her arms across her chest.

"Keep your voice down," he quickly snatched the paperwork up and threw it in the bottom drawer of his desk.

"Who is trying to fuck me on this deal?" she sat hard in the chair across from the desk and crossed her legs.

"You know what this is," He stood up and moved to lock the door.

"I thought I knew. But every time I get this shit under control, one of you sons of bitches snatches the Band-Aid off this big ass wound and everything starts all over again," she shook her head in disgust.

"Look, you have to remain calm; it's almost over," he said, adjusting his tie as he moved to the mini bar beside his desk.

"Fuck being calm; I want you to give me Kayson," she sat up making her demands.

Luccini poured himself a glass of water, put in a lime and took a seat. "I know you have been putting in work and I will give you anything else you want; but I can't give you him," he reached forward and grabbed a cigar and put fire to the end.

"You need to do this; you fucking owe me," she sat forward, breathing heavy as she awaited his response.

Luccini sat puffing thick smoke into the air as he watched Brenda's chest began to heave up and down.

"That shit ain't gonna happen. In fact, you need to leave before you say something you will regret," he stated calmly.

"Fuck that. I hand delivered everyone to you. I put my family at risk. I put myself at risk, and here I am asking you for this favor and you deny me?" she jumped to her feet.

Taking a long deep pull on his cigar, Luccini blew at the end, causing the flames to kindle bright. "I won't bend on this, Brenda. I will give you anything you want; but not him," he responded, unfazed by her anger.

"The only thing I want is Kayson's last breath. Everything else…you can shove up your ass!" she turned to the door.

"Don't put yourself on the wrong side, Brenda," he gently warned.

"You better take some of that advice for yourself. I'm already on the wrong side, muthafucka," she opened the door wide, causing it to crash into the wall.

Luccini reached over to the phone and placed a much needed call.

"Hello."

"Hello, comrade," the voice rang back with excitement.

"You are off the leash," Luccini said, sitting back in his chair.

"No problem. Who do I need to see?"

"The thorn in my side."

"But I thoug—"

"Get rid of those thoughts and handle this shit before it gets out of control," he hung up not waiting for a response.

Luccini rocked back and forth in his seat. The organization had had enough and they were getting ready to erase anything that threatened their power.

Chapter 19

The Sacrifice

"I didn't think you would see me," Yuri pulled her hotel door open, welcoming Kayson inside. She inhaled deeply as he passed her and his scent, tickled her belly.

"This is not a pleasure trip; you said you have something for me. Speak your mind," he said, moving further into the room, eyeing the decor and the layout.

"I know that you may not think that I am sincere because of how the tables turned between me and you, but I don't hold that against you. I know that was business and your family was on the line."

Yuri walked past him with her low back, tight silk jumper. Her hair was pulled back into a long wavy ponytail showing off all the features in her face. Kayson watched as she swayed from one spot to the next with the material of her clothing clinging to every curve. He couldn't front, she was definitely well put together, the Enforcer engaged in some mental gymnastics as he thought about a few very comprising positions.

Yuri turned and looked over her shoulder to catch the last piece of lust in Kayson's eyes, then his mode quickly changed and his brow wrinkled as he waited for her to speak her so-called truths.

"Would you like something to drink?"

Kayson didn't respond, he just looked at her.

"I see you're still a man of little words," she said as she moved to the love seat and perched her butt in the seat.

"What is it that you want to tell me?" he asked, sticking to his script.

"I believe that I can help you with some information," she stopped and sipped her drink. "But I need to have assurance that I will benefit very well from this transaction," she stated, looking at him like he was her next meal.

"It all depends on what you have to offer," he stated smoothly.

"My brother is in a deal with the Italians to cut your supply and work with him. They are fully aware of your dealings with father and they want to get my brother to cross you in an open meeting so they will have a reason to kill you," she ran off the information to Kayson as if she was purging her heart.

Kayson looked at her and listened to her plan as she carefully diagramed it from start to finish. Yuri had put all the players in the room that he needed to get at, and while she ran off her plan, he was designing one of his own. He could see the lust in her eyes to get her some sort of payback, and he could feel the urge inside him to have the same.

"Why now? And why are you choosing to assist me?" Kayson asked.

Yuri's face drew a blank expression and she stared at a small piece of lint on the plush carpet. Yuri tossed her logic around in her head then let it all go.

"They crossed me. My brother's greed made him go behind our back and side with your wife, which almost got my life taken. My father's ways are archaic; this family needs new leadership and new blood and I want to build that with you," she threw her proposition on the table.

"So, how much money are we talking?"

"It's just a few mill, but that isn't it; I can get money, that's not the issue. It's the power I want Kayson. I want it so bad I can taste it. I need you," she said, looking up into his eyes.

"Let me think about it. I need to run some shit around in my head."

Yuri sat her glass on the table and stood up. "Look, I know you don't trust me; but just know I would not have reached out to you if I didn't know we could both benefit immensely," she walked up on him.

"Is that right? And all you are interested in is prestige?"

"What is more important than that?" she looked up in his eyes.

"You ain't got shit coming over here."

"Oh, indeed...I would love to experience all this real deep from the back with my ponytail tight in your grip," she eased up closer breathing in his aroma. "But, don't flatter yourself, Mr. Wells; this isn't about you. It's about me," she stepped back, turning toward the door.

"I will wait for your response," she held onto the doorknob in a jester that his visit was over.

Kayson gave her a sneaky smirk as he moved toward her. "Stay in your place, little girl; play with this grown man shit if you want to." He lookd her up and down. "Standing there with your pussy all wet, I'm surprised you didn't slip and bust yo ass on the way to the door," he looked her over once more then moved past her.

Yuri chuckled. "Hurry Mr. Wells, we can't afford to lose time."

Yuri closed the door as she calmed her raising pulse. She moved back to the bar and poured herself a drink with plenty of ice. She guzzled half the glass then rolled the glass over her forehead. Kayson gave her all kinds of flames throughout her body every time he was near her. Yuri knew that she was playing with fire, but she was ready to burn on all his flames.

Yuri managed to have a few of her corrupt police connections on the island intercept three of her brother Peppa's shipments; putting him at the mercy of his suppliers. Within days she had managed to dismantal his whole plan. Peppa was out of his legue and at the end of his rope. Yuri was sitting in her father's office in the high back grey chair reading a book as Peppa walked back and forth in the middle of the floor ranting.

Mr. Odoo listened with very little interest. After Kayson had caused him to lose the respect of his peers in certain circles by allowing him to touch him and his family and still live, Mr. Odoo was forced to cave in to Peppa's desire to move dope through the ports.

Mr. Odoo looked over at his daughter who seemed to have become very withdrawn after the ordeal with Kayson. He watched as she sat quiet; while Peppa fumed, her usual quest to prove him wrong did not exist.

"Yuri, what are you thinking?" he asked, causing Peppa to stop in his tracks and look coldly at his father.

Peppa turned his gaze to Yuri who looked up slowly from her book and spoke a soothing tone.

"Father, I think we need outside help. This is bigger than us," Yuri spoke softly.

"Outside help is what got us into this shit," Peppa barked, throwing his hands to the side.

"How can you lead with such a temper?" she asked, looking at him with a face of stone. "You are too emotional. You need to move with your mind, not your blind pride," she said from her seat as if she was already sitting on the throne.

"I guess while he had you, he let you snuggle up next to him because you seem to have his tongue in your mouth," Peppa spat the words of contempt as if they had venom on them.

"I guess KoKo did you with the same dick. With your dumb ass," Yuri returned with a smirk on her face.

"Enough!" Mr. Odoo yelled out, bringing them both to a pause. "I will not have this," he asserted. "We are a family. This man doesn't get to come in here and destroy us," he raised his voice another octave.

Peppa turned his eyes to his father. "I apologize," he said and did a slight bow.

"I am sorry also, father," Yuri stood and moved to her father's side.

"We have to hold strong in times of war or the enemy will get the whole castle," he looked into his son's eyes.

Peppa calmed his spirit and nodded in agreement. Yuri looked at Peppa with teary eyes; she turned over and over in her head Peppa's words and each time, they cut deeper into her soul. Peppa had no idea that his words had just confirmed him a position as the sacrificial lamb at the birth of her rule. Yuri squeezed her father's shoulder as she claimed her spot. Blood was going to be shed and she was willing to take every life in the house.

Chapter 20

More than a night to Remember

Baseem prepared the last of his plans for the weekend and headed downtown to pick up Simone. When he pulled up in front of her office building, he got a tickle in his stomach like it was his first date.

"Nigga, yo ass is trippin'," he said aloud then chuckled at the thought of being nervous. Baseem stepped out of the vehicle and leaned up against the trunk to wait for Simone to appear.

Four o'clock on the dot, Simone emerged from the building moving fast and talking faster. She was swinging her briefcase in one hand and holding her cell phone to her ear with the other.

"Look, we have to get this together by Monday; no questions. So just get ready to be tucked inside until this project is done," Simone said to her team on the phone then disconnected as she approached Baseem.

"Hey, baby," Baseem said as he opened his arms to receive her.

"Hey, baby," she pouted. "I have bad news; I need to reschedule our weekend. I have to get so much work done. But I promise to make it up to you."

"Man, fuck that project shit. You got a date with the middle of a king size bed with a sexy ass nigga making you know you're a woman," Baseem said firmly, not trying to hear anything she was saying.

"Baby, you know I want that so much, but my team is

depending on me and this project is what I need to get to the next level," she said as his hands caressed her body speaking the words his mouth didn't have to say.

"Like I said…we got plans. Hit that chic back and delegate some shit and daddy will let you play with them for a little while tomorrow when you wake up," he smacked her butt as he released her from his arms. "Get in," he pulled the door open and gestured for her to get in.

Simone took a deep breath. "I guess I have no other choice; huh?"

"No, you do not."

Simone hit her alarm and retrieved her bag and placed it in his trunk; then she moved to the open door.

"You almost got raped in the parking lot; don't make me change my mind."

Simone's mouth dropped open.

"Close your mouth, baby; I got something for that later," he said closing the door behind her.

When Baseem got in the car Simone was looking at him with the side-eye.

"What's up?"

"What you plan on putting in my mouth?" she crossed her arms over her chest.

"I'm just planning on feeding you that's all, baby," Baseem looked at her with low eyes.

"Yeah, alright; let me find out, as you would say."

Baseem chuckled. "Don't worry, baby. I will only put in your mouth what you allow me to put in there," he licked his lips letting his eyes roam over her body.

"You so nasty."

"You haven't seen nasty yet," he said as he pulled off.

Simone buckled her seat belt and said a little prayer; she wanted to get it out of the way in case God didn't want to know her after this weekend.

Baseem turned on his satellite radio and hit cruise control.

Simone looked over at the sexy man to her left and went into chill mode. She kicked off her shoes and did just as Baseem said.

132

She gave out assignments to the team and scheduled a conference call for tomorrow afternoon because her late night and early morning belonged to Baseem.

When Baseem and Simone pulled up to the beautiful all-white country home with the huge bay windows siting on a half-acre of land, Simone put her face toward the sun and inhaled. She embraced the heat on her skin then opened the door and stepped out.

"This place is gorgeous," she said, allowing her eyes to take a tour of the land. The tall, green grass seemed to go on for miles as huge willow trees dressed the edges out in the distance.

"Thank you, it belonged to my grandparents, I just use it for peace of mind," Baseem said as he popped the trunk and grabbed their bags.

"This is the type of place you come to and just let everything go," she put her hands behind her back and clasped her fingers together. Baseem looked at her perky breast and pictured how each one would taste in his mouth. "I want you to let everything go tonight," he stepped up on her; leaned in and placed his lips on hers and sucked gently, tasting her freaky thoughts.

Simone's eye lashes fluttered as he tasted her tongue. Baseem's soft lips drew her into his every desire. Simone reached up and placed her hands to the side of his face and let her lips and tongue tell her pussy's secret. Baseem had her whole body on fire and she was more than ready to give him everything he wanted.

Baseem pulled back. "Look at you, acting like you ready," he licked her soft brown lips.

Simone looked at him with low eyes and heavy breath. "You better be gentle."

"In the morning; but tonight, I'ma eat yo ass up," he said as he passed her. "Let's go, ain't shit out here to save you; even your cries for help won't save you," he joked as he opened the door.

Simone clutched her briefcase and headed up the steps; she was about to learn why Baseem was that nigga. Baseem opened the windows and doors and placed the food in the refrigerator, then the bags in the room. Simone uncovered the furniture and folded the sheets neatly.

"I got that, ma," Baseem said as he took the sheets from her hands and placed them in the laundry room. When he returned, he had two thick throws in his hands. Baseem opened then and draped them over the huge brown couches.

"Sit down and relax; I got you, baby," Baseem said, giving Simone a sexy smile.

"Okay. Do you mind if I get some work done?" she asked, taking a seat and reaching for her briefcase.

"No work. Let me have that," he said, taking the case from her hands. "Just sit and relax and let all that office shit go. Can you do that for me?" he softened the blow.

"Yes, baby. I can do that for you," she surrendered, crossing her legs and wrapping the fluffy throw around her shoulders.

"Thank you," he winked as he walked off.

Baseem put a Nina Simone record on his grandfather's old record player and introduced Simone to the other side of him. Simone sat and watched as he began to prepare their meal. Her mouth watered as the array of aromas invaded her airways.

Baseem marinated the steak and placed it on the grill, then he cut up potatoes and put them on to boil. When he returned from outside, he had an assortment of green lettuce and carrots. He rinsed everything and diced it into a salad and placed it in the refrigerator.

"You ready?" Baseem asked as he reached out for her hand.

"I guess so," Simone said as she rose to her feet.

Baseem turned and led her to the bathroom.

Simone smiled when she saw the huge, white, old fashioned tub sitting in the center of the room.

"Have a seat," he instructed as he turned and grabbed some cleaning supplies and wiped everything down and ran a tub of hot water. Baseem lit a few white lavender candles and hit the intercom to let the music enhance the atmosphere.

Baseem went and drained his potatoes and turned the steak down low so it could smoke. When he walked back into the bathroom, Simone was looking out the window at the sun beginning to leave the sky. The various shades of red, orange and blue in the distance put her spirit at ease. Baseem walked over to her and wrapped his arms around her waist and kissed her softly on her neck.

"You need this, baby. Just let everything that exists outside of that skyline just survive until you get back," he kissed her neck again then he turned her to face him.

Simone looked up into his eyes as his hands unloosened her buttons and let her breast greet him. Baseem dropped her blouse to the floor then let her skirt follow. He stood in front of her; lusting at her beauty as his fingertips enjoyed the silky glide across her skin. Baseem settled his hands at the small of her back.

"You gonna let me have control of this body tonight?" he asked as his eyes pierced her skin.

Diana Ross bellowed out, "Good morning heartache." Baseem mumbled along with the words as he lowered her bra straps from her shoulder. Her soft nipples called his lips to them and he answered by placing his mouth over one and circled his tongue wildly while sucking tenderly.

"Ssss..." Simone bit into her bottom lip as she braced her feet to the floor. She closed her eyes and let her body feel every tingle.

Baseem placed his mouth on her other nipple and nibbled gently as his hands found their way between her thighs. Simone placed her hand on top of his as she began to feel the jolts of energy pulsating on her clit. His finger showed no mercy, pressing and circling to the beat of her every moan. Baseem grabbed her firmly around the waist and treated her pussy to a finger fantasy. He rotated between pushing his thick fingers deep inside her, to circling her clit with precision.

"Just hold on to me, baby...and let me make you cum," Baseem whispered in her ear as she tried to back up from the pressure.

"Basss..." Simone cried out as her body gave into his pleasure. She gripped his shoulders and rested her head on his chest. She pulled her lids together as intense emotion and fear paralyzed her movement. Simone wanted to push back to control the impact, but her body said surrender. She dug her nails into his flesh, bit into her lip and let go.

Baseem continued to play with her spot as her cries of pleasure rang loud in his ear. As her body jerked in his arms, he placed soft

135

kisses on her face. Simone nuzzled her face against his chest as she attempted to catch her breath.

"Give me kiss," his deep, rasp summoned her lips.

Simone lifted her heavy head and gave him what he asked for.

"That's what I'm talking about. Let me wash you so I can feed you," he pulled at her panties until they hit the floor.

Simone followed his every command as he took her from one ecstasy to the next. Baseem washed every inch of her body, caressing her muscles along the way. Simone lay back on the soft pillow and enjoyed the force of his fingers all over her body. Baseem placed her foot on his chest and ran his fingers up and down her leg and thigh.

"Baby, that feels so good," she moaned as he massaged places on her body she didn't know she had.

Baseem didn't respond; he just listened to her body and gave her what she needed. After they washed and rinsed, they put on matching white robes and Baseem finished preparing the meal.

Simone sat with her feet up on the couch wrapped in the blanket. She watched as Baseem moved around the kitchen. He poured her a glass of red wine and served it to her with a strawberry on the side.

"This is how I want my pussy to taste," he feed her a slice of mango then leaned in and kissed the juice from her lips. "Mmm...I'ma have so much fun with you tonight."

"I bet you are," she said seductively as she took the glass from his hand.

Baseem chuckled then headed to finish the meal. He mashed and seasoned the potatoes and spread them out in a pan with cheddar cheese and sour cream. Then he placed them in the oven and went for the steak.

Simone's stomach began to grumble as she smelled the steam coming off of the meat. Baseem prepared the plates, and then joined her in the living room bringing the bottle of wine along for the journey. The two of them ate and talked and laughed. Simone put her feet in his lap and chattered away while she sank her teeth in to every succulent bite. Baseem sat and listened and learned. He took note to the way she expressed every word. She was a strong and successful woman; but she was injured. He paid close attention to what her soul was crying out for and he planned every position he was going to put her body and her mind in to help heal her pain.

"Bas, you don't..." she pressed her hand on his forehead.

"Trust me, baby. I been preparing this meal, I definitely know how to eat it," Baseem said as he removed her hand and cupped her legs securely in his arms. He started with soft tender kisses and long slow licks. Simone gripped the sheets slightly, wiggling her waist as she felt his tongue flip back and forth on her clit.

"Baass..." she cried out arching her back as he stuck his tongue inside her.

Baseem used every cry and movement against her; repeating each movement until her body quivered to be free from his grip. He then placed his warm, wet lips over her sticky pearl; sucking hard between lapping the juices from between her lips.

Simone groaned from the tips of her toes to the curve of her lips as she felt vibrations of heated passion move through her body that she had never experienced before. Short, hot, breaths left her lips as she braced herself to release to him her center's sultry nectar. She squirmed from side to side as he pinned her in place; Simone inhaled deeply and let go.

"Oh, my God..." she cried out as her pussy submitted to his merciless tongue.

Baseem licked slowly as she twitched to his touch. "Mmm..." he sighed, then flipped her over on her stomach. "Lift up," he commanded, getting in position to add some panty-wetting memories to her mental rolodex.

Simone pushed up on her knees and rested her head on the pillow. Baseem parted her butt cheeks and licked easily around her wet opening.

"Ssss...baby," she mumbled as he began to pleasure her pussy on a pedestal and praised it. Simone was on the edge once again as Baseem sucked, licked and nibbled her lips and clit while giving her deep-finger thrust; tickling her secret spot within.

"I'm about to cum, baby," she panted; and as the words left her lips, her body gave in to his desire.

Baseem gripped her luscious cheeks in the palm of his hands

137

and licked slowly up and down her sweet opening and the crack of her ass, taking full advantage of the control she released to him. Simone twitched and let out a gut-wrenching cry. Clutching the pillow in her arms, she buried her face and screamed; her legs trembled beneath her as her pussy let go of years of yearning. Simone rested her body against the bed as Baseem eased her out of his grip.

Baseem got up off the bed, admiring the effect his head game had on her body. He wiped his face on a small towel and strapped up for the next level of his journey. Before getting back on the bed, he retrieved the baby oil gel from the bathroom then climbed up behind her.

"You good, baby?" he asked as he began to drizzle the oil on her skin.

"Yeesss..." Simone replied, closing her eyes and enjoying the moment as his strong hands glided along her body.

Baseem carefully massaged each body part relaxing all her muscles. Simone stretched her arms out and welcomed every touch. When Baseem got her to a point of total submission, he rested his body over hers and placed his thickness between her legs; parting them with his feet.

"Not from the back, Bas," she became alarmed at the mere thought.

"Relax, ma. I got you, baby," he comforted her as he positioned himself to enter her garden. Slowly, he pushed in; listening and responding to every moan she released and ignoring only the pleas for him to stop.

"Ahhh...not too deep, Bas," Simone panted as he broke down her tightness one carefully unrestricted stroke at a time.

"Deep dick is good dick, baby; let daddy work this pussy for you, baby," Baseem groaned as he fed her slippery inches deeper with every push. "Close your feet at the ankle," he ordered, putting his feet outside of hers when her pussy muscles snuggled around his dick causing him to pick up speed.

Simone complied to his commands and received more levels of ecstasy as he circled and down stroked deeply with every thrust.

"Ahhh...you feel so good, baby. Make me cum, Bas," Simone

let him have her every thought; she needed to make sure he could give her pussy every pleasure imaginable.

"Shit...this is what daddy like right here," Baseem let down his guard and began enjoying the feast that lay before him. He placed sensual kisses along her back; watching her fingers clench tightly to the sheets as he made up for lost time. "I gotta feel this pussy," Baseem moaned, pulling out.

"Get up on your knees, baby," he ordered as he rolled off the plastic.

Simone got into position and jumped when his hands held her in place and his inches entered her raw.

"Bas, no."

"Just a little bit, baby. Let me play in your wetness, baby," he whispered, pulling her into him slowly.

"Bas, hurry," she panted, looking over her shoulder at the passion on his face as he watched his dick slid in and out.

"I thought you wanted to cum," Baseem said as he searched for that spot that released the water.

"I do," Simone muttered, turning her head and placing it in the pillow as she felt Baseem pleasing her spot.

"Let me make my pussy cum, baby," he distracted her mind with quick short strokes against her G.

"Yesss..." she cried out and rocked back into his push.

Baseem got a little excited and went in deep and hard; when he saw his dick gloss up, he brought her back and forth into him again, ignoring her pleas.

Simone tried to bury her face, but Baseem snatched the pillows and threw them on the floor.

"Nah, ma. I need to hear that shit," Baseem handled her pussy like the beast that he was.

"Basss...I'm cumming...oh, my God!" she yelled out and reached back, grabbing his wrist to slow his stride.

"Move your hand baby and let that happen," he said, punishing her spot.

Simone again felt the currents move throughout her body; she took in a mouthful of air and released the pressure. Baseem slowed his stroke and dipped in and out of her liquid heat as she tried to recover. He thought about strapping up, but the pussy wouldn't allow him to stop. He pumped to the rhythm of her moans; holding her butter-soft skin between his fingers as he hit the pussy from the side.

"You all mine now, baby," he taunted as his stride quickened. "You gonna make daddy cum?" he asked, not missing a stroke.

"Yesss...but you gotta strap up, Bas," her lips responded, but her kitty was saying, you better not move.

Baseem pulled out and flipped her on her back; as he pushed back in, Simone dug her nails into his flesh.

"Baseem," she pouted as he went in for his attack, "Bas, be gentle," she begged as she saw the hunger in his eyes.

Baseem looked down into her face at her humble request but he showed no mercy. He placed one leg over his shoulder and went in deep; her slippery lips welcomed every stroke. He ravished what was left of her; sucking her nipples and biting into the plumpness of her breast. Baseem moved his muscular frame and long thick dick between her thighs, bringing them to the brink.

"Ssss...I'm about to come, baby; you want me stop?" Baseem asked tonguing her deeply.

Simone crumbled to his lust as he found and pleasured her spot. They moaned and grinded their centers together as the heat suffocated the air around them. Baseem pushed in deep and released as she grinded close on his pole, stimulating her clit against his pelvis until she let go right along with him. Baseem kept his mouth on hers and played with her tongue while she held him tight.

"I love you," she moaned between kisses as a tear ran down the side of her face.

"I know," he replied as he felt his dick rocking back up.

"No, Bas," she mumbled as she felt her pussy throbbing

"Haven't you realized by now I don't listen to no," he said as he began to stoke.

Simone just closed her eyes and let him have whatever he wanted. She was rewarded with a long, thick dick that could hit her spot repeatedly without question or instruction. She came and cried until he decided she was done. When Simone could no longer move, Baseem rolled over on his back, pulled her on top of him and covered her sexy limp body.

"Bas, I can't," she incoherently mumbled.

"I know. This is the position I want you in when you wake up," he replied as he reached on the nightstand, grabbed a blunt and lit up. "Rest up, ma. He ain't going to be playing when he wake up," he warned, inhaling deeply.

"Well, what do you call what just happened?" she looked up at him with low eyes.

"Foreplay," Baseem answered, blowing thick smoke into the air.

Simone felt her stomach drop. "You are taking advantage of me," she joked, resting her head on his chest.

"Yup, all weekend; and there is no one here to help you."

When Simone opened her eyes, her heart fluttered at the memories of the night before. Baseem had managed to give her body a plethora of enjoyment. She swung her feet over the side of the bed then striped the sheets and headed for the shower. Her nostrils opened wide at the smell of fresh coffee. She hopped in the shower and washed her pleasantly-pleased aching body. Simone smiled while lathering her skin. She pictured his hands, mouth, and body all over hers while showing her pussy long, deep love. She rinsed her skin and stepped out; after lotioning from head to toe, she slipped on a thong then into a thin pink sundress and headed to the kitchen.

Simone looked around the kitchen at the arrangement he set up, an assortment of fresh muffins in a basket and fruit sliced nicely on a tray. She grabbed a handful of grapes and poured herself a cup of coffee. Simone stood looking out at the field sipping hot brew when a familiar smell rose in her nostrils. She moved toward the front door and peeked out the screen to see Baseem sitting in a chair with his feet propped up smoking weed in an old fashion grandfather pipe.

"Good morning," Simone said as she pushed open the screen door.

"Hey, sexy," he responded, putting out his hand. "Did you sleep well?" he asked as she came to his side.

"Yes, too well. That bed put a spell on me," she giggled, placing her hand into his.

"Nah, that's was that real dick action; you ain't use to that," he patted his thigh for her to sit down.

"I sure do now," Simone said, perching herself on his lap.

Baseem gave her a half smile.

Simone looked down in to his face and saw so much beauty combined with so much pain. "Who are you?" she asked, stroking the side of his face.

Baseem chuckled. "Come take a walk with me," he said, motioning for her to stand. Baseem tucked his pipe away and took her by the hand. As they walked through the field, Baseem pointed out different spots on the land where he had shared special summers and occasions with his grandparents. Simone laughed as he pointed to the tree he had to get switches from when he got out of hand. They walked past the grape vines and then toward the huge willow trees.

Simone smiled from the inside out as she began to feel closer to him. Baseem shared a few more stories then stopped by the side of a brook that ran between the trees.

"This is my favorite spot. I came here many days and nights to cleanse my mind."

"You need to do more things that will not haunt your mind," Simone stated gently.

"Haven't ever had a reason to," he looked her in the eyes.

"I can try to give you one or two."

"We'll see."

"Why are you so afraid to love?" she asked, looking at the flow of the water.

"Niggas like me are different. We love when we can and kill anything or anyone that may threaten or destroy that love. Can you live with that?"

"I don't know," she stated honestly.

"I don't think you have a choice," he turned her face toward him.

"There is always a choice," she combated.

"Yup, and from the beat of your heart, yours is already made," he reached out and pulled her into his arms.

"You really think you know me," she said as she melted to his touch.

"Mannn...yo ass is an open book. When I made that pussy cum the first time, you gave me the key to all your secrets."

"Whatever," she hit his arm. "Well, what are my secrets?"

"You fell in love with me the first day you met me; and even though you didn't want to...stopping it at this point is not an option," he stated firmly.

"Like I said, whatever," she turned her face back to the stream.

"Don't worry, I won't tell," he smacked her butt then pulled out his pipe and lit it up. He held her with her back to his chest as they stared out at nature and enjoyed the serenity. "Here, take a little hit of this heat so you can get your mind right," he joked.

Simone tuned in his direction. "I don't do that," she wrinkled her noise up and pushed his hand away.

"I know you don't, but do it for me. I want all your firsts," he stared at her with intense eyes. "I'm about to give you a gift," he extended his arm, passing her the pipe filled with purple and Acapulco gold.

Simone looked up then hesitantly took the pipe from his hands. She looked at it from bowl to tip then placed it to her lips and Baseem lit up. Simone took three deep pulls on the tip just like she had seen Baseem do. Her eyes watered up and her throat did a reverse as she began to choke and cough out smoke.

Baseem laughed as he watched her hold her chest and take short breaths.

"That ain't funny. What is that?" she asked, giving him the side-eye.

"That's some grown man shit; don't even worry about it," he tucked his pipe away in the case and slid it in his pocket.

"Helloooo...I am not a grown man. I am a grown woman if you haven't noticed," Simone spoke with a frisky tongue, running her hands over her curves as she felt a tingling energy and a numbing sensation take over her body.

Baseem chuckled watching her eyelids get heavy. "You're not a grown woman yet; but I am about to make you one," he reached over and slid her dress strap off her shoulder. "Let me have this," he spoke deep as he slid the other strap off.

Simone lowered her gaze and put her hands up to her chest to catch her falling dress.

"Relax, I got you, baby; let me have all of you. Step out of this," he instructed.

Simone complied then covered her breast as she stood in front of Baseem exposed; wearing nothing but her thong and her purity. Her eyes darted from left to right surveying the area.

"It's just me and you, baby,"

Baseem lifted her chin and kissed her lips lightly; then he stared at her beautiful body as the mid-morning glow caressed her coco-bronze skin. "Move your hands," he spoke firmly then watched as her perky breast sprang from her hands. Baseem pulled off his tank and pulled her in close so that her erect nipples rested against his chest.

Simone's breaths quickened as the heat from his body caused her kitty to tingle and moisten.

"You are so beautiful. I want you to let me love you. Let me be your comfort," he said as he placed a tender kiss on her forehead.

"You have to take care of my heart," she uttered; a little over a whisper.

"I can do that, but you owe me the same courtesy," he said as he rubbed his fingers over her nipples.

"Don't take me too fast; I still don't know who you really are," Simone rested her hand on his wrist.

"Let me show you," he responded, enjoying the innocence on her face.

Simone nodded her head up and down as his hands caressed the cup of her breast.

"Climb up here so you can sit on all this power while I tell you a story," Baseem loosened his sweatpants, released the beast, and stroked himself to full capacity. He lifted her up and placed her around his waist.

Simone looked into his eyes as his thickness parted her lips, she inhaled his every breath as he moved her back and forth on him.

"Ssss..." Baseem hissed as her juices began to cover him; her tightness squeezed around his rod. Her body tried to force itself away from him as he hurt and pleased her on every in and out stroke.

"Baseem, go slow, baby," she moaned.

"Relax and enjoy this dick. You feeling these inches, baby?" he repeated as he pulled her into his him and grinded deep.

"Yesss..." Simone wrapped her legs around his waist and held on tightly as he bounced her effortlessly. The sounds of bird's chirping and the sight of pretty butterflies dancing on flowers enhanced her mood. She closed her eyes tight each time he pulled her in and she opened them on his way out. A slightly warm breeze tickled her skin as she panted and chanted his name. The echo of her cries and his grunts filled the wooded area as he pumped her pussy just right. Simone put her head back and watched the clouds move in the sky as he stirred the center of her being.

"You gotta be all mine," Baseem whispered as he bit into her neck.

Heated passion filed their bodies as they kissed and sucked each other's lips and tongue. Simone began to jump a little as she felt her orgasm coming on strong.

"Damn it, Baseem," she tisked, gripping the back of his neck tight. She again threw her head back and let the sun cover her face as she closed her eyes and released. Baseem continued to pump in her slippery nectar as she moved against him to keep the waves going.

"I wanna love you, Bas," she moaned as the sensations got stronger and more intense.

"You wanna love me, baby?" he asked, attending to her spot.

"Yes, with everything I have," she said as the sensations took over her thoughts. Simone held on to him and released again.

Baseem was in his glory; he continued to work her spot and in return, she gave him her soul. When they could no longer stand it, Baseem headed back to the house sliding in and out of her every step of the way. Simone crumbled to his power and bowed to his dicks greatness as he showed her G-spot; he was in charge. Baseem let her enjoy wetting him up, then he tasted his pussy and put it to sleep with a deep nut of his own. After a hot shower and light lunch, they fell into the bed and were out. Simone looked up from her pillow and the darkness stole her vision. She grabbed her cell phone to check the time and saw all the missed calls, text and voice messages. She eased off the bed put on her robe. She kissed Baseem's cheek then headed to the living room.

Simone opened her laptop and called her assistant. She had missed the phone conference and her part of the project. She got filled in and immediately went to work. Baseem surfaced four hours later wanting all her attention. Simone looked up from her phone and mouthed, Be good, as she typed the corrections into the document that was being dictated to her.

Baseem kissed her lips then headed to the kitchen to start their dinner. He fried some chicken and made rice and corn. Simone finished her project and joined him at the table for dinner.

"Thank you so much, Bas. I needed this weekend," she said as she placed the hot tender chicken in her mouth. Simone did a little dance as the flavors danced on her tongue. "I love you," she said, taking another bit.

"Was that for me or the chicken?" he joked.

"Both," she laughed.

"Let me find out," he chuckled.

Baseem and Simone ate and talked, then topped off their evening with his pipe, Harlem Nights, and Coming to America. Baseem held her in his arms and laughed at how high she was. Simone laughed and cried, holding her stomach as Eddie Murphy and Richard Pryor cut up. Before Baseem allowed her to rest her head on the pillow, he climbed back between her silky thighs and sealed their weekend with several mind-blowing orgasms. As they packed up the car the next afternoon, Simone stared off into the distance wondering where he would take her from here. She took in the whole area and said a little prayer that all that he was showing her wasn't the lull before a big ass storm.

* * * * *

Simone hit the alarm clock about five times before she finally convinced herself to get out of bed. She could barely lift her legs to stand and the thought of leaving the house was almost sickening. Simone wanted to pull the covers over her head and sleep for at least ten hours. She struggled into the bathroom, showered, pulled on a pants suit and made the biggest cup of coffee she could find. As she drove, her mind continuously played the many positions Baseem twisted and bent her body into. Then she thought about how many times she yelled out she was about to cum. Slight embarrassment crept into her fantasy as she stepped outside herself to see her naked body against Baseem's in the woods. Simone shook her head and covered her mouth. When Simone got out of her car, she put some stride in her step; thinking of getting to her desk and calling Baseem to hear his sexy voice.

Simone almost skipped off the elevator and to her office. She threw her bag under the desk, turned on her computer, and then retrieved her cell phone. Her heart raced as she listened to each ring, then it dropped when his machine came on.

"Shit," she mumbled then hung up. She sat the phone down and stared at it as her mind began to play tricks on her. "Nope, not going to go there," she said aloud then hit the intercom button.

"Do have any messages?" her voice rang out at her assistant's desk.

"No, Mr. did not call," her assistant shot back.

"Can you say, 'Mandatory overtime and every other Saturday?'" Simone responded joking, but yet very serious.

"Uh, negative. Your mandingo warrior has not summoned you yet, my queen."

Simone busted out laughing. "Shut up," she said then disconnected. She sat at her desk in a trance thinking about why he didn't answer his phone. A haunting thought of her girl saying, "You know how those types of niggas are," and "Watch your back" kept fighting for a place in her heart. She quickly snapped out of it and dove into her work. By twelve o'clock, she was well into her day and back to the old Simone. Just as she was preparing to leave for lunch, her cell phone vibrated on the desk. She looked down and saw it was Baseem and decided to send him to voicemail. She stood with nervous energy then waited to see if he left a message. When the icon popped up, she snatched the phone off the desk and hit visual voicemail.

"Hey, baby. Sorry I missed your call; you had a brother knocked out up in here. I'm going back to sleep. Hit me when you get home."

Simone's eyes got big and she tried to dial him back.

"Hello," he answered groggily

"Hey, baby," she responded.

"Sorry, I missed your call; you good?"

"Yes, I am now," she flirted like a school girl.

"You sound like you need to be lying next to me," Baseem said with his eyes closed, half awake.

"I do, baby," she cooed into the receiver.

"Then bring me that ass," Baseem said firmly.

"I'm on my way," she stood up, gathering her things and shutting down her system.

"You ain't getting no dick, you going to sleep," Baseem stated.

"Whatever, just open the door when I get there," she said, hanging up and grabbing her briefcase.

When she passed the desk with her bag, her assistant looked up. "Where the hell you going," she whispered looking at her watch.

"Please cover for me, I gotta go."

"Bitch, you just got here," she said then busted out laughing.

"I know, but that nigga right there," she shook her head.

"Ohhhh...you are in trouble. You better stay back from that dick," she warned.

"Girl, I can't," she said with all sincerity.

"Well then get prayed up, because he got a spell on that ass. Bitch leaving work mid-day like its half-day in kindergarten. I got you, get away from my desk."

"Shut up," Simone laughed as she headed to the elevator. On her way down, she thought about what she said as she fidgeted with the smooth leather on her Celine bag, but her tunnel vision would not allow her to care.

Chapter 21

Dinner is Served...

KoKo had been running for the last three days trying to get everything ready for Kayson's dinner party. She moved around the kitchen, checking to make sure each item that was needed for the party was purchased and ready to be prepared. KoKo pulled a few wine glasses from the box and held them to the light. The smoked glass with Swarovski crystals shimmered as she tilted it back and forth.

Kayson walked in the kitchen and a smile formed on his lips when he saw KoKo so focused on her task. The red knee-length, thin sundress clung to her frame and hugged under her booty cheeks just right. "Good evening, Mrs. Wells," Kayson joked, coming up behind her and wrapping his arms around her waist.

"Good evening, Mr. Wells; now let me go, I have a ton of things to do," she turned her head to the side and kissed along his jawbone while pulling at his wrist.

"Stop being mean to the boss. Turn around and let me taste your lips," he spun her slightly to face him.

"Real quick and then you have to leave this area; I have things to do, sir," she said, wrapping her arms around his neck and pulling his lips to hers.

Kayson kissed her deeply, caressing her butt firmly in his hands. "I need to taste you, baby," he said, pulling back from their embrace and taking her hand. He pulled her toward the table.

"Kay, we do not have time for that. The kitchen staff will be here any minute," she tried to pull her hand from his grip.

"Come sit on daddy's hot seat for a minute."

KoKo turned to look back at the kitchen door, then back at Kayson as he positioned himself in the chair.

KoKo straddle his legs and stood still watching as his fingers slid up between her thighs, slipping past the silk of her thong. She rested her hands on his shoulders as he traced her lips with the tips of his fingers; back and forth he glided them in her wetness. "Baby, why don't you wait until I finish with everyone then I can give you whatever you want in private,"

"This is the king's palace; he gets whatever he wants, where ever he wants it," he slid his hands up the sides of her dress, pulling at the string to her panties.

"Is that right?" she said, looking down into the intensity of his eyes as she felt her panties fall to her ankles.

"Come sit up here," he grabbed her leg and placed it over his shoulder; then he gave the other one the same treatment.

Kayson inhaled deep and planted a few short kisses on the lips of her pussy. Kayson was in his favorite position; to him, nothing was better than being face to face with some good, wet pussy. He gripped her lower back and nibbled on her thighs.

KoKo dug her heels into the back of the chair as his tongue connected with her clit. "Mmmm..." she moaned, pulling her dress up toward her waist so she could watch the king worship her. She wrapped her hands firmly around the back of his neck and rode smoothly to the rhythm of his tongue. The room filled with KoKo's sexy moans as Kayson slid his tongue deep inside of her. When her legs began to tremble and tighten on his shoulders, he placed his mouth over her clit and firmly sucked as she struggled to be free from his grip.

KoKo dug her nails into the back of the chair as she leaned her chest against his head. "Oh, my God," was all she could utter as she released a slippery splash all over his lips.

Kayson – knowing his pussy – adhered to what she needed after she squirted in his mouth. He pulled her onto his lap and proceeded to release the Enforcer.

"Kay, no...we don't have time, baby," she slightly resisted.

"Stop telling me no. You know that shit don't work with me.

Lift up!" He ordered, placing her onto his steel.

"Do what daddy likes," he pulled her up and down as he stiffened inside her.

KoKo pulled her feet up onto the sides of the chair placed her hands on his chest and gave him what he liked.

KoKo's attention was divided between Kayson hitting that spot, and the voices approaching the kitchen while rocking and squeezing his dick tightly between her walls.

"Baby, we gotta stop; they are going to be in here," she mumbled, bouncing slippery wetness all over the Enforcer.

"Then you better hurry up and cum," his deep voice caressed her ear as he bit repeatedly into her neck.

KoKo bounced to her pleasure as the intensity to cum and the fear of the approaching voices filled her body like hot coal as she again began to release. Just as her body shook and pressed against his chest, the first two chefs turned the corner with smiles on their faces that quickly turned into wide mouths and wide-eyed stares.

Kayson waved away the beet red faces with one hand and held KoKo's body tight against his with the other. They quickly turned on their heels and headed back to the dining area and closed the glass doors.

"You good, baby?" Kayson asked then took her head into his hands and kissed along her face until he got to her lips and sucked them tenderly.

"Yes, baby; I'm good, thank you," she kissed him with intense heat and passion. "You always getting me in some shit," KoKo chuckled.

"You love every minute of it. You like getting in the Boss's hot seat. Lift up; come give these people their instructions so you can come get the boss right."

KoKo rose to her feet. "Oh no, we have too much to do; you need to go get ready," she said, moving back out of his arms reach.

"You crazy as hell. That was mommy time, daddy gotta get his," he gave her a raised brow as if to say discussion over.

KoKo grabbed her little clip board and shook her head. "You are too spoiled."

"Yup, and you already know I will be grouchy as hell tonight if I

151

don't get my medicine. Handle your business," he smacked her ass on their way out the kitchen.

When they approached the glass doors, all eyes were on them. "Hurry up," Kayson said, nodding his head at the staff as he moved toward the elevator.

KoKo was left to face the heat. She threw her head up high and said to herself fuck it. She quickly passed out her instructions and was off to give the boss his quality time. One hour before the event, KoKo had exited the shower to see Kayson stretched out in his towel. She put on her under clothes and robe and headed downstairs to check on the progress.

When she exited the elevator, she was more than pleasantly surprised; everything was set up just as she had instructed. Everything was tastefully white. The crisp tablecloths dressed with beautiful fan-shaped napkin displays on top of the silver plates and cutlery set the mood just right. KoKo walked into the kitchen and was embraced by the warm feelings and tantalizing smells. She moved around passing out a few directives and then she was out; headed back upstairs to get dressed. The Boss didn't do late and she knew she had to be on point.

* * * * *

KoKo walked around her bedroom putting on the last of her jewelry and running the night's agenda through her mind, making sure she had everything covered.

"You look beautiful," Kayson said as he eyed KoKo's curves in her form-fitting white body dress.

"Thank you, baby, and you need to finish getting ready," she said, looking at Kayson in his t-shirt and boxers.

"I got it. People are starting to arrive. You need to head downstairs and great them; and hurry up before you release the dragon," he warned, moving closer to where she stood.

"Oh no. I gave the Boss everything he needed," she said as Kayson walked up on her and took her into his arms.

"I love when you say no," he kissed her lips.

"Kayson, be good," she whined.

"I'ma be good for now; but after this party, I'ma act the fuck up," he kissed her again.

"You can have me any way you want me," she looked up in his eyes.

"Man, fuck this party," Kayson picked her up, causing KoKo to giggle and squirm in his arms.

Kayson kissed and nibbled on her neck, then put her back on her feet.

"Kay, stop!" she pushed, and then moved to the door.

Kayson laughed at KoKo as she celebrated her ability to escape him.

"You so silly...but on the real," he switched his mode, dropping the smile from his face. "Watch everybody's response tonight. We don't trust nobody but us."

"I got you, baby," KoKo nodded then blew him a kiss. "Hurry up, Boss; you're late," she looked at her watch then opened the door.

"You wanna be late," he moved toward her.

"Stop playing," KoKo's eyes got wide.

"You so damn scary," he stopped and turned around.

"Whatever," KoKo said as she headed downstairs.

When KoKo stepped off the elevator, she could hear several conversations; and as she got closer, she could see the staff passing out drinks and hors d'oeuvres. She put a smile on her face and entered the great room.

"Good evening everyone," she said, looking at the team which was very well dressed in all-white.

"Boss Lady," Baseem held his drink up in salute and everyone else followed.

KoKo walked over to Baseem to meet the woman she had heard so much about.

"This is Simone. Simone, this is my Boss."

"Pleased to meet you," Simone put her hand out.

"You too. Please enjoy the evening," KoKo shook her hand, taking in her attire. KoKo gave her the eye. "Baseem, we have a meeting in thirty minutes," she walked off.

Baseem smirked, he knew that the silence and exit was her way of saying she approved. Simone squeezed Baseem's hand and looked up with a little discomfort in her eyes.

"You good, ma. KoKo barks louder than she bites."

Simone took in some air and tried to prepare herself for the night.

KoKo worked the room as she awaited the arrival of the heavy hitter so they could get started. She smiled and joked enough, then moved on to the next person.

"Hey, Bas," Zori said, leaning in and hugging him tightly.

"Hey, mama; how you been?" he asked, thinking of the last time they were together.

"I'm good now," she flirted. They stood in a slight eye lock until Zori broke it and looked over at Simone. "Oh, hey…I'm Zori and you are?" she asked, extending her hand.

"Hi, I'm Simone," she returned the jester with a half-smile.

"Well, I hope you enjoy the evening," she gave her the once over. "Baseem, call me if you need anything, you know I have your back," she pushed up on her tiptoes and kissed his cheek. "See y'all later."

"A'ight," Baseem said feeling the heat coming up from between Zori's legs; and to be honest, he wanted to feel it. He shook it off as he felt the heat rising from Simone's brow.

"What's up, why you looking like that?"

"No reason, I'm good," she said, forcing a smile on her face.

"*We* good, beautiful," he leaned down and kissed her forehead. "Just relax and enjoy the night."

Simone nodded her head and gripped his hand as they moved through the room. She looked at all the high-end paintings and furniture. The picture above the fireplace of KoKo and Kayson had her intrigued.

"Is that the Boss's husband and why isn't he in charge?"

"That is the Boss. But his woman is just as thorough. That is how you build a strong team; you can have a rabbit running with a beast."

"I see," she said, then turned her attention to the expensive vases and figurines.

Baseem continued to move around the room with Simone on his side then headed to one of the couches to take a seat with Chucky and Pete and their wives. Simone eyed the variety of cheese and crackers and various flutes of white and red wine. After the introductions, the mood lightened; Simone found out that she and Chucky's wife had both attended Temple and the conversation was on from there. Simone began to loosen up and feel her spot in the room; that is until the shift of energy went to the entrance when Goldie walked in the room. Baseem's eyes glued themselves to her as she moved through the crowd. She was dressed in an all-white jumpsuit with a high collar and a deep V that went almost to her navel; accented with a silver waist chain. Her breast sat up perky and her ass was more than voluptuous as she stepped in her silver Louboutins.

Goldie commanded the attention of the wondering eyes as she moved gracefully to where KoKo stood. Baseem's eyes followed her every step. Her golden locks were pulled back into a bun showing off every beautiful feature in her face, then she smiled and lite up the room. Baseem smiled unconsciously, gazing at the length of her neck as she tilted her head to laugh. Simone looked up into his eyes and a knot formed in her stomach.

Baseem blinked back to reality then looked over at Simone. "Excuse me for a minute," he patted her hand and kissed her cheek.

Simone smiled as she watched Baseem walk toward Goldie. When he wrapped his arms around her waist, Simone dropped her smile and grabbed a glass of wine and a piece of cheese.

"Where's my little friend?" he asked.

"He is fast asleep with the rest of the little royal family," she smiled.

"Tell him we have a play date," he joked.

"I sure will. Did you get the pictures I sent to your phone?"

"Yes, I did; he was rocking that Burberry," Baseem smiled.

"Because his godfather spoils him," she nudged his shoulder.

"You know that's my dude. I'll see you in the meeting," Baseem hugged her again, enjoying her fragrance.

"Okay," she turned back to KoKo to continue her conversation.

Baseem rubbed his hands together then gained control of his smile as he turned, heading back to his seat.

Simone felt his presence and looked up giving him a sexy glare. "Hey, you," Baseem said as he took a seat.

Simone just widened her smile as she brought the wine to her lips. Baseem crossed his legs and sat back, then he pulled her close to him. She nuzzled against him, enjoying the comfort of his touch. Just as she began to enjoy the moment, Kayson walked into the room causing everyone to pause and acknowledge his presence.

Baseem got up and came to attention as they awaited the Boss's first words. KoKo moved to his side and took him by the hand; then touched every eye she could. Kayson scanned the crowded room taking note of who was present and who was not, then began.

"Thank you for coming out. You know these exchanges are to strengthen from the core out. Please mix among one another and enjoy our home; dinner will be served in an hour," Kayson said to the room then gave Baseem the nod. Kayson and KoKo turned toward the elevator and exited the room.

Goldie moved next; then Baseem stepped forward and turned his finger in a circle, catching the attention of the heads of each state. Then they followed the other bosses. The men moved almost in sync until the last one was no longer visible, leaving behind the crew, staff and all of the girlfriends and wives.

Simone stared at the other women who just went back to their conversations as if nothing had ever happened. She sat her glass down and grabbed another one; sitting back against the couch, she forced a smile and tried to engage in conversation with the other women. While talking to them, she knew that this was something she was not planning on dealing with. She was growing to love Baseem, but she was not sure this was for her.

Simone got up and moved around the room as she periodically looked at her watch. She had drunk four glasses of wine and was feeling her limit. As she moved for one more glass, she saw a few of the men returning. They came back in groups of two or three until everyone was in the room again. Baseem, Goldie and KoKo emerged then Kayson took up the rear. She watched as KoKo went in one direction and Kayson moved in the other; each stopping in different sections of the room. They spoke to who they needed to, and then they headed to a set of glass doors again. The music went down and Kayson announced that dinner was served.

Baseem took Simone by the hand, lifting her to her feet; then he led her to the dining area. Simone's eyes lit up as the crystal and gold sparkled on the crisp white tablecloth and shimmered under the light. Each place was set, awaiting the guests; two spoons, two folks, two knives and a triangle shaped napkin that lay perfectly on the ivory white plate set with gold trim. Once they were seated, the staff dressed in their all-white with gold aprons began to serve the courses. Kayson and KoKo sat at the front of the room at a table alone, across from an ivory white piano. After Kayson took his first bite, every one dug in.

Simone enjoyed the royal treatment they received. Each dish was served with care. She admired he chemistry between KoKo and Kayson as she placed different items in his mouth in between him whispering in her ear and kissing her neck. She couldn't deny that they shared a bond that made everyone else in the room invisible when they were wrapped in their love. She also noticed how Baseem would steal moments to stare at Goldie as she flirted and joked with different men in the room. Simone didn't know the relationship between them, but it was something she was not prepared to be a competitor to. She ate her food in silence, taking it all in and waiting for the time to go. KoKo and Kayson stood by the entrance saying good night to the guests as they exited the room. Simone stood in the back of the line with Baseem, awaiting their turn. When she got close to them, she watched as Kayson's hand moved lovingly along KoKo's side and she smiled at his attentiveness.

"So this is Simone. I have heard a lot about you," Kayson took her hand into his and kissed it.

"Pleased to meet you," she said, removing her hand from his. "I hope you heard all good things," she looked up at Baseem.

"Yes, everything was good. I hope we meet again soon," his facial expressions became firm as he turned his attention to Baseem. "See you in a few minutes," Kayson kissed KoKo's lips and winked as he walked off.

"Absolutely," Baseem responded.

"If you will excuse me, I have to attend to the boss. Please enjoy the rest of your evening," KoKo said, then headed to the elevator.

Baseem put his hand on the lower part of Simone's back leading her out the doors. When they got into the car, Simone dropped her smile and just stared silently out the window. She crossed her arms over her chest as she began formulating the words she would use to end her trisk with Baseem. Little did she know, Baseem had a plan of his own and letting her go was not a part of it.

* * * * *

"Thank you for seeing me home. Travel safe," Simone said as she held the knob holding the door half open.

"Can I come in and talk to you for a minute?"

"I don't think that is a good idea. I have had some very good days with you, but I don't think we need to continue this," she paused, looking into his eyes. Then she took in some air and continued. "We are not in the same place in life and I do not fit into your choice of occupation. So, let's just end this here."

"Look, I am not going to lie about who I am. That would mean I can't stand by the man I am."

"I'm afraid of who I think you are and I don't want to get caught up in anything, nor do I want to be forced to sit in the faces of the women you sleep or have slept with."

"It's not like that. Each person in this is an essential part of our business."

"Well, I don't want to be a part of that; so if you will please excuse me, I am going to get some rest. Good night," she pushed the door forward in an attempt to get rid of him before her heart took over.

Baseem placed his hand on the door and opened it back; forcing her to step back a few feet. "It's not happening like that," he moved toward her then took her into his arms and pushed the door closed with his foot.

Simone grabbed at Baseem's wrist as he placed his mouth on hers and kissed her deeply.

"Don't," Simone pulled her face back while tugging at his hands. "I need you to stop."

"I sure will in a about an hour," Baseem said as he tugged at her dress, pulling it toward her waist.

"No, Baseem; let go," her mouth replied, but her body sent him a totally different signal.

Baseem answered the craving inside her as he pushed Simone against the wall and pulled at her panties. He opened his pants and let them fall to his ankles. Simone wrapped her hands around his neck as she felt him rise against her opening. Baseem pressed his body against hers as he nibbled on her neck and the crease between her breasts. He then stepped out of his suit pants and boxers and walked her slowly down the hallway, biting at her nipples through her sheer white blouse.

"You have to be kind to my heart," she moaned as he set her on fire.

When Baseem laid her back and climbed between her legs, her thighs quivered to feel him. Simone pressed her legs against him as he penetrated her heated limits.

"Bas, please be gentle," she whined as he slid in an inch at a time.

Simone laid powerless beneath him as he broke down her tightness with every stroke. She filled the room with loud grunts and moans as Baseem took her, pleasured her fears and erased her pain. Baseem looked down into her semi-closed eyes as he pushed her knees back to the mattress. He took in all her innocence as he slipped and slid in her juices. Simone knew that after that night, there was no turning back. Baseem stroked effortlessly; separating her walls and opening up her heart. He carefully positioned her in every way he could and she gave in to his power, letting down her defenses. She could only pray that he would know what to do with her heart.

The Pussy Trap 4: The Shadow of Death

Chapter 22

Art of Deception

KoKo walked into the funeral home and took a seat in the corner at the back of the room. She crossed her legs and scanned the almost empty room to see if she recognized anyone in attendance and only one face was familiar. KoKo watched as the woman, who she was told by her aunt was her sister, rock back and forth as she stared at her mother in a cheap, wooden coffin. KoKo shook her head at the view.

"Friend or family?" the tall slender man in the brown, loose-fitting suit asked as he held a small book and pen out in front of her face.

"Neither," KoKo said, looking him up and down.

"Oh, okay," the man stuttered as he drew his hands back to his side and moved away from her.

KoKo's stomach began to turn when the keys of the organ were slowly stroked. She thought about the many men she watched go down and the many she had laid down. Her heart sank as memories of Night came to the front of her mind and his last words rang loud in her head, *Take care of family if anything happens to me.* KoKo shook her head as she thought about Goldie and Jarod and guilt set in as she realized she had put them in a position where her promise may be broken by her quest for revenge.

KoKo's memory got ready to take another journey until she looked over and caught the eye of the young woman who was rocking and crying on the front row. KoKo held eye contact as the woman rose to her feet and headed in her direction.

"Hi, KoKo, thanks for coming," the woman said with a slight smile on her face.

"I'm not here for to pay my respect. I had to make sure she was dead," KoKo stated coldly.

A lump formed in Shadirah's throat as KoKo's words stabbed her heart. She took a deep breath and tried not to cry as she responded to KoKo's coldness.

"I don't expect for you to feel love for me or my mother. But I won't take this from you. I am as much a victim to their bullshit as you are," she asserted.

"You done?" KoKo asked, unaffected by the small cry for sympathy.

"You need to heal that hole in your heart and move on. I can see the pain all over your pretty face. But you will die in that rage unless you let go," she said as tears ran down her face.

"It seems like to me your mother caught that karma for me," KoKo looked past her at the coffin holding her aunt Pat's dead body.

"They crossed us all, KoKo. They crossed us all," she said as she turned to walk back to the front of the room.

KoKo heard what the woman said, but again, her hate cancelled the validity of her words. KoKo stood to leave and bumped into a well-dressed older woman with pretty coco brown skin.

"I see she has the family trade mark in that sharp ass tongue," the woman said and giggled at the heat that was shot in KoKo's direction.

"Do I know you?" KoKo asked, looking the woman over.

"No, but you should," the woman stood firmly, leaning up against her pearl handle black marble cane.

"Is that right?"

"Yes, it is. And stop using his bullshit ass phrase. That nigga's dick has been in everybody's mouth. That phase makes my ass itch," the woman said as she reached in her pocket and pulled out a business card. "Here. Come see me; unlike the rest, I am the only one who has nothing to lose or gain," she paused and extended her arm.

162

The Pussy Trap 4: The Shadow of Death

"See you around seven," she looked down at her diamond and platinum watch. "And bring me some weed; we will both need to smoke to this," the woman said with a smirk and walked off.

KoKo's brow creased as she watched the woman hobble off. She then flipped the card over that read, Pashion Allen. She read the address and recorded it in her memory then dropped the card on the empty chair and headed for the door.

"You good?" Baseem asked as he opened the car door for KoKo.

"Not yet," KoKo said as she slid comfortably into her seat.

Baseem jumped into the driver's seat and pulled out.

* * * * *

"What time you coming home? Daddy needs to nibble on your sexy inner thighs." Kayson asked as he pulled his T-shirt over his head.

"I'll be there shortly, baby, so mama can give daddy whatever he wants," she cooed into the phone as she eyed the red brick house.

"Hurry up," he commanded. "Love you, baby."

"I love you too," she disconnected the call and looked down at her watch.

KoKo checked her gun then grabbed the small black velvet bag from the armrest and hopped out the car. She walked quickly up the few steps that lead to the porch and rang the bell. KoKo waited with great anticipation as she thought about whether this was the meeting she needed to get her questions answered. She rang the bell again, then stepped back and looked up at the light in a front window then back at her watch. Just as KoKo became impatient, she heard small barks coming from the other side of the door.

"Hush and move," the woman's voice echoed from behind the door as she clicked the locks and pulled it open. "Come in, child; don't mind these dogs, they are all bark," the woman said as she turned and walked to a side room and took a seat in an ice-grey high-backed suede chair.

"Close the door," she yelled out as she settled in her chair.

KoKo closed the door and looked at the bossy old lady with the salt and pepper dreads and silenced her tongue.

"Have a seat, I don't bite," she ordered as she leaned her cane

163

against the coffee table. "And grab that ashtray on your way over," she continued to instruct.

"What else you need?" KoKo spat with a frown in her brow.

"I'll let you know. Now take a seat and let's get acquainted. And roll that heat up; it will help with this old lady's memory," she smiled and sat back.

KoKo had to chuckle herself at the woman's cocky attitude. She took a seat on the matching love seat and pulled a bag of sour and diesel mix and laced two blunt wraps and rolled them up with ease. KoKo became more relaxed as Billie Holiday played in the background and the small logs kindled in the fireplace. The home felt warm and welcoming.

As she lit one of the blunts and took a deep pull, she eyed the pictures that adorned the walls. There were pictures from one wall to the next in fancy frames of cookouts, reunions and events; also a variety of family portraits. Her eyes stopped on one in particular and her heart jumped as she realized it was her father and a woman from one of the photos she had. The woman was holding KoKo tightly in her arms and looking at her like she was her world. KoKo passed the blunt to Pashion then walked over to the photo and stood analyzing every inch of it. The woman holding her was so beautiful; she had long, pretty brown hair and a smile that exuded confidence and love; her father stood next to the woman with pride adorning his face.

"Why do you have this?" KoKo asked turning back to Pashion.

"Come sit down and let me share something with you that I believe will finally release your demons," Pashion put the blunt to her mouth. "This is some good shit," Pashion said as she tried to muffle her cough.

KoKo stared curiously at the woman with a raised brow then returned to her seat.

"Start that other one I'm smoking this one," Pashion said as she nodded and sucked her tongue, tasting the elegance of the bud.

KoKo picked up the other blunt and lit the end and sat back.

"I have been waiting for you to find me. I guess it took the grave of our enemies to bring us together," she took a few more pulls then sat it down in the ashtray.

164

KoKo remained silent awaiting the woman's revelations. She had been invited to many sit downs and each one was a dead-end. At this point, KoKo was really trying to see if she would finally get the truth.

"Firstly, I don't want anything from you and I don't need you for anything. The only reason I am sharing what I know is to clean my own hands. I am too old for this war and really if I died tomorrow, I would have only one regret," she paused. "That regret is that I never got to look you in your eyes and see how beautiful you are," Pashion smiled as her heart filled with joy.

Again, KoKo say silent.

"Just like your mother, a woman of many quiet words. Her silence caused her the only thing she truly loved, and that was you," Pashion choked back her tears as she realized she was actually sitting across for KoKo for the first time in over twenty years.

KoKo felt a lump form in her throat as the woman gave her a piece of a life she never knew and for the first time, she actually felt connected to something. Pashion looked at KoKo's face for a few more seconds then began. "I am going to tell you a story and I can only pray that by the end of it you will be free."

"Ma, I don't know what to do?" Sabrina whispered to her mother as she tried to hold the tears back from falling down her face.

"You let that nigga fuck other women, so this is the price you pay," Pashion responded as she lit a cigarette and blew smoke into the air. She was perched up on a bar stool at the Island in their kitchen as Sabrina tried every bit of patience she had left.

"Ma, you know Malik don't like you to smoke in here," Sabrina said, fanning her hand in front of her mom's face as she looked out the kitchen door.

"Fuck him, he controls your pussy not mine; and get yo damn hand out my face," Pashion spat as she continued to blow smoke in her direction. "So, what you gonna do. You just gonna let your husband have a side bitch or you gonna make him own his vows?" Pashion said, then dotted her cigarette out.

"I'm confused. You know how I feel about him. I'm not walking away from my marriage," Sabrina asserted and as the words left her lips, tears escaped her eyes. She grabbed a paper towel from the counter and dabbed at her cheeks as the reality of Malik's actions set in.

Pashion got ready to speak plain words, but stopped as Malik walked into the kitchen holding KoKo in his arms.

"What's going on in here?" he said, looking over at Sabrina's teary eyes.

"Nothing," Sabrina said as she turned to the refrigerator and pulled it open. "What you want for dinner?" she asked as she tried to collect herself.

"Whatever you want to fix, baby," Malik looked at the anger on Pashion's face, he placed a kiss on KoKo's cheek as he gagged the energy in the room.

"Can you hold her while I talk to my wife?" he asked as he passed KoKo to Pashion.

"Yeah, you do that," she said as she put her arms out and took KoKo then walked into the living room.

Malik waited until she was out of sight then began. "What's wrong, ma?" he asked as she walked up behind Sabrina.

Sabrina took a deep breath and tried to formulate her words. "Why do you need to be with her?" she asked, choking back the tears.

Malik stood silent, carefully forming his answer. "You know she handles my business."

Sabrina turned to face him. "But does she have to handle your dick?" she looked him in the eyes and waited for his response.

"You know me and Keisha are cool as hell, that's it," he lied to save her feelings.

"Don't play with me. I'm your wife. I know you better than anyone. I know you are sleeping with her. I'm not stupid," she said as her heart broke into a million pieces with every word.

Malik looked in her eyes and saw that the naive little girl she used to be was far gone and clouding her head with fantasy was a not an option.

You're right. I have slept with her; but that shit is over," he said, taking her hands into his.

"No, it's not. I can see it in your eyes when you talk about her," she pulled her hands back. "Do you love her?"

"Do I have love for her, yes. She is very loyal to the organization. But you are the only woman who has my heart."

"What the fuck does that mean?" she pushed Malik back.

"Baby, I married you. You are the only woman who has the key to all my shit; everything is in your name. You own me. You are my world; she is just a small part of it."

Keisha tilted her head to the side as her eyes lowered. "So, I'm supposed to be happy because I have your things?" she raised her voice. "None of this shit means anything if the man who gave it to me is thinking about the next bitch while he's fucking me."

Malik took a deep breath. "It's not like that," he tried to convince her.

"Well, how is it?" she crossed her arms over her chest. "You fucking me and fucking her. You tell me you love me and I'm sure you tell her the same. I have your baby and so does she. So how the fuck is it not like that?"

Malik's eyes got wide at her revelation.

"Yeah, nigga, I know that shit too," she spat with disgust.

Malik was quiet. He had been very careful about how he dealt with Keisha and the baby.

"Don't get quiet now. You wasn't quiet when you fucked that bitch raw and allowed her to have a baby outside your marriage," she shook her head in disbelief.

"I love my daughter. I am not the type of man to walk away from mine," he said as his heart pounded against his chest at the pain he saw in Sabrina's eyes.

"Then let me walk away from you," she responded as tears ran down her face.

"I will never let that happen," he reached out to her and she moved to the other side of the kitchen.

"Baby, don't do this right now. You know what this is. I would never allow anything to happen to us; which means I would never allow you to leave."

"Then let her go," Sabrina looked firmly into his eyes.

Malik took in some air then let his heart speak. "I can't," he said as he moved toward her.

"Then I guess your choice is made," Sabrina moved swiftly toward the steps; she took two at a time heading to their bedroom.

Malik was right behind her. When he entered the room, Sabrina was in full rage.

"What the fuck are you doing?" Malik came up behind her grabbing the clothes from her hands.

"Don't you touch me," Sabrina screamed, snatching away from him as she continued to pull things from the drawers.

Malik looked at his wife and for the first time, guilt hit his gut hard. She was breathing heavy and her hair was all over her head as a stream of tears ran down her face.

"I can't do this with you. I'm not sharing you with her," she cried as

*thoughts of the many times he stayed away from home and the other baby he
probably held in his arms the same way that he held their child flooded her
mind. "You took all my choices," she whimpered.*

*"I'm not letting you leave me," he spoke calmly as he moved slowly in her
direction. "Let me hold you, baby," he said as he put his hand on her shoulder.*

"Why are you doing this to me?"

"I love you," he confirmed as he pulled her into his arms.

"Why are you sacrificing our family?" Sabrina cried on his shoulder.

*"Don't worry, I won't let anything come between us. Just give me a little
time. I promise you, everything will be fine," he held her firmly against his
chest. "I got you, baby; just trust me," he whispered into her ear, placing a
single kiss on her shoulder.*

"Is everything okay in here?" Pashion asked, holding KoKo in her arms.

*"We straight, Mrs. Allen. Can you take KoKo downstairs please? We will
be right down," Malik asked as he continued to hold Sabrina close.*

*Pashion moved away from the door, pulling it closed behind her. As she
ascended the stairs, a knock rang out on the door. She placed KoKo in the
playpen and headed to the door and when she opened it, she looked into the eyes
of the man that she could only describe as the devil.*

*"Good evening, Mrs. Allen, is Malik available?" Sadeek asked, removing
his hat from his head.*

"No, he is not!" she spat, pushing the door closed.

*Sadeek stopped it with his foot then gently pushed it back open. "Well, I
guess I will have to wait for him inside," he said as he moved forward, forcing
Pashion to back up and allow him to pass.*

*Pashion let him pass, then closed the door; she followed close behind Sadeek
as he walked straight into the living room and took a seat.*

*"I guess your mother didn't teach you any respect," she said as she too took
a seat.*

*Sadeek didn't bother to respond; he just sat back and looked at her like she
was stupid.*

*Pashion lit up a cigarette and stared a Sadeek wondering if he knew that
the man he idolized and worshiped was fucking his woman.*

*"You know the thing that bothers me about you young, so-called thug ass
niggas?" she paused and took another long pull then blew the smoke right in
Sadeek's direction.*

"No, I don't; but I am sure you are going to share your so-called

knowledge," Sadeek said as he sat forward folding his hands.

"I sure am," she also sat forward and geared up to let some shit go on his smart ass. "You little niggas use words like loyalty and honor, but eat off the same plate you shit on," she said smooth looking right into his eyes.

"And your point would be?" he asked, allowing his gaze to match hers.

"You got my point. I just hope that you don't let it stick you in the ass before you feel it," she sat back, pulling deep and blowing smoke into the air.

Sadeek sat back nodding his head and processing her statement; he knew that this woman was not just talking bullshit. It was some truth to her tongue which was giving him confirmation to his own thoughts of treachery and deceit.

Pashion sat staring at Sadeek and the more she looked at him, the more she knew that he was the key she needed to unlock her own deceit.

"You ready?" Malik asked, walking into the room, pulling his arms through his thin leather jacket.

"Yeah, I been ready," Sadeek said as he rose to his feet. "Thanks for the lesson," he said to Pashion.

"Anytime," she spat back.

Malik walked over to the playpen and picked up KoKo and hugged and kissed her before placing her back down. "Stop smoking in my house please," Malik said as he turned to the door.

"You got bigger shit to worry about. The fire I put to the end of this bitch is the least of your worries," she stood up and put the cigarette out and headed toward the steps to check on her daughter.

Malik took in some air, grabbed his keys and moved out the door.

When Pashion hit the top of the stairs, she could hear small whimpers from the other side of Sabrina's bedroom door. She put her hand on the knob and turned it slowly; her heart sank as she looked at the clothes scattered around the room and her daughter wrapped in a crisp white sheet laying on her bed hugging her pillow and crying from her soul.

Pashion walked over to the bed and sat beside her daughter. "It's okay, my love," Pashion spoke calmly, placing a loving hand on her daughter's shoulder. "Why are you letting yourself go through this?"

"I love him, mommy," she said through sniffles.

"But love isn't supposed to make you sick to your fucking stomach and you can't fuck away your pain," Pashion said as she watched her daughter falling for the bullshit Malik was shoveling.

"I'm not raising my daughter alone. I can't let that other woman win,"

Sabrina said, looking up into her mother's eyes.

"Baby, it's okay to do things alone. I got you," Pashion stroked her hair.

"I know he loves me, ma. I need to play the cards I was dealt. I will be fine," Sabrina sat up, wiping her eyes. "This is the last day I cry. This is my family and I have to fight for it."

"Is the fight worth it if the prize is fool's gold," Pashion asked, hoping her daughter would hear the meaning in her words.

"Don't worry, mommy. I got this. Just promise to be here for me," she took her mother's hands into hers. "I thank you for everything; but this is my journey. I have to walk it no matter how painfully it may be at times."

Pashion took her daughter's face into her hands. "I hear you. But remember you want to give your daughter your strength, not your weakness. What you settle for, she will settle for. Show her better."

Sabrina nodded her understanding then hugged her mother tight. "Just don't stop praying for me," she said as she internalized her mother's words.

Pashion held her daughter, praying she would learn her lessons before they destroyed her spirit.

"That was the last time I held my child," Pashion whipped her eyes as she came to the end of the story.

KoKo sat looking at the pain on her face. "So, I guess that is your subtle way of saying I'm your granddaughter."

"I don't know about how subtle it was. But it is what it is."

"So let me get this shit straight. After all this time you time you pop sharing shit, for what?"

"Somethings shouldn't be taken to the grave," Pashion said looking into KoKo's eyes.

"So all this shit is about pussy?" KoKo asked with a creased brow. "So what's your contribution, who did you fuck to not get to the top?" KoKo teased.

"I didn't have to fuck anybody. But from what I hear, you fucked enough people for the both of us," she chucked.

"Sure did, that's why I'm not the broke and bitter bitch trying to erase the mistakes of the past," KoKo spat.

The smile dropped from Pashion's face. "I didn't want this for you," Pashion confessed.

"But you didn't stop it."

KoKo stood up with anger in her heart. Here she had a woman

170

she never met, telling her a dark and ugly truth about two people that she loved and vowed to avenge with every ounce of her life. KoKo reached into her pocket and pulled out a small stack of bills folded over and passed them to Passion. "I hope this covers it, I'm fresh out of love and concern," she said, extending her arm.

"Look, like I said to you when I started this conversation...I don't want shit from you. Those muthafuckas stole my child from me," she said again, wiping at her eyes. "They stole you from me. I will never forget or forgive," She paused, sitting forward and grabbing the blunt and relighting it.

"So, what do you want me to do with this information?" KoKo tucked the money back into her pocket.

"You can do what you want to do with it. I just wanted you to know that the man you been running around laying niggas in the dirt over wasn't shit."

KoKo's brow creased. "Watch your mouth."

"No, you watch my mouth and hear what the fuck is coming out of it," she pulled the smoke deep into her lungs. "You don't have a clue what you are up against. You think you are on top of this shit and you are so far away from the truth that the shit ain't even funny," she blew the heat out in KoKo's direction.

"Let me ask you something, if you know so much...why the fuck you let them take me? Why you ain't out there trying to avenge my mother's death since you got all the answers?"

Pashion just shook her head. "You are just like your father. He didn't know shit and neither do you. You didn't hear shit I just said. So I'm done talking. You can leave now; your arrogance will destroy you. I'm good," Pashion rose to her feet. "See yourself out," she grabbed her cane and walked toward the door.

KoKo stood up. "Don't contact me if shit gets tight."

"Little girl, please. This shit is tight like new pussy; and from the looks of it, you're too whipped to see that the long stroke is coming from the dick you riding," Pashion laughed. "Have a good night," she walked off, leaving KoKo standing in the sitting room pondering whether she should leave or kill the old lady.

"Let me ask you something?" KoKo walked toward her. "So why did you send for me?"

171

Pashion turned in her direction. "I don't even know you. You have been looking for me. You got all the answers to the wrong questions," she turned back around and continued into the kitchen.

"Be safe," KoKo yelled out as she headed to the door.

"Oh, no worries; they know where I'm at. And they know where you are at too," Pashion chuckled as she turned the corner.

KoKo chocked back her anger as she pulled the door open then slammed it on her way out. When she hopped in the car, she was on fire. Her emotions were all over the place; she had just met her grandmother and at the same time, received what seemed like the threat of death.

*****

Baseem had been ignoring Simone's calls all day. His stress level was on one hundred and the last thing he wanted to do was answer any questions. He started to send her to voicemail one more time, but hit the answer button instead.

"Yes," he said firmly into the phone.

"Are you okay? I am so worried. I have been calling you for days. Did I do something wrong?"

"No, you're fine. I am just busy right now. You good?"

"No I am not. I have been worried sick and all you can say is I'm busy right now," she paused trying to hold in her emotions.

"Well, now that you know I'm good, relax and I'll get with you when I finish taking care of business."

"You know what? Fuck you and your business. I can't do this. Don't call my phone back," she slammed her office phone down then sat back in her chair and cried. She told herself he wasn't shit; but sometimes a woman needs all the proof before she can let go.

Baseem put his phone on the table and rubbed his hands over his face. He got up and poured himself a shot of Hennessey then another. He had not heard from Goldie and it was fucking him up. He would take care of Simone's tantrum later; right now all he was focused on was his family.

Chapter 23

It's Her World...

KoKo walked into the uptown spa in her chocolate brown dress pants, a silky sheer blouse with a dark pink lace bra, and brown leather Louboutin sling backs. She stepped with an air of confidence and pride that demanded more than respect.

"Mrs. Carter please," KoKo asked, removing her shades.

The woman looks at Mrs. Carter's schedule then placed a call. "Hello, yes there is a Mrs. --" the woman stopped and looked up at KoKo. "Your name please?"

"Mrs. Wells."

"A Mrs. Wells," she repeated into the phone, then she looked up at KoKo as she listened to her instructions.

KoKo stood looking down on the woman as she silently took her orders.

"Mrs. Carter will see you. Please wait right here; someone will be right down," she hung up and put a smile on her face.

"Thank you," KoKo said as she stepped to the side.

Within seconds, a man wearing a tailored, charcoal grey suit came down and signaled for KoKo to follow him. They walked in the opposite direction of the main elevators to a secret elevator then hit the top floor as the doors closed.

KoKo exited the elevator following close behind the gentleman down a long hallway until they came to the only room on that floor. He opened the door and let KoKo in then closed it behind her.

"Good afternoon, Mrs. Wells," Mrs. Carter said, standing up to meet KoKo in the middle of the room.

"Good afternoon."

"Please have a seat. Thank you for coming to see me."

"No problem. How may I help you," KoKo said, taking a seat.

"My son is outta hand. I need to show him why I gave him a little bit of power and not all the power."

"What seems to be the problem?" KoKo sat back and listened intensively.

"He is moving against you and I can't afford for this whole team to fall," she said as she sat up and poured a cup of tea. "Something to drink?"

"No, thank you. I'm fine," KoKo said as she waited for Mrs. Carter to reveal her other hand.

"For your help, I will relinquish Brooklyn and give you some very prime real estate in Queens," she sipped her tea.

"I already have prime real estate in both boroughs; we good."

"Fucciano is going to flip and go with Magic. I can give you times and dates of the next meetings and in return, you offer me protection for my remaining spots and allow me to hold my status and title in this city."

"How does this help me?"

"I will buy from you and only you. I will surrender my connection with Fucciano, giving you the power of distribution."

KoKo thought for a minute then gave her verdict. "I will send someone down here in a few days with my answer and my demands; at any rate, this meeting didn't happen," KoKo stood to leave. "Have a good day," she extended her hand to secretly close the deal with a shake.

"Thank you for seeing me, I know you are a busy woman," Mrs. Carter smiled.

As KoKo reached the door, she turned and said, "What would make a mother turn on her son?"

"The same thing that would make a man turn on his mother," she paused. "Money, power or pussy."

KoKo just turned and continued out the door. She couldn't help but bubble with excitement. She was looking for a way to bust

Magic's ass and her judge and jury fell right into her lap. *Money, power, pussy,* rang loud in KoKo's head as she walked onto the elevator.

* * * * *

"What the fuck is wrong with you?" Kayson asked as the door slammed against the wall. He then moved swift in Mr. Fucciano's direction.

His staff gasped as they came to attention, alerted by his heated entrance. "Everyone, please excuse us," he instructed, holding it together graciously.

Kayson stood firm, locking eyes with the traitor in front of him.

"I gave you two directives. Never let my enemies in the same door you let me in, and never fucking cross me."

"Mr. Wells, I have not crossed you. I am a business man. I have to feed my family. I know you can understand that," he gave Kayson the smirk of a snake as he tried to calm the beast within him.

"I understand that you are playing with my muthafuckin' money. That nigga, Magic, don't get to eat off my fuckin' plate; if you feeling charitable, you let him eat out yo mouth," Kayson paused, ready to end the whole shit; but he had to move carefully until everything was in place. "Fix this shit!"

Kayson turned on his heels and headed back to the entrance.

Mr. Fucciano walked to his desk and called his partner. "We need to move forward. The cocky young man just put me in the state of mind I needed to be in. There will be no second order. Carry it out whether I am around or not," he hung up, staring at the open door. Everything was in place.

* * * * *

KoKo drove to the Loin's Den and headed straight to her office before she could sit down and wrap her mind around her meeting with Mrs. Carter she was being paged that Adreena was on her way up. She went in the bathroom washed her hands and face and glossed her lips. As she settled in her seat they came through the door.

"Hey, Boss Lady," Adreena announced as she was escorted into the Lion's Den.

175

KoKo turned in her chair to face her and a slight smile formed on her face.

"Reports," KoKo went right to business.

Adreena took a seat and ran it all down. "Baseem came to Goldie's apartment two nights ago and he left the next morning stepping like his dick was happy."

KoKo nodded.

"Magic is in love Mrs. Bre. He will roll over...no problem," she paused. "Bre went to see Long."

KoKo's brows damn near touched with that news. "When?"

"Last weekend. She managed to get away from Magic, it was last Saturday."

"Where is she now?"

"She went to Miami with Magic; he has a little spot out there. I got my people on it."

"What else?"

"Rock meets with this lady every Wednesday. I went back the next week and saw the woman. I was trying to check the guest book but the lady pulled it back as soon as my eyes touched the page, but I think it was something royal.

Dutchess rang loud in KoKo's head and heat moved through her veins.

Chapter 24

Weak in the Knees

Baseem had been spending the last week trying to re-build his relationship with Simone. She was able to get a few days of vacation time, so they flew over to Vegas so he could show her a side of life she had been missing. Simone kissed Baseem good bye and melted in his arms as he held her tight.

"Sleep well; I will see you in a few days."

"I don't want to sleep alone," Simone pouted.

"I'll make it up to you," he kissed her again. "Lock the door and hit me if you need me," he instructed, and then moved out the door, headed back to his car.

Simone locked up, then wrapped her arms around herself and squeezed as she thought about how good Baseem made her feel. He had won her heart. She was now attached to him and with that, her every move going forward would be surrounded by his influence.

Baseem drove with the night air blowing through the windows as his mind was steady with thoughts of Goldie. He had been hitting her up all week and not getting an answer. When KoKo said she hadn't heard from her in two days, his imagination went into overdrive. He pulled up in front of her building, looked up and down the block for anything that may be out of place, then he headed inside. He walked past the guy at the front desk who gave him a smile and nod as he moved to the staircase. He took a few steps at a time with several emotions rushing through his body.

Baseem exited the staircase door and bopped hard down the hallway, praying she was on the other side. He knocked hard a few times and listened hard. He heard no movement. Baseem knocked again and waited as he contemplated kicking that shit in. As he raised his hand to knock one last time, he heard a little movement. He stood anxiously waiting.

Goldie unlocked the door then pulled it slightly open. "What's up?" she asked through the small space provided.

"I was checking on you," Baseem responded, trying to see inside the house. The darkness prevented his vision as he tried to look and listen for anything out of place.

"Well, I'm fine. You can go get your work done," she said, not budging on her position.

"You alone, ma?" Baseem asked as he smelled the alcohol on her breath through the crack.

"Yes, and I'm good," she slurred.

Baseem pushed the door open and moved toward her. Goldie quickly turned and walked away from him. "I told you I'm good," she said as she walked to her bedroom.

Baseem locked the door and pulled his gun trying to see in through the darkness as he followed Goldie. When he got to her bedroom he saw pictures of her and Night spread on the floor in front of her open closet. Goldie had lit several candles and had Anita Baker playing softly in the background. Baseem eyed the other empty bottle and ashtray full of blunts smoked halfway.

"He didn't deserve to die like that," She took a seat next to the photos, taking his obituary in one hand and a drink in her other. She brought the bottle to her mouth ans turned it high in the air.

"We all know our beginning and our end in this game, ma," he spoke gently as he watched her guzzle down the brown liquor as the tears cascaded down her face. His eyes settled on the huge platinum and diamond ring on her pointer finger.

"Why are you here?" she looked up with glassy eyes.

"I wanted to make sure you were okay."

"Well, I'm good; check on the bitch you lay with, I told you I'm good," she took the bottle to her mouth then turned her gaze down to a picture of Night and one of Jarod side by side. Then he noticed that the birth date on the Obituary; it was Night's birthday and it was now apparent to him why Goldie was crumbling before his eyes.

"Let me help you, ma," Baseem reached down and took the bottle from her hand causing her to jump up in his face.

"Don't come in here trying to run my shit," she spoke loud as her breathing increased.

"Goldie, you ain't carrying this shit by yourself," Baseem tried to comfort her.

"I am carrying this by myself," she said through clenched teeth.

"Goldie, don't do this to yourself. You gotta stay strong."

"He killed my father," she whispered as a knot formed in her throat.

Baseem was quiet while he searched for the words to say. "I don't know that that man would do that. But, if he did it was to protect you. You gotta be strong and hang in there."

"For what? Huh? For what, Bas? We have lost a lot of lives." She looked in his eyes for the answers to the questions she had been running through her mind all week.

"Goldie, I know you feeling fucked up right now. But you can't shut yourself up in here and get fucked up in hopes to erase your love for this shit we in. None of that will bring Night back."

"Fuck you, Bas. You didn't hold his brains in your hands," she yelled, holding her hands up to his face. "You get to mourn. I have to suffer," her voice cracked with every word.

"Baby I got you," he reached out and took both her hands in his.

"Can you guarantee me life?" she asked as she began to breakdown.

"I can't guarantee anything. But, let me help ease some of your pain," he pulled her into his arms and held her close. He knew her words came from a very wounded place and that night, it wasn't about judgment, it was about healing.

Baseem walked Goldie to the bathroom and turned on the shower. She sat in the middle of the bathroom floor as he undressed himself then walked toward her. Carefully he undressed

Goldie as she drunkenly wobbled in his arms. They stepped into the shower and Baseem held her against him allowing the water to run over her skin.

Goldie lay in his arms and cried against is chest. "I never asked for this part, Bas," she mumbled.

"We are all in this for our own reasons. You need to find what made you fall in love with this shit and rekindle it. We in this shit; life or death," Baseem said as he rubbed the bath sponge over her back.

"I need you tonight," Goldie looked up into his face.

Baseem looked down and smiled. "You're drunk, but not enough to handle all this dick," he joked, lightening the mood.

"Fuck you, Bas," she slurred.

"Nope, because then you'll be following a nigga all over the place. Neither one of us will get anything done. Turn around so I can get you straight," he said as she moved her body to face the water in an effort to sober up.

As Baseem washed her down, he had to control his inner monster in order to not take strong advantage of the situation. They exited the shower and he helped her lotion her skin and get into her robe.

Goldie lay on the couch as Baseem moved around her kitchen preparing a meal for them. She inhaled the different aromas invading her space. Baseem walked to her side and gave her some black coffee then headed back to the kitchen.

When Baseem was done, he filled their plates with pancakes, Italian turkey sausage and egg omelets with fresh broccoli, cheese, onions and mushrooms. He placed a plate in front of her and took a seat next to her with his.

"Eat, ma; you need to keep your strength," he ordered, passing her a folk.

Goldie sat up and grabbed her plate from the coffee table; she cut into the pancakes, then the meat, and once everything touched her tongue, she began to scarf her food down without talking breaths.

"Damn, let me find out you kill niggas and you running the organization's cafeteria," she laughed at the thought.

"I am about getting this money; and that Wells' money is long. Sheeeit...I would be in that mansion cooking shit, putting it in plastic containers, laying a nigga down and then head back to the house and serve that shit. Play wit it," he said biting into his eggs.

Goldie busted into laughter at the thought. "You so stupid," she said as she felt herself sobering up.

After they ate; Baseem sat on the couch turned on ESPN and pulled Goldie close. She nuzzled against him, covering her legs with a thin flannel blanket, then placed her head in his lap. Baseem shook his head thinking about the fun he could be having if he didn't have the line of respect he had drawn for their friendship. He tucked his urges tightly away as he comforted his friend. By morning, Goldie was stretched out and Baseem was laid out next to her. She looked around the room then got up and headed to the bathroom. When she returned, she climbed onto his lap and began placing kisses on his face.

Baseem began to stir and his already semi-hard dick began to take on full capacity. "What's up, ma?" he asked, placing his hands on her hips.

"This dick, now run it," she whispered in his ear. "I need this, Bas. I need this," she panted as she grabbed his dick squeezing and stroking him to her pleasure.

Goldie was on fire, she hadn't been with anyone since Night and she was feeling the heat rising off of him and wanted to feel it deep inside her.

"Bas, Please..." she purred, grinding against his steel.

Baseem flipped her over on her back and put her legs over his shoulders. He pushed every inch in deep then stroked fast and calculated.

Goldie grabbed him around his neck and looked right into his eyes as she took that dick like a champ.

"I want it from the back," she moaned, pulling her legs away from his shoulder. She got up, bending over the couch and looked back at him with approval. "Take it," she purred and he answered.

Baseem stepped behind her and stroked to her speed, watching his steel appear and disappear; heated wetness covered him as he stood in place and enjoyed the ride. He tucked away all guilt and healed her soul with what it craved.

Goldie released and moved back into his pelvis taking all the dick he had to offer. At that moment, she was letting down all guards, it was him and her in each second with every pleasurable stroke and tomorrow would have to handle the rest.

Chapter 25

Family First...

Kayson pulled into the motorcade, parked and hopped on the elevator. The loud sounds of family boomed as she approached the entertainment room; music, television, laughter and food filled the hallway as he ascended toward his peace. Kayson took a deep breath and inhaled the aromas coming from the kitchen; it was his favorite Chicken Alfredo with shrimp and asparagus over linguini. It was about to go down.

Kayson moved into the family room and lit up when he saw Malika standing up in the playpen holding on with one hand and reaching for him with the other. Her little smile made his heart tingle. He walked over and took her into his hands.

"Hey, Daddy's girl," he softened his voice.

Malika squirmed around, giggling and touching his face.

"What's up, little solider?" Kayson asked Quran as he watched him maneuver the controller to the PS3.

"Hey, Dad," Quran's little, raspy voice responded without looking up. He made a few more moves then paused and came to where Kayson stood.

"What you do today?" Kayson put his fist out.

Quran hit his fist then ran down his day. "They made me do my work, then I ate and cleaned my room. I just got a break," he folded his arms over his chest.

Kayson was tickled, but he didn't show it. "Look up here at me," Kayson ordered.

Quran looked up in his dad's eyes.

183

"Don't ever let me hear disappointment in your voice when it comes to learning," he paused. "A wise man will be a wealthy man. But a lazy man who cannot read or write will get cheated his whole life and always be at the foot of the rich. You are a Wells; never let anything stand in the way of learning."

"Yes, daddy," he held his father's gaze.

"Always do what your mother tells you; she is in control of all the money," Kayson smiled and Quran smiled back, nodding his head.

"I love you, dad," he hugged Kayson's leg.

"I love you too, solider. Go ahead and enjoy your free time," Kayson rubbed the top of Quran's head.

"You gonna let me spank you later, dad?" Quran giggled as he jogged to the couch and picked up his controller.

"You don't want none of this," Kayson said, leaving the room with Malika in his arms.

KoKo moved around the kitchen bopping to the beat and mouthing the words to Sade's, "Sweetest Taboo": as she loaded the dishwasher and prepared to fix plates for dinner. Kayson watched her try her hand at singing and just shook his head.

"Why don't you let her do it, baby," he said, walking up behind her.

"Shut up, I can sing," she tilted her head to the side.

"I know, baby. I just don't want you to hurt yourself," he leaned in and kissed her lips.

"Whatever, Mr. Sexy. You ready to eat?" she asked, then kissed his lips again.

"I want to eat you first," he mumbled between kisses.

"Be good, your children are up and I want to be put out of commission tonight. No quickies, baby. I need you to put in some real work. Plus, I gave Mariam the evening off," she released him from her grip.

"Sheeiit...I always put in real work. That's why you be crying, begging and trying to escape," he spat back.

"Not tonight. I want every inch deep and long."

"Malika, you hear your mommy? She's a bad girl."

"I'ma be real bad tonight and I want to be chastised for it,"

184

KoKo said, running her hand over the Enforcer.

"Go ahead and wake him up."

KoKo smiled and moved away from Kayson before things got way too hot in their kitchen.

"Finish up because after we do the family thing, I need daddy time," he looked her over then rubbed her butt on his way out of the kitchen.

"Don't worry, I have plenty for daddy," she ran her tongue over her lips in anticipation of his touch.

"Do you need any help in here?" Mariam asked as she entered the kitchen with a small laundry basket of the baby's clothes.

"No, ma'am; we have it. We may need help later," KoKo said, pulling away from Kayson.

"Okay, I will be in my room," she turned and headed upstairs.

"Yo ass getting it tonight," Kayson grabbed his dick as he headed in the opposite direction.

"Whatever," KoKo said as she went back to her task.

KoKo moved around the kitchen preparing plates and washing dishes while enjoying the laughter and conversation between Kayson and the children. It was always critical that they enjoy all the time they could spend together living like a normal family, because at any second, all of that could come to an end.

Kayson removed Malika from her playpen and placed her in the high chair then took his seat at the head of the table. Quran took his seat at the other end; he just knew he was the next to sit on the throne. KoKo shook her head as she took her seat beside Kayson. They ate and laughed and talked over dinner. KoKo cut each of them a slice of Mariam's homemade apple pie, and after dinner, they each took a part in cleaning up then it was off to get the children bathed and prepared for bed. As always, Quran wanted to take a shower just like his father and Kayson assisted him while KoKo bathed the baby and got her situated for bed.

"Dad?"

"Yes, son."

"Why can't I sleep with you and mommy anymore?" he asked, playing with the bubbles on his arms.

"Because you're becoming a man now. You have to be a big

185

boy. Tuck all that baby shit," he gave Quran a firm eye. "Plus, that's my woman; you have to get your own," Kayson chuckled.

"Dad, that's not fair, you gotta share; mommy is perfect."

"How much does she pay you to talk like that?" Kayson cut off the water and grabbed a towel.

"She doesn't have to pay me. I see her work," he said, looking his dad in the eyes.

Kayson got a little choked up because for the first time he saw all of himself in the eyes of his son.

"Always be true to who you are son, and only bow to truth and wisdom," Kayson took his hand and walked him to the room to get dressed.

Quran nodded his understanding as he marched alongside his father trying to match Kayson's every jester; he wanted to be just like his dad.

Once the baby drifted off, KoKo hopped in the shower, slipped into a short, white sheer teddy, set her satellite radio, and settled in their king size bed. She lay back on the dozen fluffy pillows and stretched her arms out, then she took a deep breath and exhaled the day. The activity of chasing kids all day while executing a successful event had her completely worn out. KoKo closed her eyes and embraced the peace that had taken control of her heart and soul. She was a few seconds from dozing off when she heard Kayson's deep voice.

"Remember I told you playing sleep can't keep me from getting what I want," his voice boomed from across the room.

KoKo slowly opened her eyes and looked in his direction. "I was *not* playing sleep," she stated sarcastically.

"Come here," he motioned with his finger.

"Baby why can't you come over here?" she threw back the comforter showing him her pretty brown skin.

"Bring it to me," he gripped the Enforcer firmly in his hand.

Just as she sat up, she heard their wedding song, "Ready For Love" boomed through the speakers. KoKo threw her legs over the edge of their king size bed and sauntered over to him with her eyes moving over his sexy frame. His soft brown skin was calling her lips and hands to roam all over him. She stepped up on him, resting her breast a little below his chest.

Lately I've been thinking you're not ready for me maybe you think I need to learn maturity, India Arie sang as KoKo felt the heat rising between them.

Kayson reached up and grabbed a handful of her hair and gently pulled her head back; then he sucked the sweet spots on her neck and collar bone. "I want you to make my pussy react to every deep inch," he whispered.

"Baby," she moaned as his hand caressed her breast.

KoKo gripped his biceps as his hand slipped back and forth between her legs, wetting his fingertips. "Damn this pussy knows daddy's touch,"

"Kay," she bit into his shoulder as he pushed his finger deep inside her heated center.

Kayson placed his mouth over her nipple and tickled her spot, causing her body to jerk with every motion. With one hand firm in her back and the other feeling the grip of her sweet walls, they allowed their lips to meet. Kissing her deep, he stole every word and took in every moan.

KoKo's nails pressed against his chest as she felt her body shutter. "Kay, I'm coming she mumbled.

"Let me have it, baby," he said, gripping her hair tight. He sucked her tongue as she released her passion – warm and sticky – all over his fingers. "That's what the fuck I'm talking about. Turn around," he requested, putting her hands on the wall slightly above her head.

KoKo inhaled deeply as he pressed his body against hers.

Kayson reached around and put his hand around her throat and bit into the back of her neck. KoKo arched her back and pushed her butt against the hard rock she desperately wanted to feel.

Kayson spread her legs with his and pulled out the Enforcer and held him firmly in his hand. Brian McKnight crooned, "Never felt this way about loving you" through the speakers as he spread her butt cheeks and slid the head in and rested it at her opening.

There will never come a day when you'll ever hear me say that I want and need to be without you. I want to give my all, baby just hold me. Simply control me cause your arms they keep away the lonely. When I look into your eyes, then I realize that all I need is you in my life.

"Can daddy act up tonight?" he moaned in her ear as he slid a little deeper.

"You can have whatever you want, baby," she closed her eyes and enjoyed the feeling of him pushing into her tightness.

"You promise?" he asked, stroking slowly.

"I promise," KoKo panted, sliding her hands down the wall bracing herself; she arched her back more so he could hit her spot.

Kayson locked his hands with hers and gave her pussy what it asked for slow and deep.

KoKo moaned and pushed back into him, adjusting to the painful pleasure he gave her with every stroke. "Oh, my God, Kay; get your pussy, baby," she cried out, trying to keep balance as he picked up speed.

"Mmmm...come on baby, make that pussy grip my dick," he released her hands and grabbed her hips; changing his stroke and hitting her walls side to side.

KoKo dropped her head and pressed harder against the wall with every push. The room quickly filled with her cries and pleas as he went from slow to fuck mode.

Kayson pulled her away from the wall and pushed her forward. "Touch them toes for daddy," he pushed her forward then eased back inside her.

KoKo gripped the carpet between her fingers as he pulled her back and forth with intense force.

"Kay, wait," she cried out, placing her hand against his thigh to slow his movement.

"Be a big girl and take this dick," he reached down and grabbed her legs forcing her into a handstand.

"Kaaay..." KoKo mumbled as he took control and hit everything still and moving.

"I thought you wanted these inches deep and long," he reminded her of her words then backed up his own with force.

"I do..." she moaned as she tried to handle all that thick heat he was feeding her.

Kayson looked down and enjoyed watching all his inches wet and sticky.

"Kay, please be gentle baby."

Kayson gave her merciful short strokes, bringing his dick to the head and giving her only what she could handle.

"Just like that, baby. Make your pussy come, Kay."

"This how my baby wants it?"

"Yesss…" KoKo gripped one hand on his leg and the other on the floor as she felt the contractions take over her existence.

"Let that shit go, baby. Let me have it," Kayson mumbled as he felt her body tense up to his pleasure.

Kayson pushed in deep and let her grind on his thickness until her body shook. KoKo took a few deep breaths as she felt the blood rushing to her head and his rock hard steel beginning to ease slowly back and forth between her gushy lips. Kayson pulled out and released her legs. KoKo tried to stand on her wobbly legs while trying to catch her thoughts.

"You ready to make the Enforcer feel good?" Kayson's raspy tone played tricks with her eardrum.

"Whatever you want, baby," KoKo responded softly.

Kayson grabbed her around her back and pulled her up to his waist. KoKo wrapped her legs around him as he entered her swiftly. He threw her legs up on his shoulders and locked his hands behind her back; then he pulled her back and forth on his length. Unable to escape that knowing thrust, KoKo twisted in his arms as he pushed deeper with every entrance. Kayson grunted with each motion as her pussy got juicier with each stroke. He watched her pretty brown titties jiggle and his mouth watered to taste them. Her nipples called his name and he answered; leaning in and tracing them with the tip of his tongue.

"Ahhhh…Kaayy," KoKo threw her head back as she squeezed his strong arms. The room spun every time she opened and closed her eyes; her body was on fire and the boss was just getting started.

Kayson carried her throughout their bedroom pinning her to walls, dressers and just holding her in midair watching her wiggle in his arms with each orgasm. When he was ready to release, he threw her up on the bed, grabbed her ankles, flipped her on her belly, and climbed into his favorite position.

KoKo lay flat and exhausted as the boss continued his attack.

"I wanna give you my forever," Kayson mumbled in her ear as he slid in and out of her wet heat.

"I'll never leave you, baby," KoKo moaned, feeling his pace quicken.

"All this belongs to the Boss," he stroked long and hard.

"Yes, it's all yours baby; forever," KoKo grabbed the sheets tightly.

Kayson stroked and stroked until he felt his seed ready to release. Pushing in deep, he let go; then placed soft, wet kisses on her back and shoulders.

"I love you with every part of me," Kayson said, feeling himself rock back up.

"I know, baby. I love you too."

"Always be honest with me, baby. I need all of you all the time," he nibbled on her neck ready to go another round.

"I promise," KoKo confessed.

"You know you in trouble; right?" he asked as he plotted his next move.

Knock. Knock. Knock. A little tap rang on the bedroom door.

"Who is that?" Kayson yelled out.

"Me," Quran answered.

"What's up?"

"I need mommy," he yelled through the door.

"That's your blocking ass child," Kayson said, reluctantly pulling out.

"No, that's your little partner," KoKo giggled. "Here I come, baby," KoKo yelled out looking around for her robe.

"Nah, you sent that little nigga a bat signal. I was about to tear that ass up," Kayson pulled the blanket over his body.

"I sent a what?" she burst out laughing.

"Never mind. Next time Mariam needs a vacation, she gotta take your blocking son with her. Got a Nigga's dick hard and wet and ain't no pussy on the end of it."

"You so nasty," KoKo said, opening the door to see Quran with the look of death on his face. "What's wrong, papa?"

"My dreams ain't right, mommy," he said, rubbing his eyes.

"Come on," KoKo took him by the hand, leading him back to

his room. Quran had been having the same dream about killing his grandmother. KoKo lay next to him in his bed and rubbed his back until he began to doze off. For once in her life, she thought that she had something pure; something great that she had created. But regardless to how hard she had tried to keep him safe, he still ended up tainted.

After checking on Malika and changing her diaper, KoKo jumped in the shower then climbed on top of Kayson.

"Rock up, baby…so I can put daddy to sleep for real," she purred, sucking that sweat spot at the base of his throat.

"Look at you running up on this dick," he said as he rose for the occasion.

KoKo slid down on him letting out a soft moan then went to work. Kayson put his hands behind his head and watched her zone out and enjoy her favorite toy. Within no time, the Boss took over and put KoKo totally out of commission. He stared at her sleeping peacefully. From the outside it would appear that they had not a problem in the world; but on the inside, he knew there was no peace, and not even sleep was refuge, even the dreams of their children were haunted by murder and death.

NeNe Capri

192

Chapter 26

Ambush

Baseem walked into the lobby of Simone's office building with one mission on his mind. He was trying to lock her down and moving slow was getting him nowhere. He needed to seal the deal and he knew just what he needed to do.

"Simone Bivings," he said to the receptionist, lowering his gaze as he peered into her eyes.

"Is she expecting you?" the young woman looked up at him with a slight thirst.

"I hope not," he said, pulling a few hundred from his pocket and sliding it toward her.

"She has a meeting in thirty minutes; but if you hurry, you can catch her," she smiled as she slid him a visitor's pass.

"Thank you," he said, taking the pass and heading toward security.

"My pleasure," she responded, looking around her high desk; her eyes roamed over his frame as he walked away. All she could do was shake her head.

Baseem exited the elevator, walked down the long shiny hallway and through the small crowds that moved around busily making sure their clients' money was in the right place at the right time. When he looked over at her secretary's desk and saw an empty chair, he moved swift to her door, walked in, and closed and locked it behind him.

Simone looked up from her computer and her mouth almost hit the desk. "What are you doing?" she mouthed.

"Shhhh..." Baseem put his finger up to his mouth as he walked around her desk.

"Yes, I'm listening," she said into the receiver as Baseem pulled her from her chair.

Simone stared him in the eyes as she divided her attention between his forceful hands that where caressing her body and her client on the other end of the phone.

"Yes, I can put together a portfolio that will double that amount in thirty days," she said as Baseem sat her on the desk and pulled her legs apart.

Siomone's eyes got big when he sat in her chair and reached up under her skirt. "Please hold," she managed to say as he reached over and hit the hold button.

"What are you doing?" she pushed at his hands.

"About to have lunch with you...get back to your call; you missing that money," he said, pulling at her panties.

Simone was about to say something when her phone buzzed, reminding her that a caller was on hold. "Hello, uh...yes. I need to set up a meeting so we can go over the strategy. Is Friday at twelve good? " she asked, hoping to get rid of the caller; however, he went on a rant. She pressed the phone to her ear looking down at Baseem's tongue as he ran it over her clit nice and slow.

"Okay," she responded hurriedly to the caller while trying to fight the sensations Baseem was sending all through her body.

Once he had her squirming, he locked her legs in his grip and went in placing his mouth over her clit and sucking hard, causing her legs to shake. It was just as he thought; her ridged ass was very orgasmic. He was about to give her exactly what she needed.

"I have an emergency. I have to call you right back," she hung up not waiting for a response.

Simone placed her hand on top of Baseem's head and tried to wiggle away as her contractions came on strong. "Oh, my God," she moaned as she began to release in his mouth.

Baseem continued to suck as her juices ran down his chin. He looked up and smiled as she tried to regain her composure. He ran his tongue up and down her lips, playing in her sticky pleasure. Baseem rose to his feet and kissed her passionately.

194

Simone put her head back and let him have whatever he wanted.

"Mrs. Bivings, your two o'clock meeting is about to start and your client is on his way up on the elevator," her secretary yelled through her intercom.

"Okay," she reached over and hit the button as she tried to push Baseem back and get off the desk.

"You lucky as hell," Baseem said as she hurried around the desk to the small bathroom in her office; closing the door hard. Baseem grabbed a tissue from the box on her desk and dabbed his chin, then sat back in the chair. "Mission accomplished."

Simone stood in the bathroom trying to internalize what had just happened. She had to smile at his cockiness. She shook her head as she washed up then hurried out of her bathroom. "You are so wrong," she said, walking around her desk trying to grab her files.

Baseem smiled as he headed to the bathroom. When he returned, she was standing there with her hand on her hip. "Your pussy tastes good, baby," he said, walking up on her and taking her in his arms; kissing her again.

"Baseem, please...I have to go," she said, then heard a knock on her door. "See," she said with raised eyebrows.

"You so scary; you need to let me get back under this skirt," he stole another kiss while sliding his hands over her butt.

Simone pulled back, grabbing his wrist. "Behave," she warned, snatching the door open and moving into the hallway. As she reached her assitants desk her appointment was coming down the hall fast and focused.

"I'm ready. Sorry for my lateness. I had to finish up with a client. Good afternoon, I'm Ms. Bivings," she said extending her hand.

"Good afternoon," Mr. Fucciano said as he took her hand into his then placed a single kiss on her knuckles. "No problem at all. I just srrived. I heard you are the best I will follow your lead," he tipped his hat.

"Great come this way," she instructed.

"I'll catch you later, thanks for lunch," Baseem said with a sexy gaze then kissed her lips.

"Have a great day sir." She said to Baseem as she turned in the opposite direction.

"Come this way so I can show you what to do with this money," Simone walked into her office with a very satisfied smile on her face.

*****

Baseem hopped in his truck smiling from ear to ear. He picked up the phone and dialed Kayson.

"What's up?" Kayson asked as he stacked bills in his wall safe.

"Something big just fell in our lap."

"Is that right?"

"Hell yeah. I know how they moving that money," he said as he bent the corners.

"Meet me in Jersey," Kayson said as he closed the safe.

"Heading to the tunnel now." Baseem hung up as he tried to calm his excitement. After all this time Mr. Fucciano was right up under their nose.

Chapter 27

Calculated Movement

Yuri stepped quickly through the casino lobby heading toward her suite. She marched proud in her all-white pants suit and emerald green six-inch stilettos and her medium sized silver briefcase. She had met Kayson at this spot three times while moving the money she got from the hits and making the final adjustments to the plan. This night was set to be the final meeting before things became turbulent.

Yuri tipped lightly to her room thinking about the meal she ate with Kayson the last time he was in town. She reminisced about the way his soft lips approached the folk and moved perfectly. Yuri took pride in being able to make him laugh which gave her a small glimmer of light and she was going to test his gangsta tonight.

Yuri walked into the room, hit the lights and placed the briefcase on the table and her light jacket on the chair. She moved to the bathroom to freshen up before the Boss, who doesn't do late, was at her door.

When Yuri exited the bathroom, she rubbed her hands together in anticipation. She tried to shake her nerves, but couldn't; just the idea of being next to him had her feeling like she was a virgin all over again. As she moved to the wet bar to pour herself a drink, a pattern of knocks rang out on the door.

"Shit," Yuri jumped, and then headed to see who was there. She looked out the peephole then unlatched the locks as the butterflies in her stomach did the shimmy.

"Good evening," she said softly as he passed through the doorway.

"Good evening," Kayson responded, heading into the room.

"Please have a seat," she offered, closing the door.

Kayson moved to a chair at the dining table and sat back.

"I have everything on the table and I believe after that, we are done until the next deal," she said as she moved to the bar to get a drink.

"Be you with me tonight," Kayson said, stopping her in her tracks.

"Excuse me?"

"Why you use liquor to mask your mode? Just be you," he said from his seated position.

Yuri walked over to where he sat and stood directly in front of him. "Can I sit on your lap while I'm trying to be me?" she rubbed down the side of his face speaking a little over a whisper.

"This is a big girl's seat; you gotta be able to handle about this much dick to ride this ride," he held his hand far apart.

"I think I can handle it," she said, straddling his lap and pushing her clit right up against his thickness.

"Why is it your personal quest to fuck me?" Kayson rested his hands on her thighs, looking deep into her eyes.

"I want to feel you inside me," she rubbed her hands over his, then brought her nose under his chin and breathed in his aroma. "I want to know why these women bow to you. I want you to make me understand why that bitch is so loyal to you," she whispered in his ear as he allowed the Enforcer to join her illusion.

Yuri grinded slowly against him, stimulating her clit till it began to throb. She looked him in the eyes as the tension from his zipper and throbbing dick caused little contractions to take over her clit. Yuri grinded a little faster as the excitement of his size forced her movements.

"Is that what you think? You think dick makes them obey me?" Kayson asked, allowing her hands to have the pleasure most woman only dream of.

"I know that's what it is," she wrapped her arms around his

neck and pressed her breast to his chest. Her whole existence was on fire as she was finally in the position she had been fantasizing about for months.

"Let me show you something," Kayson said, removing her arms from his neck just as she was on the brink of wetting his jeans. He rushed her over to the wall placed her hands on the wall above her head and spread her legs.

Yuri's breaths quickened as his hands did whatever they wanted with her body. Kayson rested the rock right between her butt cheeks and she arched her back to feel his heat.

"You think you can handle being on a Boss's team?"

"Yes..."

"You gotta be willing to do whatever I need, whenever I need it," his words eased over her ear and neck as her mouth craved to taste him.

"Whatever you need," she panted as his hands rose up her stomach and rested on her breast.

"And you think that he can make you do what I need you to do?" he asked as his hand griped the opening in the back of her jumper and pulled it at the material tearing it and exposing her perfect caramel ass cheeks. Her all-white G-string rested between the crack accentuating her sexy.

"I know he will," she mumbled, gasping for air as his hand slid up her chest and around her throat.

Kayson pulled at her panty string causing it to pop back in place. Yuri welcomed the sting and tooted her booty a little more; she wanted him to know he could get it.

"You ain't ready for this, baby," Kayson stated firmly. "This dick gotta be earned," He said, leaning into her. "That bitch, as you like to call her, is not loyal to me because of what I do with this dick. She is loyal because of what I won't do with it," he released Yuri from his grip and stepped back.

Yuri turned around holding her clothes together.

"I'll be in touch," he turned around real smooth heading to the door. "Hold on to that money for me. I'll tell you when I need it," he continued out the door.

Yuri watched as he exited the room and instead of feeling

199

insulted, she felt an intense thirst for him. After tonight, she knew that the power he possessed wasn't just between his legs and she wanted him to pour it all over her entire existence.

Chapter 28

Heated

Kayson drove through the streets of New York looking at the people hustle around trying to get closer to their dreams. He thought back to when he was in the streets hustling around from one block to the next. Now he had a team of men ready to give their lives for that same hustle. Kayson thought about how he had moved so far away from the hustle and now he was back street level.

"This can't be what this shit is about," he thought as he realized he was back to where he had started from. The streets knew his reputation well; but they didn't have a recent reminder that he built this shit. Kayson vowed that from this day forward, he was going to let it be known who the fuck he was.

He pushed on through the streets watching as the sun began to leave the sky. He was trying to find some calm to release the anger in his heart. He brought up memories of the children which brought him a small amount of solace and in those seconds, the flashes of the next nigga fucking his wife almost damaged the love he had built for her. He then saw KoKo's smile followed by the sound her of laughter; which moved the images and his reason why he breathed each breath came clear to his mind. His anger began to slowly simmer and just when he started to relax the crease in his forehead, his cell went off.

"Hello."

"Where you at Boss?" Baseem said into the receiver with a little urgency in his tone.

"Why what's up?"

"We gotta call a meeting. These niggas think we playin'. We got a little rivalry in the ranks."

"Where you at?" Kayson asked, turning the corner.

"We at the pool hall."

"I'm on my way."

"Nah, we good; we got it. I was just putting you down," Baseem tried to redirect the energy.

"I ain't ask you shit. Be ready to open the door when I get there," Kayson disconnected the call.

Kayson walked through the door of the pool hall and everything fell silent. He looked down at his watch then scanned the room. "I'm the only muthafucka in this room that can afford to play games. A broke man is always working on strategy, but a comfortable man will always stay broke," he shot his eyes around the room once more connecting with his head men.

Each man could feel his gaze piercing their soul; without hesitation, they began to move toward the door. With each step, the adrenaline pumped heavy in Kayson's veins. He walked through the conference room door and silence fell across the room. His eyes scanned the long, wooden table looking at each man in attendance. He became uneasy when he realized half of the faces he didn't recognize. Baseem had been working with the men and from what he could tell, niggas hadn't got the memo on who was the boss and who were the employees.

"I usually don't come down this muthafucka over bullshit, but is seems like the niggas running the shit are apparently fucking up," he cut his eye around the room.

"Boss, I'll take care of it," Baseem tried to save face.

"Should have had that thought before you rang my fucking phone," Kayson said, giving him a cold stare then he turned his attention back to the table where niggas where sitting way too comfortable. On the right was uptown and on the left was downtown; each man had their territory, but the sides were mixing and some blood had shed; a definite offense on his team.

"Now I hear that we may have a few unhappy campers. If you got something on your heart, speak so I can get the fuck outta

202

here," he looked around the room again.

At first silence ruled the space, then Brim, the dude who ran downtown, got a little fidgety in his seat.

"I got some shit on my heart," Brim spoke from his reclined position.

"Is that right?" Kayson spat, moving closer to where the man stood.

"Yeah, it's right," Brim spat, looking up at Kayson like he was the butler. He leaned forward and grabbed the bottle of 1800 and poured himself a drink. Slowly, he lifted the glass to his mouth and took a sip.

"Since you came all the way down here to find out what is going on with the little people, let me school the Boss," he spat sarcastically. "We down here making shit happen and you sitting back collecting the profit and allowing these young disrespectful niggas to run their mouths and get outta hand," he wrinkled his brow.

"Bitch nigga, who the fuck you talking about?" Tweet bucked up.

"Shut yo young ass up; this grown folks talking, lil nigga," Brim spoke loud and aggressive.

"Nigga, fuck you; you gotta give respect to get some," Tweet sat forward.

Kayson looked back and forth between the two men as the tension in the room began to heat up.

"Nigga, say some more shit and I'll blow yo muthafuckin' head off," Brim reached toward his back.

"You ain't said shit," Tweet reached to his waist.

"Sit y'all bitch asses down!" Kayson barked. "You muthafuckas must be crazy," he moved a little closer to Brim.

"Fuck that nigga," Brim rose to his feet.

"Fuck me too; huh?" Kayson asked, walking up on Brim.

"I'm way pass giving a fuck; I'm in these streets. You muthafuckas sitting back while we on the front line. Fuck that! If you can't run this shit, let another muthafucka handle it then," Brim pounded his fist on his chest.

"You want my crown, take it!" Kayson walked up in his face

203

and beamed deadly eyes into his soul.

"You ain't said shit," Brim grabbed his gun by the handle and began pulling his arm around.

Before he could get his arm all the way to the front, Kayson pooped his ass in the nose breaking it on contact. Brim's head went back as the blood poured. Kayson put his hand around Brim's throat and pushed him back into the chair. As he squeezed on his windpipe, he reached over and grabbed the bottle by the neck and began beating him in the face with it. Every time Kayson drew back the bottle, flesh tore away from his face and skull. The bottle cracked and broke at the neck and Kayson dug it into Brim's right eye, taking it right out the socket.

Kayson released his neck and let Brim's lifeless body slid to the floor. Breathing heavily, he turned to look at each member in the crew. "Does any other muthafucka got some shit they want to put on the table?" he caught the eyes of every man in attendance. Blood dripped from his hand and sweat ran from his brow.

Tweet felt the adrenaline flowing through his body; he knew and heard many things about Kayson, but this was the first time he was able to see a real Boss.

With a smirk on his face he responded, "I got mad love for this hustle and I respect everything this organization stands for. You got my total loyalty," he stood up and saluted Kayson nodding his head in agreement. Tweet was fearless and he had a deadly team of four that loved the kill more than they loved life. Kayson had also heard a lot about Tweet, but a lot still had to be proved.

"We will see," Kayson spat back. Kayson looked around the room first connecting with Baseem then with the other men in the room. "Let me spit some hot shit at y'all niggas real quick," he threw the broken bottle with Brim's eye attached in the middle of the table. All eyes connected with the gruesome sight then looked back at Kayson. "In every business there is a Boss and then there are workers. In this muthafucka, I'm the Boss and y'all work for me. I respect every sacrifice you have made to sit next to my throne. But on the level that we are on, I need niggas to be on point and ready to live today and die tonight. I ain't running no fucking nursery school; we got niggas on our ass. I done had the niggas I eat with spit in my food, and I will not have a repeat of that shit. I will back you; but if you're wrong, I will cut your fucking throat," he paused. "That nigga right there…" he pointed at Brim's bloody body. "…his heart pumped bitch. If you got bitch in you, hang out with some pussy; the only bitch I like on my team is the one in my bed," he turned to Baseem. "This right here is your shit. Get this shit under control!" he ordered as he walked toward the door.

Baseem looked on as Kayson moved out the room.

"I've been a little too comfortable with everybody; so from this day forward, I'm in yo ass. If you sneeze, I'ma bless you; it's killing season and anybody can get it. Tweet I want your team with me. The rest of you niggas get back to work."

Tweet jumped up and his team followed. He ran his ship like a well-oiled machine and wanted desperately to get buck. He had gotten the break he was looking for and he was getting ready to show the game what happens when a nigga's hunger is on starvation mode. "Let's make these niggas bow," he said to Baseem as the heat of his promotion pumped thick in his veins.

Baseem was impressed, but not fooled. He knew he needed to keep an eye on a thirsty nigga; but an ambitious nigga…he needed two eyes and glasses for one of those. Even when a nigga was trying to kiss your ass he could still miss some shit, and he was not going to let anything sneak in and crumble the castle.

✱ ✱ ✱ ✱ ✱

Kayson moved money and people around until four thirty in the morning. When he walked into the house, the quiet calmed his soul. He realized that he needed that peace and calm to survive. Kayson looked in on his children, walking into each of their rooms and kissing their forehead. He stood the longest in Malika's room; she had stolen his heart and he knew he needed to tie everything back up and get his family back out of the country.

Kayson closed the door to the baby's room and headed to the master bedroom where he knew KoKo lay waiting on him. He had to remind himself that KoKo was who she was and that sometimes the hustle in her was stronger than the one he had within himself. But the reality was her ass was not in charge. He needed to set a standard in their relationship so there was no confusion about who had the dick and who had the pussy.

Kayson walked into his bedroom allowing his eyes to roam the room. KoKo had lit the fireplace, causing her silhouette to dance on the wall behind her. His eyes settled on her vest and gun on the chair and boots by the closet door. Kayson looked over at the bed at KoKo's body with the silk sheet clinging to her frame. She had been on the hunt, but was back laying comfortably in his bed; conformation that everything she was, belonged to him. The idea of that made his dick jump. He moved to the closet, stripped down and hit the shower.

When he entered the bedroom wrapped in a thick dark green towel, he had one mission on his mind. He needed to break KoKo's ass down; he had created a monster and it was time to make her submit and follow. Kayson dropped his towel to the floor, pulled back the sheet and laid next to KoKo's body and inhaled her scent. Honey vanilla rose up in his nostrils as his hand slithered over her body. KoKo began to heat up as she felt his fingertips on her nipples and his dick rock up between her butt cheeks.

"I know yo ass got somebody on the connect."

KoKo remaind silent.

"Why I gotta keep finding shit out that you aint telling me?" Kayson asked as he grinded against her.

"Baby, I'm sorry," she moaned as his hand slid between her thighs.

"Say that shit so I know you mean it," his warm breath caressed the nap of her neck and his soft lips followed.

"Baby, I'm sorry," she raised her voice a little as his finger traced her clit. She opened her legs wide, giving him full access to her purring kitty.

When she was on the brink, Kayson climbed between her legs and kissed her deeply. KoKo rocked back and forth, wetting the tip of his dick with her slippery lips.

"Let me have you, baby," she begged, gripping the back of his head as his mouth rested over her nipple sending heat through her body.

"Why you so hardheaded?" Kayson asked as he teased her throbbing hole with the tip.

"I'ma do what you say, baby," KoKo whined, pushing her pussy to him with every movement; anxious to get him inside her.

"You gonna do what I say?" he asked as he began sliding her those inches a little at a time.

"Yesss..." KoKo moaned as he pushed through her tightness.

"You promise," he teased, pulling back to the tip then rubbing it against her erect clit.

"Yes, I promise baby. Put it back in," she pleaded, biting into his neck.

Kayson pushed all the way in hitting the bottom, and then he bounced off her walls using her cries of pleasure to guide his push.

"Feel good, baby?" he asked, pinning her legs down while stroking her deep.

"Oh, my God, you in my spot, baby," KoKo threw the pussy at him causing the slid to be hot and sticky.

When Kayson heard her breathing change and felt her pussy lock around him, he pulled out.

"Baby what you doin'? I'm about to cum," she cried out, panting and gripping his back.

"You like disobeying me. You can't do what I ask you to do. So, I can't do what you ask me to do," he peered down into her eyes. "Your pussy feels good as hell; hot, wet, and tight to my fit. I wanna fuck you till you can't see straight. But never forget I taught this pussy to do what it do; so, you can't fuck me," he hardened his gaze with an intense crease in his brow. "And since you like doing things on your own..." his eyes roamed down her breast toward her heaving stomach. "...start with doing the rest of this on your own," he rose up on his knees, stroking his thickness in his hand. Kayson winked as he eased off the bed and stood to his feet. "I'm about to leave town; I'll catch up with you in a couple of days," he paused. "Remember, regardless to how much praise you get on these streets, I'm the Boss up in this muthafucka. You better get right," he turned toward the bathroom.

KoKo sat up and crossed her arms on her chest. "This nigga is crazy. He got me fucked up," she got off the bed and followed him into the bathroom. "Is this how we doin' this shit?"

Kayson turned toward her staring into her eyes as he ran the soapy cloth over the length of his dick. KoKo put her hands to the side and tilted her head waiting for an answer. Kayson rinsed his skin, and then turned off the water.

"The conversation was over when I left the room. Go get yourself some rest," he moved his naked body past her, heading to the closet to get dressed.

KoKo stood in place, ready to go in; but she knew the fire was already hot. She dared not make Kayson explode. It panged her heart that she had caused doubt to creep into her husband's mind. She stood there hating that now there was a tear in their trust.

"If you need me, call the emergency phone. Other than that, start cleaning yo shit up," he moved out with a black back pack on his shoulder.

The Boss had had his say, but Miss KoKo was infamous about disobeying. But with the shit he just pulled, the thought of getting even pushed logic to the back of her mind. And she knew just how to do it.

*****

"Shit!" Magic yelled out throwing his mug against the wall. "How the fuck does this nigga have both connects in his pocket?" Magic asked Leger as he tried to calm himself down.

"I have beed tapping all my sources and nobody won't deliver without Kayson's permission." Ledger reported.

"This shit is crazy. First this nigga gonna push our ass in a fuckin' corner, then he gonna tie a knot in production. I gotta do something about this shit, he fuckin' with my money," he said as he sat hard in his chair.

Ledger ran off a few more facts about the crew and they went back and forth about how to slow Kayson and his team down.

Breonni tipped away from the door and down the hall back to Magic's bedroom and closed the door. She hurried to her cell phone, ran into the bathroom locked the door and cut on the shower. She croched in a corner and called KoKo.

"Hello."

"Hey, it's confirmed they have been cut off," Breonni stated lowly.

"Are you sure?"

"More than sure, and the Boss needs to watch out they are plotting some shit. I will fill you in when I see you."

"Okay, get up outta there. Call me when you leave his house,"

"Got you." she hung up adjusted her call log and jumped in the shower. She needed to get away from there as soon as possible.

NeNe Capri

Chapter 29

Breaking the Boundaries

Baseem's mind raced on his way to Goldie's apartment. Again she had been out of touch and he needed to check on her and the baby. He had called several times and when his calls kept going to the voicemail, he jumped in his car and headed to her house. When he pulled up and saw her car had not moved he became uneasy. Baseem pulled out his heat that was tucked in his waistband then exited the vehicle. As he moved to the front door of her apartment building, he was praying hard to the gods for everything to be okay.

"Good evening, Mr. B," the night receptionist said from his desk.

"Good evening, Brian. Has Miss Brooks been out of her apartment today?"

"Ah no, sir," he thumbed the log pages. "In fact, she has not been out in two days, sir," his slight British accent returned the information.

"Let me have the spare key," he put his hand out, not waiting for a response.

Brian saw the silver tip of his gun and the slight fear in Baseem's eyes and knew he was not trying to hear about policy and formalities. He reached over into the drawer and handed Baseem the key.

"Thank you. If I don't call down here in ten minutes, you know what to do," Baseem said as she continued to the elevator.

When he exited, he drew his weapon and moved stealth down the opposite wall; carefully training his ear toward her apartment.

Baseem took a breath, slowly turned the lock, and eased the door open an inch at a time.

His eyes darted through the crack for any figures or moment. It was pitch black and the only sound was the one from the living room television. He eased a little further until his body was completely inside, then he closed the door gently.

Moving from one room to another, he kept his gun drawn for any surprises. When Baseem got to the baby's room, his heart sank when he didn't see him in his crib. He looked down the hall at Goldie's door and his chest got tight. *I can't do this*, the voice rang loud in his head as he moved toward her bedroom. Baseem's breathing quickened as he turned the knob.

Once the door was open, his eyes did flips around the room trying to identify every inch. The bed was tattered and there were cups and tissue and trash throughout the room. He tipped to the bathroom and when he saw Goldie's body spread out on the floor his legs got weak.

"Oh shit, Goldie," he moved to her side and shook her shoulder.

Goldie's eyes fluttered open and a look of relief brought a slight amount of color to her face.

"What happened, ma?" he asked, looking over her body for wounds or injuries.

"I'm fucked up," she slurred.

"Where is the baby? How long have you been laying here?" he asked, pulling out his cell. "Hello, yeah...she's here, I'm straight. I will call back down there in a minute," he said to Brian and then disconnected the call.

Baseem turned her over on her back and looked her over again. "What's wrong?"

"I'm sick I couldn't move," she said, putting her head back and closing her eyes.

"Where is the baby?' Baseem repeated.

"With Mariam."

"Why you ain't answer the phone?" he asked, feeling her forehead.

"It died, I can't find my charger."

"Aight. Let me get you straight."

"I need something to drink."

Baseem looked around and spotted a towel; he rolled it up and put it behind her head. "I'll be right back," he got up and headed to the kitchen. After fumbling around he saw some straws and poured her some water.

Baseem kneeled down and assisted her with a few sips. She was weak, but she was alive and that alone was comforting.

"Lay back. I got you, ma. Let me get some things and I'll be right back," he stood up, pulled out his cell phone and began his mission. He gave Brian a list for the store, cleared everything with Kayson then checked on the baby. Once he had secured the perimeter, he began his mission. He covered her up with a sheet then went to work. His first step was to open the windows and get some air in there.

"What the fuck," he yelled out when he found a small bit of throw up next to the bed. He shook it off and began grabbing things, shoving them in a garbage bag. By the time he had the sheets changed and trash secured, the bell rang.

Baseem tied up the bag and headed to the door. When he pulled it open his package was right there waiting. He paused, reached in his pocket, and pulled out a few bills.

Brian was standing there proud and happy with a small smile on his face. "Here you go, sir," he held out the bag. "And I'll take that," he reached out and took the money from Baseem's hand and the trash from the other.

"Thanks again."

"Anytime, sir. Please give Miss. Brooks my best," he turned and walked away from the door.

Baseem closed and locked the door then placed the items on the kitchen counter. He turned on the front eye on the stove, grabbed a pot and put the chicken noodle soup in it. As it came to a boil, he read the directions on the Nyquil then made a cup of hot tea and poured some inside.

"This will fuck a cold up," he chuckled then headed to the bathroom.

Kneeling again by her side, he shook her awake, lifted her head and got the medicine moving into her system. Once she drank half a cup, he sat her up then ran her a shower.

"This is not a good look," he joked.

"Fuck you, Bas," she mumbled then gave him a slight smile.

"Not looking like this you won't," he returned.

Baseem pulled his shirt over his head and then lifted her to her feet.

"I can't. I'm dizzy as hell," she shook her head slowly.

"I got you, ma," he said, sitting her back down.

Baseem stripped down to his brown skin then pulled her into his arms. He pulled her out of her pajamas then carried her naked body to the shower.

Goldie leaned against his warm, smooth chest as he ran the soapy cloth over her back. The hot water felt so good going over her skin and his firm, yet gentle, touch soothed her aches and pains.

"Thank you, Bas," she mumbled as he turned her around and put her back against his chest.

Baseem carefully washed her body and fought to keep his dick from stiffening. Goldie had the perfect body; fat juicy ass, small waist and perky firm breast. God, you got jokes he said to himself as he completed his task.

Baseem stepped out with Goldie in his arms; he grabbed two towels and dried her off then himself. Goldie put her head back on the pillow as he laid her down on the crisp clean sheets. Baseem searched the draws, found a little black nighty and slipped it over her head.

"You always take good care of me; thank you."

"I told you I got you."

Goldie snuggled up like a baby and passed out. Baseem tucked his towel around his waist and collected the sheets and clothing. He placed them in the machine then headed back to the room. After getting her to take a few sips of water, he then got in the bed next to her. Goldie cuddled up against him and moaned a little before she drifted off again.

* * * * *

When Baseem got to his car and turned on the phone there

were several messages from Simone. He listened to them then hit her number.

"Hey you. You alright?"

"I guess."

"What does that mean?" he asked as he pulled from his parking spot.

"I can't understand why I only see you maybe twice a week and then when I call you, you don't answer," she said as she took a seat on her bed.

"You know I be traveling, but you got me right now," Baseem spit that slick shit.

"You think you are so cute," she addressed his confident attitude.

"Don't worry ma, I got you. I just have to move around for a few more days."

"I am going to hold you to that," she smiled lightening the mood.

"What you got on?"

"Why?"

"Take all that shit off, I'm on my way," he hung up giving her no time to respond.

Simone's kitty jumped as she looked down at her phone. She placed it on the nightstand then did just as she was told. It had been days since she saw him and she could not wait to fell his touch.

Chapter 30

Reflection

KoKo moved slowly around the bedroom in her bra and panties. She sat down then lay back on the bed and stared at the ceiling.

"Why you naked?" Kayson asked as he moved over to where she lay.

"Just taking a quick minute to get my head straight for your little field trip," KoKo said as she rolled over on her stomach placing her hands under her chin.

Kayson walked over and laid on KoKo's back. "Why I gotta convince you to handle your business," he spoke into her ear then planted a few tender kisses on her neck.

"You know I don't do bitches," KoKo stated firmly.

"I know you don't do bitches. But you are a boss and you gotta handle your business," he said as she stretched her hands out over her head and parted her legs with his.

"I have a feeling you are going to try and convince me that this whole dinner thing is a good idea," KoKo purred as she felt Kayson maneuvering her thong to the side.

"And I have a feeling that after these back shots, you are going to get along with your friends a whole lot better," he responded as he slid between her slippery wet lips.

"Mmmm..." KoKo let out a soft moan as she felt his inches go deeper.

Kayson gave her exactly what she needed to get her mind right.

He stroked and gave her one power orgasm after another.

KoKo stepped into the shower and quickly washed herself from head to toe. She dressed herself, grabbed her clutch, filled it with a few hundred and a black card; then she tucked her guns and stopped briefly, kissing Kayson's lips.

"Be good," he warned.

"Be awake when I get in," she threatened, giving him a wink as she turned to walk away.

Kayson chuckled and smacked her butt. "Oh, I'll be all the way up."

KoKo just giggled and shook her head on her way out the room.

When KoKo arrived at the restaurant, all the girls where already there and seated. She walked with a little swag to her step as she felt the slight throb of her kitty against her jeans.

"The next bitch can't even open the door for my man."

"I be like...no, thank you, I got his knobs," Deena chuckled as she brought her folk to her mouth.

"Girl, bye...these lurking ass side bitches is winning. You gotta have eyes on all sides of your head," Goldie chimed in.

"Well, I'm good; I ain't worried about the next chic. If she can take him, she can have him," Simone responded, sipping her virgin drink.

KoKo sat back and looked around the table as her confidants tossed around dumb ass statements; she could do business with females, but friendship was annoying. They always said some shit to rub her the wrong way. She crossed her legs and took her glass by the stem.

"Why you looking like that, KoKo?" Deena asked with a side-eye. "Oh, that's right...the Boss ain't leaving his First Lady," Deena joked, perching her lips to the side.

Goldie shook her head...she already knew.

KoKo took in a little air then enlightened her understudies. "Bitch, I wouldn't lose no sleepover a nigga even if he held my eyes open," she spat locking eyes with Deena. "It just baffles my mind that a bitch could convince herself that the next bitch took her man," she paused and sat her drink on the table. "A man doesn't leave his woman for the next chic. That Nigga was already leaving regardless; the fact that she welcomed him with open arms and legs into his transformation is called convenience, not a reason. These bench-able bitches need to sit down and take notes because if he left you then you been out the game. The other bitch just so happened to ring the buzzer."

KoKo reached in her clutch and pulled out a couple thousand, laid it on the table, then rose to her feet and her bodyguard came to attention. "Continue to have a good evening, ladies. Remember: if a bitch gets your spot, it was never really yours in the first place. Be easy," KoKo moved around the table headed to the exit.

"I respect that bitch. Her pussy got value. She is the truth; y'all bitches better take notes," Adreena teased. "Let me get y'all another drink. You bitches done dried up with that piece of advice," she laughed as she flagged down the waitress.

* * * * *

Adreena was parked outside the restaurant waiting for the last lady to pull off. She reached over into her glove box and pulled out some hand lotion and applied it as she planned her route back to the Lion's Den. She was prepared to pull off when she looked up and say Pete movng through the parking lot like he was on a mission. Adreena slid down in her seat and watched. When she saw Magic pull in she knew shit had just changed.

"Well what do we have here?" she mumbled.

Pete got in Magic's car and sat for about fifteen minutes then hopped out and jumped back in his turck with a small bag. When Pete pulled off so did she, his ass was about to be in for a rude awakening.

Chapter 31
The Revelation...

Baseem sat in his rental car watching as KoKo stepped out of Rock's house giving him a hug and then moving toward the cab that was parked in his driveway. He slid down in his seat as she scanned the block before jumping in her ride and taking off. Baseem started to grab his gun and run up in Rock's house and blow his brains out. But his cooler head took over and moved his hand to the gear shift and his foot to the gas pedal. He knew that Kayson needed to know what was going on then make his own moves; he was not about to murder over the next nigga's pussy.

After following KoKo to the Atlanta airport, he watched her head inside then he pulled off. After making the runs through the city and setting things up with Chico, he too was on his way back to New York; he needed to get the secret off his chest. Kayson had had two men he loved and trusted betray him, and he was not going to be the third.

Kayson was seated at his desk going over in his mind what needed to be done next. He knew that he needed to make moves that were well calculated. Kayson looked up from his desk to see Baseem walking into his office with a stern look on his face.

"Reports," Kayson said, getting right to the point.

Baseem took a seat across from him and took a deep breath. "You know I don't get in the next nigga's business, but me and you are way past business," Baseem stated then chose his words wisely.

"Don't worry about what I'll be thinking, say that shit," Kayson's nostrils flared as he braced himself for the information that Baseem was about to give him.

"I saw some shit that has me uneasy. I don't have proof of what is going on, but the shit don't look right," he paused. "Your wife is meeting with some nigga down in Georgia. I know he is into real estate, but I haven't collected enough information on this nigga to hold him in contempt."

"What did you see?" Kayson sat forward.

"Just picking up or dropping off, but the shit just looks strange. I started to confront the nigga, but I needed to let you handle your own house," Baseem looked into Kayson's face for confirmation.

Kayson nodded his head as he took in what Baseem had just revealed. His heart knew that KoKo would not violate his love and trust, but he also knew she would disobey and do shit that was questionable in order to get what she wanted.

"Thanks, I got it from here. Handel shit on ground level and be ready to leave town in a week. You can let yourself out," Kayson said, rising to his feet heading upstairs to where KoKo was with the children. Baseem's revelation wasn't new information. KoKo had revealed to him that she was with Boa and the dude Rock in Georgia, but he was sure she had put that shit in the grave along with their enemies. But obviously, she had some secrets and he was about to make her realize what holding secrets meant in his world.

Baseem immediately felt a surge of guilt as he watched Kayson leave the room. On one hand, he had a brotherhood with Kayson that he would rather die than violate. Then on the other hand, he had a brotherhood and trust with KoKo that he cherished. But at the end of the day, him and Kayson had been crossed by people that they loved and he was not going to let anything slid because on the real...even though he loved her, he would take her life before he would let her get his taken.

* * * * *

Adreena sat a few cars back until she saw Pete pull into a diner in Hoboken. When he jumped out and went inside she pulled into the lot and parked two cars down. Carefully she tucked her gun and moved to the entrance of the diner. Once she spotted where he was seated she requested his section. Adreena sat quietly behind him looking at a menu and waiting to ear hustl. Seconds later she looked up and saw Chucky coming that way. She lowered her gaze as he slid in the both. Their conversation began and when she realized what was going down her blood started to boil. These two niggas had been filtering information to Magic and plotting to have the crew hit so they could join him.

"Would you like anything ma'am?" the waitress asked standing with her pen and pad ready to go.

"I thought I did but I just got sick, can you bring me a sprit to go?" she asked rubbing her stomach.

"Right away," she took the menu and left the table.

Adreena put a twenty dollar bill on the table then moved to the door. When she got to the car she took off her jacket screwed the silencer on her gun then stepped out the vehicle and waited.

Pete and Chucky emerged from the diner picking their teeth and laughing as if they had just gotten over. When they got to their car they were alerted by the sound of a woman crying. Pete went to one side and Chucky went to the other.

Adreena was croutched down between the two cars crying and mumbling incoherently.

"You good ma?" Pete asked reaching down to her.

Adreena continued to mumble.

"Let's see if we can get her to stand up," Chucky said moving in to help out.

"What's wrong? Did somebody hurt you?" Pete asked.

Adreena mumbled. "I can't belie…"

"I can't hear you ma, did you say you can't believe?"

"Yes. I can't believe you crossed us muthafucka."

Adreena grabbed him by the collar then shot him three time in the stomach. When he fell to the side she drew on Chucky shoting him in the thigh, and twice in the chest. When he hit the ground she jumped to her feet hopped in her car and peeled out headed straight to KoKo.

Chapter 32

Fed Up

Kayson walked off the elevator on fire. He moved through the rooms looking for KoKo like an angry bull. When he walked in the bedroom, his eyes met with KoKo and the color drained from her skin.

"What's wrong?" she asked, trying to gage his mood.

"Get Mariam to come and get the kids. I need to speak to you," Kayson walked into the closet and then walked back in the room.

Mariam walked into the room with a bright smile on her face. Her eyes connected with Kayson then KoKo and she knew there was a problem; as usual, she did only her job.

"Hey, little face," Mariam said as she reached out for Malika.

KoKo passed the baby to Mariam as Quran stood staring at his dad.

"Go with Mariam," Kayson gave him a stern look.

Quran nodded his head and walked out the room. When the door closed, Kayson began.

"You got something you need to tell me?" he asked, moving close to her.

"No, why? What happened?" KoKo looked in his eyes.

"I'ma need you to do me a favor and not treat me like a fucking bitch ass nigga," Kayson based as he moved a little closer; now towering over her.

"What is wrong with you; why you cursing at me?" KoKo got a little indignant.

"I'ma ask you one more time and I want you to dig deep and don't fucking play with me," he said as his breathing slightly picked up.

"Baby, I have no idea what you are talking about. If you have something to ask me, just ask me. I have never lied to you," KoKo was now getting upset. And just as the words left her mouth she knew exactly what he was talking about but she damn sure was not going to be the first to say the words.

"You fucking that Atlanta nigga?" he rubbed his hands together as he tried to keep calm.

KoKo took a deep breath. "No, I am not. Did I? Yes. But that was before you came home."

"If you fucked that nigga and it ain't shit between y'all, then why the fuck you keep running to him when shit gets tight?"

"Baby, it's not like that. I have some business with him and I need him for some things that I have to take care of," she tried to defend the situation.

"What the fuck could you possibly have to take care of that you need a nigga you were fucking to help you with?" he gave her the side-eye.

"Kayson, please don't do that. I slept with him once. I had no idea that you were alive and at that time, that man risked his situation to make sure I was good and assured my freedom. I have a few things pending in Atlanta that I have to wrap up, then it's over."

"Fuck that, it's over now," he turned to walk away.

"Kay, I can't just walk away from this. I need a little more time please."

"You end it or I end it," he turned back in her direction.

"I can't."

"You can't? What the fuck you mean you can't?" the crease deepened between his brows.

"I'm sorry, but I have to see this through," she folded her hands over her chest.

"Is that right?" he raised one eyebrow.

KoKo stood quiet; she knew that if she said the wrong thing shit could go from bad to disaster in a matter of seconds.

"I'll tell you like this…you won't be prepared for what I have to do," he turned to walk out the room.

"Baby wait," KoKo moved swift and positioned herself in front of their bedroom door.

"Don't fucking, baby me and get yo ass out the way."

"We ain't doing this shit. I'm your wife; you don't have anything to worry about," she put her hands up to his chest.

Kayson quickly moved her hands. "Don't fuckin' touch me."

"Are you serious right now?" she was now heating up.

"Move," he gave her the stare of death.

"You fuckin' walking out on me?" KoKo asked as her heart felt as if it would leave her chest.

"It's all good; call that nigga to get you through it."

"It ain't shit between us but business," she based at him.

"And obviously it ain't enough between us," he pushed her to the side and snatched the door open.

KoKo grabbed his arm and he pulled away.

"That's what the fuck we do now? We walk out on each other?" she came up behind him.

Kayson turned on his heels looking down on her with his intense hazel eyes. He spoke slowly but firmly. "Let me explain something to you so you don't get it fucked up. The only reason I didn't knock you the fuck out is because I love you. And the only reason that nigga is still alive is because I don't kill niggas over pussy. However, my advice to you is to leave me the fuck alone before I break rule number one," he looked at her, nostrils flared and fist bald up tight as he struggled with his emotions.

"All the shit I have done for us and sacrificed so that we could be straight, and you turning on me?" KoKo got choked up.

Kayson cracked a slight smile. "I taught you a lot; but obviously I didn't teach you enough. But it's all good; you'll have plenty of time to learn this lesson," he turned his back and moved toward the steps. Kayson was heated, for the first time he felt a small amount of hatred in his heart toward KoKo. He had forgiven her for all that she had done while he was gone because he justified it with his own deception which made them equal. But the fact that she was working close with a nigga she fucked was not sitting well

227

on his conscious; and he was about to break his rule number two.

KoKo stormed back into their bedroom and marched into the closet and grabbed her gear and suited up. Then she placed a call to Goldie. She knew that there was only one thing she needed to do; she had to say fuck strategy and go at these niggas' crowns. It was true, she had sacrificed a lot; but the one thing she was not prepared to sacrifice was her love for the Boss.

Chapter 33

Next Move

"Are sure this is what you want to do?" Mr. Raja asked as he pulled the documents from his briefcase. He had finalized the turning over of twenty-five percent of Odoo Enterprises to Wells Incorporated.

"For the hundredth time. Yes, I have it all under control." Yuri responded taking the papers into her hand.

"I hope for your sake you do. That man is nothing to play with," he warned.

Yuri signed her name next to her father's forged signature and then slide them back to Mr. Raja. He signed then Yuri took the contracts and placed them in a folder she had prepared for Kayson.

"Thank you for all your help." She extended her hand and they shook to conform the deal.

"I will be in touch," he said rising to his feet. Mr. Raja grabbed his hat and jacket and walked out of Yuri's office.

Yuri called Kayson and requested his presence. When she hung up she quickly showered and put on something sexy, lit a few candles, turned on some music and waited for his arrival.

Kayson rang the bell twice and stood back and waited.

Yuri stopped on her way to the door to look in the long hallway mirror before proceeding. She adjusted her breast in the tight red form fitting dress then ran her fingers through her long wavy hair. Taking in some air she unlocked the door and pulled it open. He kitty jumped at the mere sight of him.

"Welcome to my home. You know you are always welcome." She moved to the side.

"Thank you," Kayson said as he entered.

"Everything is in the here," she commented as she walked towards the hallway leading to her office.

Kayson followed her lead allowing his eyes to feast on her beauty. The material of the dress clung nicely to every curve and sway of her figure. He blinked back the fantasy as he entered the room. Kayson eyed the candles and knew she wasn't trying to let him out of there without giving him some pussy.

Yuri walked over to her desk and picked up the file then turned to Kayson. "Everything is here. I can't wait to see the look on my father's face when he realizes he works for the Boss." She smiled locking her low gaze with his.

"You did good," Kayson said taking the folder into his hand. He looked over the documents and nodded his approval.

"Would you like anything to drink?" Yuri asked in a low tone.

"No thank you. I have a flight to catch." He turned down her offer.

"You are always about business. Life is to short, you need to live a little," she smiled at him showing her sexy dimples.

"I do live. I am just very careful of my actions," he responded.

"I wish I would have met you years ago. We could have took over the whole fucking world."

"I aleady have someone who I have taken over the world with."

"Oh yeah, Miss KoKo," she stated sarcastically.

"You already know," he responded.

"Kayson. Let me ask you something. What does she have that I don't?" she moved in a little closer.

"There is to much to list," he stated smoothly placing the folder down on the table.

"She would never know. I just want one night." She took him by the wrist and rested his hand on her breast.

Kayson stared into her eyes as she began to caress his dick. He slightly obliged her by squeezing her breast and rocking up so she could fell the beast off his leash.

"You have to be careful of what you chase. Sometimes it

catches you first," he smoothly stated as she heated up.

"I wanna suck your dick. I need to taste all of your power," she panted.

Kayson slid his hand up her chest and rested it on the back of her neck. Slowly he pulled her to him then kissed her deep.

Yuri's head became light as he released her from his embrace. "I need to feel the back of your throat." he said as he released the Enforcer from his zipper.

"My pleasure," she whispered as she moved to his waist nibbling on his chest and stomach on way down. Yuri squatted in front of him and just inhaled his scent before taking his pulsating rod into her mouth. Slowly she inched down on him tightening her jaws a little along the way. Yuri was in heaven and in Yuri's world, God couldn't compare to Kayson.

Kayson looked down with a scrawl on his face. This bitch was on her knees trading away her family's fortune just for a chance to suck his dick. She was lower than a snitch she was the worst kind of woman. The women his mother warned him about, those that would try and use pussy to bring him to his knees.

Yuri moaned and sucked holding on tightly to his thighs.

Kayson's dick stiffened to capacity as he thought about ending her treachery. He reached in his back pocket and retrieved a piece of fishing wire. He watched as she bobbed and slobbed all over him. Kayson, fought back the urge to cum as murder took over his mind. His nostrils flared in anger then he wrapped the wire around her throat. Yuri's mouth opened wide releasing him from her jaw grip. She grabbed at the wire as it cut into her skin.

Kayson held on tight as she slipped into the darkness. When he dropped her body to the floor he tucked away his steel then grabbed the wire from around her neck. He retrieved the paperwork from the coffee table and formed an evil smirk as he exited. As Kayson headed to the airport he couldn't help but celebrate. He had did it, and within a few more days he would own everything.

* * * * *

When Kayson landed he tucked the paperwork safely away then headed straight to the pool hall to meet Baseem he walked in to see

231

him sitting at a table by himself with a bottle of Jack Daniels and a single glass.

"What's up?" Kayson asked as he approached the table.

"Just trying to wrap my mind around all this shit we into," Baseem slurred.

"This shit is about to be over. We just need a few more days," Kayson said then headed to the bar for a glass. He returned, filled his glass to the top and took a seat.

"We got hit uptown and downtown, we have a few men down. But, I got people on it no worries. I just needed to sit the fuck down and remember what we are doing this for," he took the glass to his lips.

"And?"

"They found Pete and Chucky in Hoboken."

"Yeah, they was living foul. I had some people on that. They say some bitch hit them." Kayson stated smoothly.

"Where was your wife last night?" Baseem asked raising his brow.

"You never know. Her ass be in the shadows laying niggas down." Kayson said taking his shot to the head.

"I got Tweet and his crew looking into it. I told everybody to be cool until we can get a handle on this shit. We got to much money at risk."

"Okay keep me informed." Kayson paused to gage his mood. "What else is on your mind?" Kayson asked taking his drink down and poring another.

"I fucked around and caught that shit from you," Baseem said then reached over and grabbed his blunt and lit it up.

"What the fuck you talking about?" Kayson asked raising his brow.

"That love shit." He shook as he said it.

"Oh shit, not you. Let me find out Mr. Fuck that bitch, done caught a feeling or two. Which one is it this time?" he laughed.

Baseem again shook his head. "Goldie."

"Nigga you going to hell," Kayson joked.

"I know I been fucked up about that shit. You know Night is my brother, that shit just happened," Baseem spilled his guts as if

232

he was sitting in confessional.

"Which part, the you just so happened to fall in her pussy part, or you just so happened to fall in love part?" Kayson continued to fuck with him.

"Man fuck you," Baseem slurred.

"Nah, on the real. It's all good. I know my brother, he would want his son to have a good father and he damn sure wouldn't want no duck ass nigga hitting his pussy in his absence," Kayson tried to lighten his mood. "You got my blessings. Just don't hurt her."

"I got you." Baseem knocked fist with Kayson.

"What about Corporate America?"

"Me and little mama cool but she ain't the one." He pulled thick smoke into his lungs and blew it in the air.

"That's good to hear, cause KoKo sent that pussy after you," Kayson said then sat back.

Baseem dropped his smile. "Get the fuck outta here."

Kayson shrugged his shoulders. "She had to make sure you was straight."

"Nigga you serious?"

"Don't even sweat that shit. KoKo hooked yo ass up," he chuckled

"That's fucked up, but thank her for me." He lifted his glass into the air. "I owe her ass." He continued then swallowed the rest of his drink and refilled his glass.

"Boooyy... I done lived to see the day this muthafucka done fell in love," Kayson burst into laughter. "I told yo punk ass."

"I know that shit had me depressed at first. I didn't know whether use a bullet or poison."

They both laughed hard at the visual.

"You got that shit. You'll be straight. I don't have any advice for you thou, you know KoKo be driving my ass fuckin' crazy. All I can say is good luck nigga."

"That's fucked up." Baseem just put his head down and chuckled.

Kayson and Baseem sat for the next hour joking back and forth then silence fell over the room. They had both retreated into their thoughts and then Baseem spoke. "Every day we touch something that threatens to take the lives of the people we love."

Kayson took a few swigs and tossed some thoughts around of his own. "We have been marching for a long time and we are at the end of a long ass journey. Just a few more days Bas. Just a few more days." He took one last gulp.

"I'm marching with you until the last muthafucka is dead." Baseem nodded taking the rest of his drink to the head.

"I already know," Kayson confirmed Baseem's loyalty.

They finished their drinks then cleaned up and headed for the door.

"So what do we do with this nigga Magic?"

"Oh, I got some shit planned for him. He is going to curse the day his grandmother was born by the time we get done with him."

* * * * *

As Kayson drove through the unforgiving streets of the city thinking about being fifteen years old and full of life hopping from one train to the next, running the city with an unseen hand a smile came over his face. In those days war was fun, you could set one strong example and everyone else would fall in line. But today, you had to kill half of a man's family in order to get him to bend. Kayson was losing good men that trusted him with their lives, and bringing their wives and families stacks of crisp hundred dollar bills and his condolences wasn't enough to erase their pain.

Kayson walked into his basement and looked around the room with a heavy heart. As his eyes wondered over each area, a flood of memories took over his mind. Many nights he had stood in that room with men he loved and trusted; and now each one of them were only a memory of the men that once were his right hand and confidants. Kayson pulled his shirt over his head and removed his boots. He walked to the bar and poured himself a drink then took a seat on the deep red sofa. He grabbed the remote and turned on the satellite radio.

His mind was heavy and his heart panged with the idea that he and his wife were now as close as strangers. Kayson had sacrificed so much and lost so many in his quest to clean the blood off of his name and keep his family safe. His thoughts always went to, Was it all for nothing? He had a wife he could no longer communicate with, which threatened the very fiber of his family and weakened the reason for which he breathed each breath.

Kayson took a few sips of his drink, sat it on the coffee table, then put his head back and closed his eyes. His soul needed peace and there was no way to go forward without having his home in order.

KoKo had sat up in the bed and listened intently when she heard the alarm being reset. She grabbed her gun and moved to the monitors. When she saw Kayson seated on the coach in the basement, relief took over her mood. She put her gun back in place, threw on her white silk robe, tied the belt in a bow and headed to where he rested.

When KoKo walked off the elevator, she knew what needed to happen. Her pride had destroyed some of the love in her marriage and she was tired. Her soul had taken all it could bear, and it was time for her to set herself free.

Kayson opened his eyes and lifted his head to see KoKo standing in the doorway with her arms folded over her chest. He sat up and just stared into her pretty brown eyes. There was only a few feet between them, but it felt as if they were worlds apart.

"I don't want to fight with you anymore, baby," KoKo said a little over a whisper as tears weld up in her eyes.

"Come here," he commanded.

KoKo paused for a moment then walked over and took a seat next to Kayson on the couch. She lowered her gaze to the floor. Playing with different ways to speak her thoughts, she finally decided to just let it flow easily.

"Every day I wake up with regret and each time I look over to where you use to lay, my heart aches knowing that my pride, ego and need for power and revenge is the reason why I am without your touch," she paused to wipe the tears that had forced their way down her face.

"I know I am head strong and I move on impulse, but I promise you at no time did I ever risk the virtue of our friendship or our marriage," she placed a hand on his leg.

"I agree, I should have never continued to see Rock after you

235

came home. But this burning in my belly to see every person involved in the death of my parents suffer consumes me; but I cannot let it make me lose you," she looked up into his eyes.

Kayson allowed her words to sink into both of their spirits before he carefully chose what to say next.

"First, let me say this…loosing me is not an option; but losing yourself is what you will regret forever," he took her hand into his and gently kissed it. "Baby, I understand your pain and I wish I could carry every demon for you. But if we both destroy our souls, what will we have left and what will we give our children?" he asked, placing his hand under her chin. "You gotta let me handle this from here forward."

KoKo nodded her head up and down as she agreed to allow him to lead. As soon as her mind accepted the change of power, she began to feel light, as if her burdens were all lifted. Kayson leaned in and placed his lips on hers; the salt from her tears seeped into his mouth as his tongue parted her lips. KoKo tilted her head as his mouth and hands began to take control of her every thought. Kayson eased her legs apart and slid his fingers deep inside her. KoKo let out a soft moan as he began to pleasure her spot.

"Baby, let me fix us," Kayson's warm breath nuzzled behind her ear sending chills down her spine.

"I'm ready to submit to your power. I don't want to lose what we have," she moaned as the reality of what happened caused a pain in her chest. She needed relief. She needed to feel that heat between her thighs that only the Boss could ignite. As if Kayson could read her mind, he leaned in and placed his mouth over her right nipple and gently tickled it with the tip of his tongue. His warm, soft lips and tongue caressed her nipples until her pussy lips became slippery.

"Kaayyy…" she whined, gripping the back of his head and neck. "Baby, I need you," she panted.

"You need me, baby?" he asked, again placing his lips on hers and easing between her thighs. "Release the Enforcer," he mumbled, biting and nibbling on her lips and chin.

KoKo caressed his steel, enjoying every inch before pulling open his zipper, taking it into her hand, and stroking him slow and firm. She eased his jeans and boxers off his ass and slid them down his legs with her feet. When Kayson bit into her neck, KoKo dug her fingertips into his back releasing his heat. Kayson positioned the Enforcer at her moist opening and let just the head get a taste of her nectar.

"Let me make love to your heart," he stared into her eyes. "I need to feel inside you, baby. Let daddy fix your soul," he began pushing into her tightness. Kayson wanted to go slow and give a little at a time, but he only found satisfaction when he hit bottom. Being serenaded by Marsha Ambrosius set the tone of the physical conversation.

Gonna be a late night, early morning when I get you home. Gonna give you good love, give you what you want and, gonna do it all night long. Baby, let me do you all night long.

"Kaaay…make your pussy obey," she begged, moving with precision with every long deep stroke.

"This pussy is obeying daddy right now. Look how she drips with my every push," he settled in a push up position and gave each wall diagonal pressure, causing her pussy to soak his thickness.

Slippery wet whispers formed from the heat between the lips of her eager flower, filling the room as he played with his favorite spot deep in her core.

"Fuck me, Kay," she demanded him to be deeper and he complied to her every cry.

Kayson rose up on his knees, pulling only her waist to him. KoKo rocked her hips to the rhythm of pull and push.

"Look at daddy's baby; get that dick," Kayson fixed his eyes on the divide of her juicy lips every time he brought her waist down on his dick.

"Get you pussy, baby," she continued to ride.

"You want me to get it, baby," he squeezed her tightly and slid in and out with precision; not missing any angle.

"Baby, you gonna make your pussy cum," she cried, watching the sweat run down his chest as his muscles flexed as he performed the wicked pleasure she craved.

"Cum for me, baby. Cum for the Boss; let me have it, baby."

KoKo gripped his wrist as her waist moved faster with every wave.

"Get it, baby," Kayson pounded the spot causing her to bite her lip and dig her fingers deeper into his skin.

Kayson looked into her face. KoKo's eyes were closed tight, while trying to tame the intense orgasm that was building to its height. However, he needed them open. He needed her to let him all the way in.

"Open your eyes," he commanded.

KoKo slightly raised her lids to see him peering down at her with more intensity than she could handle. She wanted to close them, but the fire behind the hazel took control of her ability to look away.

"Look at me," he started his last lesson, he needed to teach her. "You belong me; all your dreams, all your nightmares…let me have em', baby. Release your demons, Ce'Asia. Let me have everything. Give me your hate and give me your love," his deep, rasp moved in her chest while he held their gaze.

Her body began to shake and move against him as he took over her spot and gave it what it needed. Tears flowed from the sides of her eyes as she released months of pain and regret fueled their movements; they consumed each other's every breath and every emotion. In those seconds of flesh to flesh and heat to heat, KoKo finally tapped into the peace her soul had been longing for.

"Uh huh," he mumbled, pulling her faster, intensifying every nerve in her body.

"Let that shit go, baby. Let it all go. Release it, baby. Let me have every part you."

Feelings of intense relief moved from the tips of her toes to the head of her clit. Surges of energy moved in her stomach, pushing loud grunts from her lips right before she lost the ability to speak. She glared into his hungry eyes and released to him her center, her inner conflict and in return, he released the essence of life deep inside her womb.

KoKo held on and rode until only her legs shook as her body went slightly limp. Kayson pushed deep inside her and held her in place as she squeezed him tightly between her thighs.

"I love you, baby," he said, leaning in; ready to go quench his thirst.

"I love you more; thank you, baby. I got your back," she said, kissing his lips.

"I know," he kissed her deep and then dug deeper. "Remind daddy why he fell in love with you," Kayson spoke into her ear as his dick came back to full attention; growing between her walls.

KoKo moaned as he filled her up. "I know what the Boss likes," she struggled to take in the air between his steamy wet kisses. Filled with unbridle passion, she moved with a slight wildness beneath him. Sweat, tears and flames sparked between them as they both closed their eyes tight and let the love and lust exchanging back and forth take over every movement and emotion.

Tonight he was feeling all her womanhood; KoKo was ready to surrender and he gave her every reason to let go. Vows were made, but that night they had actually sealed their love and their bond.

Chapter 34

A Wells Man

KoKo and Kayson spent the rest of the weekend speaking the words that had gotten missed early in their relationship. The love that they shared was undeniable; but their physical connection most times overshadowed the opportunities they needed to bridge the gaps in their heart between one pain and the next. Both of them carried dark secrets and hatreds that threatened to destroy them, but this time, Kayson would get to release some of the burden on his spirit.

KoKo laid in Kayson's arms listening to his heartbeat and he told her his story. First, touching on a subject that had become taboo in the Wells' house, but he needed to clean his mind of some demons.

"Ever since I could sit up straight, my mother would always pump into my head, *You're a Wells man, and there is no man greater than you.*" he paused as he summoned his mother's voice.

KoKo rubbed his chest and listened attentively as he released to her his anguish.

"I never really knew what that meant until I looked my father in his cold eyes and the reflection of deadly power stared back at me. I was around eighteen years old and he came to visit me at a spot I used to have meetings at up in the Bronx. Aldeen and I were chopping it up when he walked through the door and everything inside me changed.

"What the fuck is wrong with you?" Aldeen asked, turning slightly to see

what had instantly changed Kayson's mood.

Kayson didn't speak, he just held a firm eye with the well-dressed stranger as he approached the table.

"Can I help you?" Kayson broke the silence.

"No, but I can help you," Tyquan returned as he unbuttoned his suit jacket and pulled out a chair.

"What makes you think you will be here that long to need a seat?" Kayson asked with a wrinkle in his brow.

"A Wells man does his best negotiating seated; because when he stands, things can get deadly," Tyquan returned. He looked around for the waitress, then flagged her over. "Let me get two shots of Bourbon," he said, giving the young woman a slight grin.

"Will that be all?" she asked, gazing into his dark hazel eyes.

Tyquan motioned her to bring her head to his mouth then poured something sexy in her ear; something that filled her panties with wetness.

She pulled back slow and looked at her watch. "Twenty minutes."

"Fifth teen," he said firmly, dropping his smile and turning his attention back to Kayson.

"Now that we have all the formalities out the way, let me get to the point. I know you know I am your father."

"You ain't shit to me. You gave me a ride into this muthafucka and for that, I thank you. But we don't have anything past that."

"We have more in common than you know," Tyquan looked over the features in Kayson's face and he filled with pride seeing the exact replica of himself with the heart of a lion.

"This is the last time I plan to ask. What do you want?" Kayson folded his hands on the table and tilted his head.

"It's time for you to come work for the family," Tyquan threw his proposition on the table as if he and Kayson were on any terms.

Kayson chuckled looking over at Aldeen. "Is this nigga serious?" he chuckled again. "Look, I appreciate you taking the time out of your busy schedule to hand deliver a fucked up proposal. But I must disrespectfully decline. I got my own shit. What the fuck can you give me that I can't get for myself?"

"Son, I'm not your enemy. I'm just a man on a mission; either you see a spot or you don't. Either way, the sleep I was planning on getting won't get lost on your decision."

242

"You got some real balls coming here. I don't need anything you have. You can keep all your shit," Kayson said, sitting back with his hands on his chest.

"Balls? Fuck I need balls for to come see you?" he too sat back and crossed his legs.

Kayson's eyes lowered as his jawbone tightened. *"You got one minute to get the fuck outta my face and then…"*

"And then what?" Tyquan raised his voice. *"That hate, that fearlessness that runs through your veins is because of me; you are who you are because of me!"* he hit his chest. *"Remember, I kill muthafuckas too,"* he too lowered his eyes and rested his hands in his lap.

"I am who I am because of me! I didn't learn shit from you but how to walk away. I don't hate you and I don't love you; so either way, I will put you on your ass, nigga," Kayson barked sitting forward.

Tyquan chuckled as he looked at his watch; the diamonds sparkled in the eye reminding him this was not the time. He quickly took those few seconds to talk himself out of killing his only son. *"I only came to you to invite you into the fold. But, I can see you're not ready,"* he adjusted cuff links.

"I'll never be ready for anything you got going. I don't give a fuck if the offer came with a lifetime supply of free pussy. I'm good."

Tyquan rose to his feet fastening his suit jacket. *"I remember when I used to run my mouth and kill niggas on a humble. But today, I exercise patience. An angry man will destroy himself and die blaming his enemy. But me, I out think the angry man and when I come for him, he knows I am his enemy,"* he stopped to stare his son in the eyes.

"Then we both better watch our backs," Kayson spat.

The young honey brown skin woman came up to the table with the drink in her hand. Tyquan turned to her, taking his eyes from her toes to head. *"Sit it down, they might get thirsty before I do,"* he smoothly directed giving her his intense stare. *"I'm ready to go,"* he commanded her attention.

"Me too," she seductively returned.

"Meet me at the door," he excused her, then watched the jiggle of her ass with every stride.

"You think it's that easy, you can just say no? You're a Wells man; you inherited the same evil as the rest of us," he brought his attention back to Kayson. *"And just like every other Wells man, you will take your seat at the table either by will, or by force."*

"Then I choose force."

243

"I knew you would," Tyquan smiled.

"Your time is up," Kayson spat, losing patience with the whole situation.

"Is that right?"

"Without a doubt," Kayson responded with full confidence.

"I'ma love watching you break."

"You better raise up before I break my foot off in yo ass," Kayson's trigger finger twitched and so did Tyquan's.

"My young bull. You have Boss in those veins. I gotta go stroke a cat, but I'll see you again soon," he walked off with a sinister grin. He had succeeded at his task, he needed to get in Kayson's mind.

Kayson had opened one of his old wounds; he sat for a minute staring off at the wall, caught up in that moment in time. KoKo looked up into his blank stare and could now connect with his pain. He too was chasing demons and trying to come to terms with the deceit in his past.

"Baby, it's time for you to let go too," she gently stated. "There is nothing either of us will gain by holding onto the past."

"I have already buried the past; and the present has a toe tag waiting. There's a few things in our world that cannot be settled with just letting go. They need to be handled aggressively and with malicious intent."

Chapter 35

The Black Out

KoKo struggled into the house with several bags; Kayson had called her for an emergency meeting while she was out preparing for her trip to see the children. She threw the bags down on the couch and walked to the kitchen. As she looked at her watch, she caught an immediate attitude when she realized she was going to be later than she thought.

KoKo poured herself a glass of water, drank it down and then sat the cup in the sink. She then hurried to her room to change clothes. On the elevator, KoKo thought about how things had gotten so off course; and more importantly, how was she going to get things back on track. The doors came open and she dashed out heading quickly down the hall. When she approached the door, Kayson was standing there in a thick black towel; skin creamy brown and glistening with tiny beads of water on his chest and shoulders.

"Why you not dressed?" she asked, giving him the side-eye.

"Because tonight I gotta take care of my wife," his deep sexy baritone caressed her eardrum as he reached out and took her hand.

"So, I take it there is no emergency meeting?" she asked, following close behind him.

"Is needing to see the quiver in your thighs when I slide in that spot an emergency? Not to every nigga; but to a Boss, hell yeah," he said, stopping right before the entrance to their bedroom.

* * * * *

KoKo smiled when she saw the display that Kayson had prepared for the evening. Her eyes moved around the dimly lit room, adoring the various different sized black glass candles. The fire sparkled and danced on the wood as to the tune of passion. The thick black mink comforter was laid out perfectly between the two couches in the sitting area. There was a small silver tray of Kayson's tricks covered with a black silk scarf sitting in front of the fireplace.

"I know you're scared; and you should be," he stared intensely into her eyes.

"You about act up, baby," KoKo purred.

"I think I'm about to break about three different laws, in five countries with you tonight," he reached out to her, pulling at her shirt until it was over her head. Kayson released her belt buckle and she wiggled her juicy booty as he pulled her jeans down to her ankles.

KoKo stepped out of her jeans and shoes and allowed her eyes to enjoy every inch of his body. Her mouth watered to taste him. KoKo watched as his finger gently traced along her breast and up her neck. Kayson placed his finger under her chin, tilting her head so he could taste her lips. KoKo's hands slid inside his towel and down the length of his dick. Heat moved from the pit of her stomach to her kitty, causing her clit to tick against the lace of her thong.

"Nah, daddy calling the shots tonight, baby girl," he took her hand into his and led her to the bathroom.

"You're the Boss, baby," KoKo said a little over a whisper.

Kayson developed a maniacal grin on his face as the plan turned over in his mind. The bathroom was set up the same with black Burberry scented glass candles setting off the aroma of pleasure throughout the room.

KoKo scanned the area then asked Kayson, "You got me nervous, Boss; what you got planned?" she looked over at the black straps mounted to the wall across from the in-floor Jacuzzi.

Kayson caught her gaze in the mirror and enjoyed the nervousness on her face. "Oh that? That's called lights out," his

246

emotionless reflection increased her fears.

KoKo swallowed her spit hard, and then took a deep breath. Kayson grabbed the remote and put "Famous" by Keith Robinson on, hit repeat, the turned it up.

I wake up early to loving you; I get my hands dirty to loving you. When it's all said and done, I want to be famous, famous, just for loving you.

He dropped his towel to the floor and stepped into the shower; causing the water to push warm from the sprinklers. He put his hand out and reached for her. KoKo stepped out of her red lace thong then walked into his arms. Kayson held her tightly in his embrace then blessed her lips with his. The warm water ran over their lava hot bodies as their hands had a festival of touch all over each other's frames. KoKo gasped as Kayson bit into her neck over and over as his hands slid between the lips of her pussy.

"Kay," she moaned as he gave her the pleasure only he could.

"I want you to submit everything to me tonight," he whispered in her ear, grabbing a handful of her hair, squeezing tight as he flipped his tongue slowly between her lips.

KoKo closed her eyes and climbed inside their love and let go; the heat that poured from his body to hers caused her stomach to quack with a craving to feel him.

"I'll give you whatever you want, baby," she said as he pulled his mouth back.

Kayson caressed her breast in his hands, gently squeezing her nipples as he nibbled her ear lobe while whispering in her ear every position he wanted her in. His slippery wet hands slithered along her stomach, resting between her legs.

"You ready to let daddy turn them lights out?"

"Yesss," KoKo submitted as he took her waist then stepped out the shower with her firmly in his grip. "There is no telling daddy no tonight," he said as he placed her next to the tub.

KoKo looked over her shoulder and the seriousness in his eyes glued her lips shut. Kayson instructed KoKo to sit on the thick fluffy towels on the edge of the Jacuzzi. KoKo complied, placing her feet in the water, she then watched as Kayson prepared his night of terror. Kayson took KoKo by the wrist and put her right hand first in to the black leather strap that he had mounted to the wall.

"Pleasure ain't pain, until pain turns into pleasure." He pulled a little tighter.

"Mmmm…" KoKo looked at the Enforcer just inches away from her face and her tongue said, taste him. She extended the tip of her tongue and ran it over the one eye staring back. KoKo gave the head a single kiss allowing a moan to pass her lips.

Kayson smiled and licked his lips at the invitation. "Don't worry, ma; I'ma let you at the Boss," he tightened the strap causing KoKo's breathing to pick up slightly as he grabbed her other hand and placed it in the leather restraint. Kayson traced his finger over her lips as he eased past her. KoKo watched as he left the room and her nerves took over when he returned with the silver tray. Her eyes wandered over to the silk scarf, wondering what was underneath it.

Kayson removed the scarf and grabbed a pink strawberry liquid in a tube then positioned himself right over her head. He looked down at KoKo's luscious lips then opened the bottle and drizzled the sticky liquid down the length of his dick, and watched it drizzle onto her lips and down her neck and breast. KoKo opened her mouth allowing the liquid to coat her lips then slide down her throat as she pushed her tongue up to trace the head of his dick. Kayson rolled the tip of his dick back and forth over her lips and tongue, and then slipped a few inches in her mouth.

KoKo held on to her wrist restraints as she welcomed him into her mouth and sucked and licked him sideways enjoying his taste. Kayson rocked all the way up against her jaw and she tightened them with every push; moaning and humming matching his every hiss. Kayson stood with buckled knees as his wife enjoyed the taste of his power. He held her head steady as his urge to release took over.

KoKo pulled back and gave him a naughty squinted gaze. "Let me have it, baby," she said, then pushed her mouth forward, taking him to the back of her throat. She gave him that ball-tingling jaw work; rotating her neck and making sloppy as she begged for his essence.

Kayson held back until he was satisfied; then he rewarded her good deeds with something warm and tasty to the back of her throat. KoKo rewarded him back; slurping down his treat, then sucking the head of his dick just right to hear the moans of the aftershock.

"The Enforcer said, thank you," Kayson pulled back, rubbing the tip over her lips and chin then moved to his next phase.

"Mmmm..." KoKo licked her lips as she watched him move throughout the room. Kayson's silhouette played tricks on the walls, causing even his shadow to taunt her. She sat awaiting what was going to blow her mind.

Kayson grabbed a small, black velvet bag; then he stepped down into the tub towering over her. KoKo looked up unto his hazel eyes and chill bumps covered her heated flesh. Anticipation took over her emotions as he kneeled between her thighs. She gripped the leather straps as his hands slide up her thighs.

"I wanna make this pussy know I own it," he stated firmly.

KoKo gasped as Kayson pressed the tips of his fingers along her soft skin while staring into her eyes. His warm breath left his nostrils; tickling her collarbone as he leaned in to nibble on her chin and bottom lip. His fingers slipped between her wet lips then deep inside her.

KoKo took in a mouthful of air as he moved his fingers inside her.

"Ohhh...baby..." she whimpered as he pleased her while planting sensuous kisses all over her face.

"You gonna let daddy put those lights out," he moaned into her ear as he reached for his instrument of pleasure.

"You can have whatever you want, baby," KoKo moaned as her body filled with passion.

He turned on the water and grabbed the head from the base and adjusted the stream of water to flow lightly. Kayson allowed the water to trickle over her lips and run down on her nipples, then he blew cool air, causing them to stand at attention. Kayson placed his mouth over her smooth erectness and sucked gently.

"Ssss..." KoKo hissed as Kayson attended to her other nipple, his butter soft tongue circled as the suction of his jaws sent tingling

249

sensations from her toes to the crown of her head.

Kayson sat back and watched as the water drizzled down her stomach and ran down between the lips of her pussy. He adjusted the water to a higher speed and focused the stream on her clit; he parted her lips with his fingers, allowing her throbbing clit to get his full attention. KoKo squirmed as the pressure beat down on her causing her body to jerk with every pounding sensation on her clit.

"Kaaay…" she mumbled, biting down onto her bottom lip as she rested her head against her arm.

Kayson showed no mercy. He turned up the speed and placed himself between her legs, forcing her to keep them open. Again he leaned in and sucked her nipple and bit into the flesh of breast, causing her to release hot passionate moans as her body twitched to his every sensation.

"I'm about to cum, baby," she moaned out.

"You can't come yet," he bit into her neck and shoulders as she trembled and shock locked her legs to his waist.

KoKo let her head fall back as her she tried to catch her breath. Kayson allowed the water to continue to rain down on her, enjoying the way her pelvis jerked and her stomach heaved as she resisted the greatest pleasure.

"Kay, I wanna cum, baby," KoKo moaned, moving with the pressure to keep the sensation on her spot.

"You wanna cum, baby," he asked, smirking wickedly as he thought about how he was getting ready to put her all the way out of the game.

"Yeeess… I need to cum, baby," she mumbled.

"Give me a kiss," he demanded, placing the spout down into the water.

KoKo slowly lifted her head and licked her lips as she brought them to his. Kayson placed his mouth on hers and slid his tongue down her throat while the Enforcer parted the others. Slowly he stroked in her slippery heat as he tonged her deeply.

"You ready to play?" he broke the kiss briefly then grabbed her hair and pulled her back as he reached for the tiny silver bullet. Kayson carefully pushed off each wall as he adjusted the speed on the bullet for the intense pleasure he was getting ready to rock KoKo's whole soul with.

"I wanna play," she moaned as she felt Kayson's inches fill her every inner curve.

Kayson placed the vibrating silver on her clit and quickened his stroke. "You gotta hold that shit, baby," he began his game.

"Ahhh…" KoKo moaned as jolts of energy moved through her body.

"Don't cum," Kayson taunted, pressing harder on her clit. He pushed his thick pole all the way in and grinded deep. He pulled all the back to the head and mercilessly teased the opening while continuing to make that clit act up.

KoKo's legs shivered on his waist as she tried to hold back. Her hands gripped tightly around the straps and her teeth chattered as her whole body was at odds with Kayson's commands as she begged to release.

"I need to cum," KoKo cried out as her juices began to flow.

"Hold that shit," he growled, stroking in her spot and sending vibrating currents through her clit.

"I can't," she gripped tighter and moaned louder. The vibration on her clit and the precision of his stroke had her body shaking to be free.

"Yes you can. Breathe with me, baby; just feel me. Let me have control of your whole body," Kayson instructed. "Just feel me, baby," he stroked and worked her button looking into the slits of her eyes.

Kayson pulled back and moved the bullet, lacing his mouth over her clit and sucked her firmly between his lips and tongue. Kayson ran his tongue slowly down the lips of her pussy; nibbling lightly between firm sucks. KoKo jerked and pushed back away from him as he teased her clit with the tip of his tongue.

"Baby, please…I wanna cum," she cried out while moving her pussy to the rhythm of every sensual lick.

"Hold it for me, baby," he paused briefly to instruct, then went back to work. Kayson gave no mercy as he sucked her to the edge of no return, then put the pussy on pause as he sat up and slid back in; placing the bullet back on her tender clit.

Tears weld up in KoKo's eyes as she tried to control her breathing and her urge to let go. "Kaaay...I can't hold it," she said as she felt him pick up the speed of his thrust.

"Yes, you can," he gripped the small of her back, tilted her waist and dove in and out of her liquid heat, maintaining the vibrating pressure on her clit.

"Ahhh...Kaaay...." KoKo moaned, gripping the leather and closing her eyes tightly. Unable to control her breathing any longer, she panted and squirmed as she received his long deep strokes. KoKo's body rebelled as her pussy began to respond to the pleasure he provided. Her ability to stay lucid was coming to an end as she began to squirt her warm juices all over him. Her body quivered and her head dropped to the side as she lost slight consciousness.

"Ssss..." Kayson slid his thickness back and forth between her wet lips as he brought her face to his. "I thought you wanted to play," he teased, kissing her lips.

KoKo just rested limp in his hands, unable to verbalize a response. Kayson continued his stroke, looking down at his dick repeatedly parting her lips.

"Can you untie me, I want to touch you," she mumbled, barely audible.

"I can't, I'm still having fun," he turned the vibrator up another speed and lowered it between her legs and started the process all over again.

KoKo went in and out of consciousness as Kayson took her to the edge of ecstasy and back. He made her hold all the passion in and then release repeatedly until she could no longer move. Kayson planted his hands on both sides of her ass cheeks, adjusted her to his waist, and pumped hard with precision until he felt the urge to release.

When Kayson finally allowed himself to cum, KoKo felt like she was no longer on this planet. Her head was leaned all the way back and her body twitched every time he moved. He carefully untied her wrists and laid her back. KoKo's limp body lay motionless on the thick white carpet while Kayson looked at her sexy curves with a satisfying smirk. Kayson stepped out of the tub and pulled KoKo up and into his arms. When he got to the mink rug, he laid her down and climbed between her thighs and covered them with the cashmere blanket.

"Kay, I can't," she placed her hands on his chest in effort to slow him down.

"I ain't hearing that shit," he said, sliding in and stroking slow. Kayson crawled in and out of her moist walls, making her vocals drip with pleasure.

"Baby," she moaned as he hit her spots.

"I always know what my baby needs," he spoke softly in her ear. "You still want me to stop?" he asked, keeping a steady pace against her G-stop.

"Ahhh..." she released the sound of desire from her gut.

Kayson listened to the every plea that left her lips and answered with thick thrusts filling her pussy with ten inches of delight.

"I love you," KoKo moaned, biting into that tender spot under his chin.

"Ssss... I love you more," Kayson responded as he enjoyed her wiggle work.

KoKo listened to the music and crackle of the fireplace, accompanied by his slippery push in and out her lava hot kitty. She twisted her waist to his thrust and squeezed her muscles firmly around his dick. The almost silent grunts that left his lips as he kissed hers, confirmed that she was giving him his pussy just right.

The two of them became lost in each other by every passing moment as they inhaled and exhaled one another's hunger.

*****

Kayson rose up the next morning and prepared breakfast for KoKo and the kids. He placed KoKo's meal on the plate and tray then brought it to her in bed. KoKo sat up and smiled as she pulled the sheet up over her chest.

"Awww...thank you, baby," she cooed as he placed the tray on her lap.

"I want you to get some rest. I'm taking the children out with me."

"Yeah, where?" she said, taking the fork in one hand and a strawberry in the other, biting into it allowing the juice to drip from

253

her bottom lip.

"I gotta go see Unc," he responded as he leaned in and kissed the juice off her lips.

"Mmm...you taste so good, baby," KoKo said, running her hand down his chest sending him an open invitation to more of what she gave him last night.

"Behave, the Boss got little people to hang with; I need all my strength," he leaned in and kissed her sweet lips once more. "Eat your food because you will need your strength later," he said before standing up and heading to the bathroom.

"Oh, I will be ready," she said with a slight smirk as she cut into her omelet and turkey sausage.

Kayson showered and got dressed, then he retrieved the children from Mariam.

"Are you sure you don't want me to come with you, Mr. Wells?" she asked as she placed Malika in his arms.

"Nah, I got it. But if I'm not back by dark, you know they got me," he said smiling at his baby girl.

Malika giggled, nestling in his neck and Quran took his hand feeling like a little man. Kayson loaded the children into the truck and was on his way. He moved through the streets and toward the Lincoln Tunnel so he could head into Jersey for lunch. He arrived at Benihana, parked and gathered his legacy from the back seat. Quran's little eyes were on everything as they entered the restaurant. Malika just put her little thumb in her mouth and laid on his shoulder. When they were seated and the chef got started, Quran almost stood up in his seat. The chopping of knives, spatulas and high flames had his whole attention.

Kayson smiled at the beautiful children he was never expected to live to produce, and his chest became heavy. He thought about his mother and her treachery and how she died at KoKo's hand; then his mind went to Aldeen and Wise also taken by her hand. He satisfied his mood with the idea that everything that KoKo had done was for the safety of everything that they had built; and most importantly, for their children. However, he never thought that he would be sitting at a table with his children and not have either one of them around to share the moments with. Kayson was taken from his reverie buy the vibration of his cell phone. He pulled it from his side and hit answer.

"Hello."

"What's good, Boss? I'm just checking in," Baseem said as he bent the corners.

"I'm straight, just spending some time with the family. You good?"

"Yeah, about to go pick up Simone for lunch; just making sure you straight."

"A'ight, enjoy the day, see you tonight," Kayson disconnected the call and turned his attention back to the little people just as the chef began placing the food on the plates and sliding them in front of them.

"Don't touch it yet," Kayson said firmly.

"Yes, dad," Quran answered, looking at his father's eyes for approval.

Kayson tipped the cook and began to feed the baby. Quran waved his little hand over the smoke then fumbled around with the chopsticks.

Kayson had to laugh. "You want me to do it?" he asked.

"Nah, I got it, dad. You know I can't let these sticks beat me," he said as he fumbled some more, finally getting a piece of diced chicken in this mouth.

"See? Wells men never quit," he said with pride as he went back at it.

"Indeed," Kayson confirmed, full of pride.

He sat and talked and laughed with Quran. As he continued to say the things that tickled Kayson to the bone, all he could do was shake his head. They finished up and headed back to the car. Once they were fastened in, it was on to the Heavenly Rest cemetery. Kayson drove onto the grounds and pulled down the rows of tombstones. He pulled across from his uncle's spot. Kayson sat staring out at the patch of earth with the cold stone which read, Rabb Ali and his stomach became queasy. He looked in the mirror at the children and caught a slight bit of solace as he watched Malika kick her feet and slightly nod to the cartoon he had playing on the small screens in the headrests.

Kayson stepped out of his truck and gathered the little ones. Quran held his father's hand as his little eyes danced about the area. He kicked a few rocks as they approached Rabb's grave. Kayson held Malika firm in his grip; as he got closer, he squeezed down on Quran's hand. Quran looked up to see his father with teary eyes; his little brow wrinkled as he tried to understand this side of his father.

Kayson picked up on his gaze and looked down into his little soldier's concerned eyes; he quickly gave his son an assuring smile.

"It's okay for a man to cry. This man right here who we stand before was like a father to me."

Quran looked up to Kayson and then back at the tombstone with the picture of a man that his father obviously loved and respected.

"Was he brave dad?"

"Very brave," he gripped Quran's hand.

They stood together not speaking a word but saying volumes. Malika picked up her little head and smiled at Kayson rubbing her little hands on his face.

"Daddy's girl," Kayson said as he kissed her caramel cheeks. Quran looked up at his dad and sister

"You can kill a muthafucka without blinking, but you can't stand at the feet of your fallen without tears in your eyes," the female voice came from behind Kayson.

Kayson turned toward the voice and when his eyes settled on hers, he slid Malika down into Quran's arms and placed them behind his back.

Quran hugged his sister tightly as the blood in his little body began to stir.

"I knew I would find you here sooner or later. But don't be alarmed, I would never hurt children. It is only the parents I am after," she said while keeping her hand firm on her gun.

"You got a lot of nerve coming this close to me," Kayson said as he began to plot on how to get his hands on her.

"Kayson, I want you to call that woman off," she said, then glanced down at Quran. "Your children are beautiful," she said as she tried to look past him.

"You need to get the fuck away from my family," Kayson said as his patience began to wear thin.

"You don't know what you are up against."

"Bitch you gotta gun on me while I'm with my children. No. You don't know what the fuck you up against," Kayson based.

Quran flinched as he felt his father's anger emit from his very pores. He thought about the .22 his father kept attached to his ankle strap then wondered how he could get to it. He slid him and Malika to the ground and rested his head against Kayson's calves.

"Walk away from this and walk away from her," she warned as she began to back away.

"I suggest you do the same with my father. The fall out is going to be a muthafucka," Kayson spat back as his hand twitched to let that heat loose.

"Walk away, Kayson. If you value what is left of your family, walk away," she said as she a dark green Infinty with dark tinted windows speed up and stopped in front of her.

Brenda snatched the car door open and yelled out one last time. "Walk away," she jumped in the car and sped off.

Kayson took a few deep breaths and scanned the area. He reached behind him and picked up Malika and Quran and ran to his truck. He placed Malika in her seat, quickly fastened her in, and then jumped in the front. "Get strapped in, Quran," he ordered as he too sped off.

Kayson hit the Bluetooth, called Baseem, and put some things in motion. By the time Kayson pulled up to the mansion, the crew was in place and on high alert. Kayson pulled into the garage and jumped out.

Baseem moved to the truck, removing the children as Kayson moved toward the elevator. Six of the scariest dudes you ever want to come across followed close behind him; and four more followed Baseem to another truck.

"I need you to fly the children and Mariam out of the country. My people will be waiting for you at the airport," Kayson said as he waited for the doors to open.

"On my life they will make it there safe," Baseem said as he loaded the children into the truck.

"I'm betting on it," Kayson said, staring at Baseem as the doors closed.

When Kayson exited the elevator, he headed for the basement safe, unloaded some stacks into the duffle bag then headed upstairs to get Mariam.

"It's time," he said, standing in the laundry room door.

"Yes, sir, Mr. Wells," Mariam dropped the fluffy white towel on the pile of folded laundry then hurried to her room to grab the three bags from her closet that she kept packed for her and the children.

"Where is Mrs. KoKo?" she said as Kayson took the bags from her hands.

Kayson didn't answer, he just moved to the elevator.

Mariam didn't say a word; she just crossed her finger over her chest and kissed the cross that hung around her neck.

With Kayson's family tucked safely in the truck, his team loaded in the three identical trucks and everyone pulled out.

The met back up at the airport and pulled onto the black top. Kayson jumped out and moved swiftly up the stairs to the plane and gave the pilot the instructions. He placed the bags in the cabin then headed back to his family.

Baseem was standing with Malika tight in his arms and Quran firm by his side. "Any other instructions?" he asked.

"Yes. Make sure nothing happens to my children and return safe," Kayson said, leaning in and taking Malika from his arms.

"No doubt."

Kayson escorted the children while Baseem took Mariam by the arm. Two of his trusted men loaded on with them.

"I am putting this mission in your hands," Kayson looked at his longtime friends and the intensity in his eyes chilled them to the bone.

They nodded in agreement then shook hands with Kayson. Kayson kissed his baby girl then placed her in Mariam's lap.

"Do what you are told; take care of your sister. No questions. You will see us in a few days," Kayson turned his attention to Quran.

"Yes, dad," he said, looking in his father's eyes.

Kayson buckled him in, kissed his head and bumped his fist. He moved past the crew and headed back to the truck. When he got behind the wheel, it was more than time to go, it was time for death.

KoKo moved through the mansion franticly looking for the children and Mariam. She went from one room to the next and when she saw the children's lunch untouched and laundry incomplete, she began to panic. KoKo turned to head back upstairs and bumped into Kayson.

"Oh, my God, you scared me. Where are my children?" she looked in his face for answers.

"They are safe."

"What the fuck is that supposed to mean?" KoKo tensed up.

"Baby, just trust me," Kayson said in a soothing voice.

"Kayson, it's not about trusting you. I need to know where my children are," she slightly raised her voice.

"Come with me," he said, taking her by the hand.

KoKo moved behind him, getting angrier with every step. "Kayson. Baby, stop," she paused and pulled her hand from his. "Where are my children?" KoKo got a sick feeling in the pit of her stomach.

"I told you they are safe. Just come with me," he reached out to take her hand again.

"Don't fucking touch me," she backed up. "Kayson, I can take a lot of shit, but I can't live if something has happened to my children. Where. Are. They?" KoKo's emotions began to take over her logic.

"You think I'ma let something happen to the kids?" Kayson was now raising his voice. "What the fuck is wrong with you?" he asked, moving closer to her. "Like I said...they are safe. Somebody came to see me today; they knew exactly where to find me. Until the kids are at their destination, don't nobody know where they are. Now, stop your fucking tantrum; man the fuck up, shut the fuck up, and come with me," he grabbed her by the arm and moved her to the basement.

When they entered the room, KoKo eyes had settled on the two black duffle bags with pump shot guns and an AK sitting next to them. She scanned the stacks of money that were on the bar then looked back at Kayson.

"Sit down," Kayson instructed.

KoKo took a seat as she watched Kayson place the bills into a Gucci tote.

"I need you to tell me everything that happened with my mother and then I want you to tell me what you are doing. Don't leave shit out because if I find dirt in your nails that you didn't tell me about, my disappointment with you will be unrecoverable," Kayson said as he poured himself a tall glass of something brown.

KoKo tensed up a she watched him take the liquor to his mouth. She was avoiding having this conversation and now it seemed as though getting around it was not on the list of options. Kayson sat his drink on the table and sat next to KoKo with his ear turned toward her lips.

"Speak," he said a little over a whisper as he folded his hands in front of him.

KoKo took in some air, swallowed hard, and began. "Your mother was not who we thought she was," she paused being very careful of her words. "While you were gone, I sheltered her. I gave her Quran and I loved and trusted her the way I thought you would expect of me in your absence. And then she crossed me," again she stopped to consider Kayson's mood.

"Continue," Kayson spoke through his pain.

"I found out your mother faked her rape to manipulate you, and she slept with my father's killer to destroy him," KoKo decided to just push the words out of her mouth and let the situation take care of itself.

Kayson kept his gaze forward. "You proved all of this before you moved; right?" Kayson for the first time questioned KoKo's judgment.

"Of course. I would have never made that kind of move if I didn't have accurate proof. Kayson, she said the same lines to me that one of the members of Terrance's team heard her say when she put the hit on my father, and as for her role with Raul," she paused. "You need to ask your father," she said and placed her hand on his leg.

"Kay, I would never do anything to hurt you."

"Yeah, but some shit you did had our children in danger," he said, reaching for his drink and taking it to the head.

"Shit I did?" she wrinkled her brow. "We both have put in that work that would make a nigga kill anything associated with us. How can you sit there and put this shit on me?" KoKo moved her hand.

Kayson sat his glass down and weighed his accusations. "Who is Brenda?" he asked, and then looked over into her eyes.

"I don't know, why?" KoKo asked, searching his face for answers.

"She showed up while I was visiting Rabb's grave and put a gun on me and the children. I can't rest until I lay that bitch down. Do you know anything about her?"

"No, I do not. What did she look like?"

Kayson paused, took a deep breath, turned back forward and took the rest of his drink to the head. When he sat the empty glass down he spoke. "You," he said, then turned to face her.

KoKo had no words; she just sat silent as she tried to read Kayson's mind for answers.

"Anything else?"

"No," she stood firm.

"No more secrets. I need to know what the fuck is going on at all times; all this behind my back shit stops now," he stared at her hard. "Starting tomorrow, you no longer have a lead role in this play. I need you to fall all the way back and follow," he gave his orders as if she was one of the crew.

"I don't have a problem with that," KoKo said as an eerie feeling filled her body. She choked back the tears as she began to feel as if she had betrayed him.

Kayson picked up immediately on her feelings and even though he wanted to grab his wife and hug her and tell her everything was good, he couldn't. Kayson needed to teach his soldier a lesson and the best way to teach it was harsh and server; he could put Band-Aids on the cuts later, but right now he needed her to know this shit was not a game.

"I will see you in a couple days. Close this house down; secure

261

the streets and your team, then meet me in Dubai," Kayson got up and finished loading the money in one bag and the guns in the other two.

"Move like muthafuckas is on yo ass and get to me safely. I will have the kids call you when they land," he headed for the door.

"Kayson," KoKo yelled out.

Kayson stopped but didn't turn around.

"I am holding you to the same standards about our children that you hold me to," she rose to her feet. "Trust and believe if they are harmed, I will not stop until they kill me," she said firmly at his back.

"I am counting on it," he said, then kept it moving.

Chapter 36
Twisted Motives

KoKo moved quickly around the volt gathering the folders and thumb drives then she stacked them along with the cash into four big black duffle bags. When she got to the bottom of the drawer she saw a white envelope addressed to Kayson's mother. She reached down and retrieved it and tore it open. She scanned the words on the page and her heart jumped when she got to the end of the document, which named her as the beneficiary to all three insurance policies and the Chief Executive Officer of Wells Incorporated owning fifty-five percent of the company. Here it was finally right in her face, she had been searching for the reasons behind her parent's death and the many attempts on her own and Monique had the proof the whole time. *But why is it in this drawer?* she thought as she read on.

"Bitter bitch," KoKo mumbled as she thumbed to the last page.

KoKo got sick to her stomach when she read the amendment that said in case of death everything transfers to Kayson and Quran Wells. The document was signed by Monique and Tyquan and notarized and witnessed by Brenda Watson.

"What the fuck?" she said as her eyes lowered into slits.

*****

Lu sat straight up in her bed and listened attentively. The light squeak of the floorboard caused her heart to pick up pace. She slowly slid her legs from between the sheets and put them over the edge. Carefully, she slid her gun from under the pillow and removed the safety. She stood up and remained still trying to gage the location of the noise. Lu moved toward the door, staking one calculated tip-toe after the other. She posted up by the door frame and held her gun tightly in both hands.

With caution, she peeked out into the darkness and looked up into the mirror above the fireplace. She listened again then stepped out the door. Lu pressed her back against the wall and when she got to the end, and then she peeked out. Just as she was about to continue, she flew across the floor sending her in one direction and her gun in the other.

The object moved closer to her, leaned down and grabbed her by her collar and punched her repeatedly in her face. Lu felt her jaw crack as her head slammed to the floor. The man stepped over her body, snatched her by the arm and drug her in front of the sofa then tore at her gown. She forced her eyes to open as they begun to swell. Lu cringed when she realized it was one of Fucciano's bodyguards. When he bent down over her, she began to kick her legs and swing her arms with the little bit of strength she had left.

"Please don't do this," she cried as he held her to the floor and placed sloppy wet kisses on her face and breast.

He hit her again; this time breaking her nose. She put her hands up to her face as he leaned back on his knees and pulled open his pants. She looked over to the side in order to save her soul from the visual of the man taking away her control.

The man put on a condom and leaned back in. "You wanted to fuck us; right?" he asked as he pulled off her panties.

Lu didn't fight as he put his semi-flaccid penis near her opening. She took a deep breath and with the last energy she had, she reached under the couch, pulled out her pug noise, and let off one in his chest. The man fell to the side, crashing into the coffee table. She let off another shot then kept on squeezing until her gun was empty.

Lu crawled over to the kitchen and reached in a drawer and pulled out a burner.

"Hello," KoKo said into the receiver.

"They came for me. I'm good, but y'all need to be careful."

"No worries; I will take care of it," KoKo disconnected the call then placed one to her cleanup team.

When Lu hung up, she grabbed the towel from the refrigerator and held it on her nose and waited for the Calvary.

* * * * *

Brenda hurried around her hotel room stuffing her clothes and shoes into her two Gucci bags. She stoofd in the middle of the room twisting her ring on her finger as she tried to remember if she had covered all her bases. The wait was coming to an end, she had been preparing for this moment for years and now she was going to get everything she had coming to her.

Knock...Knock...Knock...

Brenda paused staring at the door as if it would open itself. She hurried to answer and her eyes widened when she saw KoKo through the peephole. She took a deep breath and pulled the door open and looked KoKo over.

"You are very hard to catch up with," KoKo said breaking the pause in Brenda's movement.

Brenda looked at her then shifted her weight to one side. "I have always been right there. Do come in." She moved to the side.

KoKo walked in the door looking Brenda up and down as she passed.

"You are way too late. Everything that is done is done. Coming to see me will not change what is already in motion." Brenda closed the door and walked in KoKo's direction.

"You sure about that?" KoKo asked as he pulled the envelope from her inside pocket. She stopped over by the desk and held it in her hand. She stared hard at Brenda as she approached her then eyed the packed bags around the room.

"This is business little girl. You are taking this way to serious," Brenda smirked as she tightened her robe stooping only feet away from KoKo.

"You got something you want to tell me?"

Brenda paused looking at the envelope in KoKo's hand, she knew exactly what it was.

"That fuckin' Monique always leaving a little trail of bread crumbs. Sentimental bitch." She shook her head in disgust. "Look, I am sorry about the way a lot of this went. I wanted it to be a smooth transition. I wanted to have this over with years ago. But Noooo...that nigga is soft on you." She said with hatred dripping from her vocals. "Your father was the same way. They needed him to let the bitch Sabrina go so he could be with my daughter, raise my grandchild and run all of this." She pressed her finger against her chest. "She wasn't built for this. Sabrina was weak. This should have belonged to my daughter. She saved Malik's life and he gave it to another bitch," Her voice elevated slightly.

KoKo did as Pashion had told her and just listened. The pain in her heart was about to show her hand.

"Sacrifices were made. Some good. Some not so good. However, it was all to keep the cycle going."

"What cycle? You muthafuckas have been trading the lives of your children for money."

"You are never too young to get in the family business," Brenda stated coldly.

"Bitch you are a snake."

"Maybe, but I get results." She paused and crossed her arms over her chest.

Brenda looked into KoKo's face and delivered her final blow.

"I remember sitting in a meeting once and while negotiating a deal, the prospect kept asking me 'how am I going to do this done'. It was simple, when you know a persons' weakness you can destroy them." The side of Brenda's mouth turned up when she released her last word. "I made sure he had everything he needed to erase all my problems."

KoKo's head began to throb at the temples as she thought back to the informants words about to meeting to kill her father. Monique had said those same words which caused her her life. And now the words were slithering out of Brenda's mouth. It was her, she had helped set it all into motion. KoKo's breathing picked up at the thoughts of the lives she had taken in search of that one trader. Heat surged through her body as flashes of Star's bloody lifeless body played loud in her head. She reached around and grabbed a blade from her waist band.

KoKo leaped forward and snatched Brenda by her hair then put the blade to her throat. She held a firm gaze as she walked her to desk and slammed her in the chair. KoKo held the sharp edge under her chin glaring down into her face.

266

"Bitch you better not move," KoKo growled through clenched teeth.

Brenda gripped the edge of the chair as beeds of sweat began to form on her brow.

"Please. I know everything. We can have all of this together, I will offer you the same deal I offered everyone else." Brenda looked up with pleading eyes.

"And I will offer you this," KoKo put the knife at the base of her head.

"Please don't," Brenda pleaded.

"It's already done," KoKo said as she stuck the knife repeatedly in the back of Brenda's skull.

Brenda fidgeted in pain until her movements ceased.

KoKo let her head drop forward on the table, and then she wiped her blade on the bright white robe then stood firm in place. KoKo stepped back a few inches then closed her eyes and took a deep breath of relief. Tears weld up in her eyes as she realized she had fulfilled her promise to her parents. It was over and it was done, by her hands.

* * * * *

KoKo had just got word that the Lion's Den had been shot up, killing five people and wounding several others. To add to the bullshit, Goldie called from Atlanta reporting that ATF were all over Golden Paradise asking questions and pulling video, forcing her to close everything down. KoKo quickly had everyone moved and all the money secured. Shit had escalated faster than she thought and her main goal was protect the family and then hunt Magic's ass down.

KoKo moved into Bre's building, collected her and was back in the car before the driver could turn around. They drove in silence until they pulled up to Goldie's apartment building.

"Look, I am putting my people in your hands. Don't cross me," KoKo said, giving Breonni a look that said, *Test this shit if you want to.*

"KoKo, I got you," Breonni said as they exited the vehicle.

KoKo stepped to the doors, gave the door man the nod and headed for the steps.

Breonni didn't miss a beat, she was right on KoKo's heals.

When they reached Goldie's door, she already had it open and was on point with her gun at her side.

"My nigga," KoKo joked in her Denzel Washington voice.

"You already know," Goldie looked out the door as Breonni walked in then locked it and moved to her bags. She placed one bag on her shoulder and passed one to Breonni, then tucked her gun in the small of her back.

"Let's do this, Boss Lady," Goldie said co-signing her mission.

KoKo grabbed the last bag and they were out.

When they got downstairs, KoKo's assassins were all standing next to the van ready to handle the task at hand. The women were taken to the airport where they all loaded the plane. After a five-hour flight and a long ride through the mountainous terrain, they arrived at a big brick house with a small farm house behind it in a huge field out in Montana. KoKo's bodyguard jumped out and escorted the ladies into the house as the other four men grabbed the bags.

Breonni looked around at the fully-furnished room and mapped out all exits and entrances as she moved further into the house. The men moved throughout the rooms checking everything over. Once they were sure it was secure, they posted up around the room and waited for the next instructions.

KoKo looked around the room into each person's eyes before she began.

"I want you to guard these ladies with your lives. No one knows you are here but me and you will know when I am coming; other than that, hit a muthafucka high and low," she looked at her men with a firm, unwavering gaze.

"They ain't gonna want this shit right here," Solomon said, holding his Desert Eagle tight in his grip.

The other three men nodded their understating as the intensity of the moment pumped heat wildly through their bodies.

"Let me speak to the ladies for a minute. Y'all take your post," KoKo ordered and each man moved to their position.

KoKo walked to a back room and Goldie and Breonni followed. When the door was closed, she laid down the law.

"Goldie do not take any calls from Baseem. Breonni cut off all communications with Long," KoKo said, giving her a stern look.

Breonni's eyes got wide when she mentioned Long's name; she had been given an order to leave him alone ans she had disobeyed and was now wondering how much KoKo knew.

"Somebody ain't right. I need these dicks dry and confused so I can see what the fuck is going on around here."

"You think Bas got cross in his blood?" Goldie's nostrils flared at the mere thought.

"I'm not saying that. But I have to isolate this shit before it gets way outta hand. I need Magic feeling that burn so he will move different; somebody is feeding that nigga. He sweet on that pussy you been giving him. I need that nigga off balance once them scales are tipped he *will* fuck up," KoKo stated firmly.

"I am down for whatever; shit, you can have my phone. Everybody who needs me is in this room," Breonni said, pulling her phone from her pocket.

"Nah, you hold that. I have to be able to get to you in case the people I trust can no longer be trusted," KoKo said, not blinking an eye.

"Got you," Breonni said as she blocked Magic and Long's numbers from her phone.

Goldie took her phone and did the same. "When will we see you again?"

"Not sure. Just hold shit down and be ready for whatever. If shit don't feel right, you know where to go," KoKo impressed.

"Yes I do," Goldie confirmed.

"Everything you need is either in here or out in the farm house. Let them get what you need; stay in the house. Familiarize yourself with the weapons. There is a sawed-off under that kitchen table and one under that rocking chair. There is also a gun in the bathroom drawer and kitchen drawer and one under the pillow in each bedroom. Don't hesitate to tuck a nigga ass in," she stated strongly. "Anything else?" KoKo asked. When the ladies didn't speak, KoKo knew it was time to push on. "A'ight, let me get back to the streets," she moved toward the door.

"Be safe, mama," Goldie said, feeling bad that she was not

going with KoKo.

"You do the same, and protect that baby. Night saved me and my son's life; I have to give him the same favor."

Goldie got choked up and moved to KoKo and hugged her. "Thank you for everything, KoKo."

KoKo patted her on the back as if she was a small child. "It's all good, ma. Y'all get settled in and no worries. I got this," she assured her as she pulled back.

"Here we go with the mushy shit. Y'all fucking up my gangsta," Breonni spat, moving past KoKo and Goldie.

KoKo chuckled. "Sheeit...you better be happy to see me affectionate; that might have just been that last part of me that is human," KoKo said looking at Breonni with a cold stare. "See y'all in a couple."

Breonni felt a heaviness in her heart as KoKo hit the door. Her words sunk deep into the pit of Breonni's stomach. She knew that as scary as it may seem, the reality was that they were all on the edge of the grave, praying that this day was not the day death picked their number.

* * * * *

KoKo, Adreena and several of the soldiers marched up into Magic's little social club and walked right up to the bar. She leaned in and asked the bartender's name.

"I'm Wynter, how may I help you?"

"I need you to get that muthafucka, Magic. Not now...but right now!"

"He's not here. Can I help you with anything," she asked as she wiped the counter down.

"Bitch, if I have to ask you again, we gonna be wiping up your teeth with the rest of the shit on that rag," KoKo threatened.

"Let me call him," she said, reaching for her cell phone.

"Put that shit on speaker," she ordered.

KoKo watched as she dialed. He picked up and the woman told him they needed him at the club right away. He agreed to come and the call was disconnected. KoKo waited and watched the room. The tension was high and the anticipation was so thick it was suffocating.

Ledger and his nephew li'l Will emerged from a back room and walked right up on KoKo.

"Do I have business with you?"

"Not sure yet. But I'm sure we are all about to find out. KoKo turned to Ledger then pulled out and shot Will in the head.

Ledger's heart dropped at the same time lil' Will's body hit the ground.

"What the fuck is wrong with you," he pulled out and put his gun right at KoKo's forehead.

Wynter pulled a small pump shotgun from behind the bar and put it to Ledger's head. "You must be tired of living," her voice echoed from behind him.

KoKo's men put chrome to the security and waited for the next man to make a move.

Adreena moved from one man to another, collecting guns and placing them in a black duffle bag; then she joined KoKo's side.

"Bitch, I am not breakable," She said holding her gun firm.

"Give me the one who calls the orders!"

"You must be out your mind," he stood firm.

"This is your last chance. Give me the man who calls the orders."

"Fuck you," Ledger said as he began to press his finger on the trigger.

Before he could move another inch, Wynter blew the side of his head off.

"What the fuck is wrong with you?" KoKo yelled in her direction. "How you gonna shot this nigga when I got heat to my head?"

"My bad. The bitch was having a hard time making up his mind," she tucked her gun. "The floor will put it back together for him," she looked at KoKo. "But I can tell you one thing, these scared ass niggas are about to tell you everything you want to know. I'ma pour some drinks while you handle your business," she sat her gun down and proceeded to pour several shot glasses of Ciroc then passed them out.

KoKo just shook her head. She had created a team full of monsters and they stayed on green light. All she could do was move to the next step. For the next two hours, her men laid a few dudes out and the rest gave up everything they knew in exchange for their freedom from the game. When she and the team walked out the door, they had all the information that they needed.

The team jumped into their trucks and KoKo, Adreena and Wynter hopped in KoKo's whip. KoKo adjusted her mirrors and waited for her men to take the lead. As soon as their cars turned out, two explosions rang out into the night. The car holding her men flipped falling only inches in front of her truck. KoKo jumped out of her vehicle and looked at the smoke and fire that pushed its way into the sky.

"What the fuck!" she yelled out as she pulled her gun and turned in all directions."

Shots flew in their direction, causing them to hit the ground taking cover. KoKo looked at the fear on Adreena's face as bullets whizzed past her on all sides and a slight panic set in. She reached out for her hand, and just as Adreena moved to come where KoKo was taking cover, her head was blown off her shoulders. KoKo jumped back to her spot and waited for a pause, and then she jumped up and lit up the night in the direction of the gunfire.

"Punk muthafuckas!" she yelled out as she let off. When she ran out, she ducked back down and Wynter got her some in.

Wynter crawled low to the ground as she tried to get closer to KoKo, just as the gunfire began to slow down. Just as the ladies were reloading their guns, they heard car tires screeching. KoKo looked out and was hit in the face with a butt of a gun. The man put the barrel in Wynter's face and they were both grabbed from their position and hoods placed over their heads as they were tossed into the van.

* * * * *

Kayson stood over Magic in the open field with fury in his eyes. The dim light from the truck illuminated the area as crickets played in the distance as Magic lay bloody and unconscious only seconds away from coming face to face with evil.

"Wake his bitch ass up," Kayson ordered.

"No problem Boss," Baseem replied with a wicked smirk as he opened the bottle of alcohol and began to pour it over Magic's face.

"Ahhh…" Magic was jolted from his sleep screaming as the liquid seeped into the gashes on his face. He breathing heavy he struggled to look around in the darkness and slight panic creeped in his chest when his eyes met with lava that was pouring from Kayson's.

"Thanks for agreeing to meet with me," Kayson said coldly as he pulled the hood back slightly from his face.

Magic's eyes moved back and forth from Baseem and Kayson then down at his battered body he wanted to move but couldn't, both of his arms and legs were broken and twisted in different directions. He began to shake as the realty of his condition played loudly in his mind.

"Usually I would just blow your head off and get on with my day. But you one of them niggas that need special attention. So, here we are," Kayson stood with his gun rested easy at his side.

"This shit aint gotta be like this," Magic mumbled as his body throbbed in pain.

"That's what the fuck we tried to tell yo ass months ago. Dumb muthafucka," Baseem growled then spat in Magic's face.

Magic turned his head cringing it slide down the side of his face.

"So how you want this?" Kayson asked as he pulled one in the chamber.

"I'll pay you man," Magic stuttered as tears ran from the corner of Magic's eyes.

"Baseem which hand you think he tried to stick in my pocket?"

"Left," Baseem said smoothly.

Kayson shot him in the left elbow almost severing it from the bone.

"Ahhhh…Please…" He pleaded staring into Kayson's unforgiving glare, but knowing his plea would be denied.

"I offered you money. Denied. I offered you territory. Denied. You told me to kiss your ass and suck your dick," Kayson's voice echoed into the darkness. "Nigga you tried to fuck me." Kayson let off a shot hitting Magic in his dick.

"Ahhhhh…!" he yelled out in agonizing pain which caused him to blink in and out of consciousness.

273

"Now you got a pussy muthafucka," Kayson said then positioned himself right over Magic peering into his blood shot eyes, he needed to steel his heart and his soul. He stood and watched the agony and terror on his face and as his body shook; Kayson formed a smirk on his face.

Magic choked up blood onto his face and gasped for breath as his lungs struggled for air. His glossy gaze became empty of life as the chilly whispers of the grave called his name.

"Never send for death unless you really want to see its face," Kayson said then emptied his gun.

Chapter 37

The Shadow

KoKo was kneeled in a puddle of water and her own piss and blood. Her hands were tightly tied behind her back and her head was pounding like she had been hit with a hammer. KoKo forced her vision to look down at the bottom of the hood, trying to see if she could make out any images or her location.

"That bitch needs to die," the female voice growled with anger.

KoKo turned her head slightly in the direction of the voice.

"Just be patient. We need the rest of the guests to arrive so we can start the party." Mr. Fucciano stated with a smirk hugging the corner or his mouth.

KoKo heard the accent and knew exactly who it was, but everything was still a puzzle to her.

"Here you go," KoKo heard a strong deep voice ring out, and then she felt something being thrown in front of her.

KoKo gazed down to see it was a body, but she couldn't make out who it was.

"She tried to hang in there, but I guess her heart ain't as strong as her Boss's," he taunted. "The other one we let go, but not before having fun with her," they laughed in unison.

Vomit rose in KoKo's throat as she realized that one of her girls was lying there, but she couldn't tell which one. "Please don't let it be Goldie," she mumbled thinking of her promises. Tears wanted to escape her eyes, but she wouldn't let them fall; they had stolen enough and weren't getting shit else.

Within minutes, she heard what sounded like a garage door

opening then many different patterns of footsteps.

"What the fuck?" she heard Kayson say from only feet away from her.

Kayson and Baseem stood with their arms out as they were patted down. Kayson put his arms to his side and scoped out the surroundings as he moved closer to where they stood. Baseem was close behind counting the heads and visualizing how face he could blow them off their shoulders.

"Welcome to the party, Mr. Wells; as you can see, we started without you." Dutchess stated with a smile on her face.

Kayson eyed the room locking eyes with his father and his made bitch; then Mr. Luccini and his team and Mr. Fucciano and his team. He looked at the men that were lined up around the room holding semi-automatic weapons and then back at his wife. But nothing touched him more than the sight of Goldie laying there lifeless.

Baseem's heart pumped hard against his chest when he looked down and saw Goldie lying in a puddle of blood in front of KoKo. His hands shook as he looked at her beaten body and face. Kayson didn't say a word; he just stared at Mr. Fucciano.

"The problem with men like you is, you always believe you can't be touched," he said as he loaded his colt revolver.

"Please excuse my son, he was raised by a whore so he is very tender on bitches," Tyquan stated, lighting the end of his cigar.

Kayson wanted to reach for his gun and make it rain bullets and body parts; but the safety of his wife and family was far more important, so he remained silent; waiting for his opportunity to pounce.

"I am surprised that the man with many profound words has nothing to say." Mr. Fucciano moved over to KoKo. He pointed the gun at her head and continued. "The worse thing a man can do in this business is expose his heart," he pulled the hood off KoKo's head, grabbed her hair tightly in his palm and pressed the gun to her temple.

Baseem jumped and Kayson grabbed his arm to stop him. "Just wait," he said on a low tone.

"Let your dog loose, Mr. Wells. I have been dying to see his face. I believe the young woman called out for him several times," he continued to taunt them.

"You wanted me. Now you have me," Kayson based and his deep voice bounced against the brick walls.

"I don't want you, Mr. Wells. I want everything that they think you are."

Kayson looked over at KoKo and his heart felt as if it crumbled in his chest. One of her eyes was swollen completely shut and the other was on its way. The beauty that usually set the room on fire was covered with cuts and bruises. There she was tied up like an animal, damn near naked and kneeling in her own piss and blood.

Kayson didn't say a word.

Tyquan looked on in anticipation. "Let me at least introduce you to your replacement," Tyquan said, looking over to the shadow.

When the man walked out, Baseem felt his hand ache for his gun. He tightened his fist struggling to wait for Kayson to give the order.

"I don't need an introduction. This nigga knows who I am," Rock said as he took his place near Tyquan and his mother.

"Oh, you've met?" he asked with a smile on his face.

"Nah, let's just say we ate from the same plate once," he said, looking down at KoKo.

"Did I forget to mention that he is a Wells?" Tyquan asked, pulling on his cigar.

Kayson looked at Rock then at KoKo; he swallowed his spit, forced a smile to his face, then went in. "You think this shit can break me? Muthafucka, every man on my team knows what it is. If they gotta be sacrificed, then that is what the fuck it is." He looked down on her once more.

"Oh, so your wife doesn't matter?" he asked, pulling one in the chamber.

"She is replaceable pussy," Kayson spat. "Now if it's business you called me down here for, then do what you gotta do so we can get to it."

"You hear that my dear? He is willing to have you replaced," he pulled KoKo's head back and looked down into her beaten face, trying to steal her emotions, but there were none left.

Anger filled KoKo's chest as the words left Kayson's mouth. She looked up into his unwavering eyes and the coldness that stared back at her chilled her to the bone.

"Don't play with that bitch. Kill her," Dutchess said as saliva filled her mouth. "We have been playing with these two long enough." She tightened her jaw then slammed her fist in her palm.

"Don't worry Ma, let this happen. Plus she is used to being on her knees. After this maybe me and my brother can both bend her over." Rock threw his offer at Kayson.

"I might have got excited about your offer, but I'm playing with the memory of your mother sucking my dick." Kayson stated smoothly looking Rock in his eyes.

Rock's Brow creased. "Is that right?"

"Let me know if you need the details." Kayson spat venom in Rock's direction.

"Look at this both my sons soft on the same bitch. Who knew," Tyquan chuckled. "I guess I didn't give y'all enough Boss in your blood."

"Just be patient. I'ma show you my Boss in a minute," Kayson said then turned his attention back to Mr. Fucciano.

"I hate to break up this little reunion but we have some bitches to kill," he stated in his thick accent while holding the gun to KoKo's temple.

"Well get to it. I'm losing money," Kayson spat with clenched teeth.

"Since she don't mean shit to you. Why don't you pull the trigger?"

"No problem." He moved in her direction.

"Noooo…he does not get to end her life on his terms. She killed my son." Dutchess yelled from Tyquan's side. "This isn't the plan. What are you doing?" she asked rushing over to Mr. Fucciano.

"Bitch, you were never in my plans," Tyquan said then shot Dutchess in the back.

Dutchess fell over holding her gut tight. She looked down at the blood seeping through her fingers and opened her mouth to scream but could not. "You promised me," she gasped as her chest heaved for air as it filled with fluid.

"Bitch, ain't no honor amongst thieves," he said then put one in her head. He turned back in Kayson's direction. "Don't worry son, she deserved death." Tyquan said emotionlessly to Rock as he stared at his mother's dead body.

Rock bit into his bottom lip and squeezed his sweaty palms tight.

"I got shit to do; so if you're going to kill her then do it and get it over with," Kayson said without emotion as he stared down on KoKo with evil in his eyes.

KoKo's brow creased then she lowered her head. Thoughts of her children filled her mind as she closed her eyes and prepared for her final seconds.

"Take her life then. And it will seal all our deals," Mr. Fucciano said. "Plus, she's damaged goods; no man should want to eat anything another man has chewed up and spit out."

"Kill me," she whispered.

Mr. Fucciano looked down at her. "What was that?"

She lifted her head and looked up at Kayson. "Kill me!" she yelled, causing her voice to send a chilling echo throughout the room.

"Bitch, fuck you," Kayson growled.

"No, fuck you! I would rather die now then live a thousand deaths by your side. Now do it, punk muthafucka!" she screamed.

Mr. Fucciano handed Kayson his gun and stood back with victory and pride beaming from his eyes.

Tyquan stood and watched each piece move across the board like a well-tuned orchestra. He was almost there, he could taste the money on his tongue.

"Like I said, no problem." He then raised his hand and put the gun to her forehead. "Sleep well, bitch," he uttered, then pulled the trigger.

KoKo heard his words then the shot; but the numbness that moved through her body blocked out all images. She looked down into Goldie's face as she blinked back tears of regret. Her eyes fluttered as the many emotions coursed through her veins. She was ready to surrender her soul until she heard several other shots ring out which jolted her from her daydream. Mr. Fucciano fell beside her, then Baseem put one in each of his bodyguards and they fell like hot bricks. Mr. Luccini smiled as he watched the competition go down in a blaze of gun fire.

Kayson reached down and untied his wife and pulled her to her feet. Baseem took off his jacket and put it over KoKo's battered body. Kayson peered down at Mr. Fucciano as he took his last breaths. His eyes were filled with fear and confusion and he surrendered it all to the Boss.

"Are you ready to do business, Mr. Wells?" Luccini asked from his left side.

Kayson stood briefly staring down at Mr. Fucciano then he spoke. "It was always business." He raised his head then glared an evil eye in his direction. "These niggas right here tried to make it personal." He waved his gun in the direction of the dead bodies. "At any rate, I'ma Wells man; we don't share our throne." He put one in Luccini's throat and one in his heart. He then turned his gun on Rock.

For a brief moment Rock felt safe until Mr. Luccini's men took their places behind Kayson leaving Rock standing alone.

"So, is this what it is KoKo? I handed you all these muthafuckas." Rock said as heat moved through his body.

"Muthafucka, I don't know you." KoKo spat adjusting her weight on her wobbling legs.

"I think you know me very well." Rock grabbed his dick.

"Nigga please. That soft meat between your thighs don't excite me. I have a pussy of my own," She spat out blood in his direction. "But you can share it with Diablo, she loves to eat pussy." KoKo revealed that she knew Rock put Diablo on her Night. She grabbed the gun from Kayson's hand and pumped Rock's chest with some hot shit. "Slimy muthafucka."

Rock's eyes widened then his body jolted from side to side as each bullet entered then exited. He hit the floor and his feet twitched as the energy left his limbs.

"Congratulations son, we did it," Tyquan said clapping his hands and moving towards Kayson.

Kayson's brow creased and lips tightened. "I told you ain't no fuckin' we between us," Kayson growled as he eased the gun from KoKo's grip.

Tyquan's semi-smile turned into a frown as he stopped in mid-stride. "Sheiiitt...Nigga you better remember that I made you. I kept you safe all these years. It's my power that keeps you on top." Tyquan based in Kayson's direction.

"You let them touch my wife," Kayson said through clenched teeth.

"You better make that bitch man up, she knows what this is. She signed up for the same shit we did." He unfastened the buttons on his blazer. "It's about this money son. Her pussy was meant to be played with, you fucked around and fell in love."

Kayson pulled KoKo behind him and tightened his grip on the gun as he moved closer to his father.

"What? You can't touch me. All this shit belongs to me. All of it." He yelled as he began to move in Kayson's direction sliding his hand to his lower back.

The two men closed in the space between them with hatred and rage. Each standing in front of a throne that they refused to surrender. Kayson drew his gun and Tyquan drew his. They stopped only inches from each other with their heat rested firm against their thigh. Kayson looked into his father's dark hazel eyes and cringed to at the thought of them sharing the same blood. Tyquan also cringed to know he was standing in front of a younger more deadly version of him with a fire burning in his soul for power and revenge.

"You don't mean shit to me. But on the strength of my mother I would not kill my father. But today, I break all promises," Kayson spoke firm as the heat from his eyes pierced into Tyquan's soul.

Tyquan's hand shook as he began to settle with the idea of death. There was nowhere to hide, his temptations and greed had delivered him right into the palm of its merciless hands.

Tyquan swallowed his spit chuckled then stated his peace. "These muthafuckas right here." He waved his hand at the men that stood behind Kayson. "They fear you. I don't give a fuck what you call yourself. I gave you all this fuckin' power." He leaned in causing their noises to almost touch.

"All this belongs to me. I say when it's over. You owe me muthafucka," Tyquan grabbed Kayson by the neck of his shirt. Kayson grabbed his wrist and at the same time both men brought their guns to the air. Kayson put his gun to Tyquan's mouth and Tyquan rested his at Kayson's temple.

Kayson heard the ringing of bullets being lodged in chambers and ordered. "Everybody stand the fuck down!"

Baseem slightly lowered his weapon and the men did the same.

"Is this what you wanted?" Kayson yelled.

"Hell yeah. I want to see who you are," Tyquan growled back. "You ain't no boss. You hide behind the skirt of a bitch," Tyquan spat.

"I am trying not to blow your muthafuckin' head off," Kayson said through clenched teeth.

"Do it. Do it. Do it!" Tyquan yelled back as the two bulls locked eyes and grips.

Kayson battled with the pain of taking his own fathers life and the reality that he was trying to also take his. He had almost decided to give him mercy until he felt the gun tap his temple. He quickly pulled his head to the side and let one off in Tyquan's mouth. Blood and teeth splashed back in Kayson's face but he didn't as much as blink. Kayson grabbed his father in the throat and let off two more as he took his body to the ground.

Tyquan shook as the silver heat coursed through his organs and his air shortened.

Kayson stood up tall over his father glaring down at him. He then glanced around at all the death that scattered the room and pride swelled up in his chest. He had finally put their enemies to rest. Today everything would start over; he needed to put his wife and family back together piece by tattered piece.

Kayson turned and looked into the eyes of his men and then passed out orders. "We start this shit over today." He paused staring into their eyes. "My wife is no longer in charge she will be my personal advisor but that is it. Y'all bring everything to me and me only. And your disobedience comes with a penalty of death." He paused again.

Each man stood firm and nodded confirming their allegiance. The silence was thick in the room as Kayson held their gaze. He then moved towards KoKo.

"Your done baby. I can't live with you on this end of our business. Am I clear?"

"Yes, and you owe," KoKo said unable to hold eye contact with Kayson.

"I'ma spend the rest of my life paying you back." He pulled her into his arms and KoKo rested against his chest.

Kayson turned and looked at Baseem who was now kneeling next to Goldie trying to lift her into his arms.

Baseem rose up to his feet and held Goldie close to him. Tears ran from his eyes and onto her face. He whispered in her ear as he caressed her golden blood soaked locks. His heart sank to the bottom of his dark black soul with every word he uttered.

"No regrets Bas. She chose her path, and now you have to choose yours," KoKo stated with ease looking over at Baseem.

Baseem choked back his tears and inhaled deep. He thought back to the day Kayson saved his life and the many days he took the lives of others. Death was his destiny and he would live from this day forward in its painful shadow.

"My loyalty. My honor and my gun will always be for y'all," Baseem looked at KoKo then firmly into Kayson's eyes.

There was an eerie moment of silence then Kayson spoke. "Today our allegiance is stronger than ever," Kayson held their stare. "We will take all the pain and hatred we have for our enemies and put it in our sons. They will settle every score we leave behind."

Kayson knew that there was no getting out and there would always be someone lurking to be at the top, someone to challenge his power. He vowed to protect his throne by all cost and only relinquish it to the grave. Until then, they would all live each day in the shadow of death.

Made in the USA
Middletown, DE
07 August 2023